THE VALANCOURT BOOK OF
VICTORIAN CHRISTMAS GHOST STORIES

VOLUME THREE

THE VALANCOURT BOOK OF

VICTORIAN CHRISTMAS GHOST STORIES

VOLUME THREE

Edited with an introduction by
SIMON STERN

VALANCOURT BOOKS
Richmond, Virginia
2018

The Valancourt Book of Victorian Christmas Ghost Stories, Volume Three
First published December 2018

Introduction © 2018 by Simon Stern
This compilation copyright © 2018 by Valancourt Books, LLC

Published by Valancourt Books, Richmond, Virginia
http://www.valancourtbooks.com

ISBN 978-1-948405-20-1 (paperback)
ISBN 978-1-948405-21-8 (hardcover)
Also available as an electronic book.

All Valancourt Books publications are printed on acid free paper that meets all ANSI standards for archival quality paper.

Set in Dante MT

CONTENTS

INTRODUCTION

THE VICTORIANS INVENTED MANY THINGS—the penny post and the telegraph, the sensation novel and detective fiction, bicycles and petrol and antimacassar oil—but they did not invent the ghost story. Yet we associate the ghost story with the Victorians, in part doubtless because of Charles Dickens's efforts to craft the form when serving as editor of *Household Words* and *All the Year Round*, and his ability to recognize its appeal for readers during the Christmas holiday—another Victorian achievement, not invented but perfected in the nineteenth century. Writing nearly a quarter-century after the close of the Victorian era, M. R. James proposed a formula that indicates what made Dickens and his contemporaries so successful:

> Two ingredients most valuable in the concocting of a ghost story are . . . the atmosphere and the nicely managed crescendo. Let us . . . be introduced to the actors in a placid way; let us see them going about their ordinary business, undisturbed by forebodings, pleased with their surroundings; and into this calm environment let the ominous thing put its head, unobtrusively at first, and then more insistently, until it holds the stage . . . Then, for the setting. The detective story cannot be too much up-do-date: the telephone, the aeroplane, the newest slang, are all in place there.

Although James advised that the author might "leave a loophole for a natural explanation" (as we see in some of the stories in this volume), he preferred to keep it "so narrow as not to be quite practicable."

This recipe, particularly the concern with atmosphere, helps to explain what many Victorian writers seem to have understood intuitively. The paraphernalia of everyday life pervade any number of Victorian ghost stories, and if to their first readers they offered the pleasure of the mundane slowly and almost imperceptibly inching into the eerie, to modern readers they offer the additional pleasure of a densely and vividly imagined material world whose comforts and accoutrements are fascinatingly different from ours and yet invitingly homey.

The same considerations help to account for the continuing attraction of the Sherlock Holmes stories: what makes them so compelling has to do not only with Holmes's talent for creating a biographical sketch out of seemingly insignificant trifles, but also with the kinds of trifles he relies on—such as hats and gloves and walking sticks. Even when something drab, like mud, provides the telling clue, it turns out to be the mud near the Wigmore Street Post Office, a localized detail that invites us to place ourselves in the topography of Victorian London.

The ghost story, like the detective story, creates its effects by asking us to imagine a world stocked with desks and paintings and all the furnishings of a world that is sufficiently far removed from living memory as to provide a reliable occasion for nostalgia, yet not so far removed as to seem unenticing. And in both genres, what attracts the reader is not only the profusion of material objects but also their tactile qualities: just as the glove becomes meaningful because of its frayed edge and indentations, the ghost story's plush sofas and ancient, creaking chests figure not just as items in the background but as palpable objects with a sensory allure.

If these tales owe some of their enduring appeal to the opportunity to imagine, in fine-grained detail, the comforts of Victorian life, those sensations gain additional force in the Christmas ghost story, with its elaborate descriptions of the food and drink, games, and bedclothes that so many of these stories rejoice in offering for the reader's delectation. We might think of them as a particular kind of sensation tale, one that occasionally recalls the sensation novels of the 1860s and '70s by introducing a backstory featuring matters like adultery and illegitimacy, but that more typically invites the reader to experience the contrast between the Victorian home's cheery interior and the piercing cold of the snow and ice outside. In his essay "Gaslight, Fog, Jack the

Ripper," Joachim Kalka points to this contrast as the defining feature of the period, remarking that, "For us, the primary quality distinguishing the nineteenth century . . . is a great, cozy sense of security brought out all the more vividly by the evocation of the uncanny." The Christmas ghost story compacts all of these features and heightens their effect by eliminating the boundary that insulates the cozy domestic interior from the bitter cold: instead of scaring up an external threat and imagining the home as the safe harbor, it terrorizes the inhabitants with spectral beings who wander between those two spheres.

Not every story in the following pages exemplifies these features—this year's anthology showcases the diversity of Victorian ghost fiction by including examples of the comic and even satirical modes, as well as the suspenseful variety—but many of them combine drama and fantasy in a way that uses visual and meteorological effects to appeal to the reader's senses and to heighten the reader's pleasure. "The Ghost of the Cross-Roads" opens on a lavishly described Christmas feast (with "the whole Pie family" running the gamut from "plebeian Apple to rich Mrs. Mince") and then immediately presents us with a violent ice-storm, before introducing a wayfarer who has just barely survived the storm and the dreadful adventure that makes up the gist of the tale. "19, Great Hanover Street" and "Walnut-Tree House" give us richly described premises that come under threat in precisely the way that James recommends. Similarly, "Old Simons' Ghost!" is a wonderful tale of a miser who comes back to reclaim his property, on Christmas Eve, from the long-suffering clerk who tries to take possession of it. On the other hand, some of the stories imagine hauntings that take place entirely out of doors ("The Haunted Tree," "Haunted Ashchurch," "The Nameless Village") or hauntings that target specific individuals ("A Dead Man's Face").

Other stories use the form more playfully, such as "The Ghost's 'Double'," which starts conventionally enough, with a bachelor reclining by the fireside in a room whose décor is conducive to "suicidal depression," only to find himself haunted by two competing ghosts with apparently incompatible agendas. "The Barber's Ghost" and "The Wicked Editor's Christmas

Dream" take the comedy even further—the would-be victim of the barber's ghost proves to be a pragmatic sort who turns "the late discovery to his own advantage," and the wicked editor is compelled to undergo a dismal literary tour seemingly based on Scrooge's experiences, with the significant difference that he is given no reason to reform.

It is perhaps salient that most of the comic ghost stories date from the end of the century, when the familiarity of the genre in its traditional form, carrying the accumulated weight of many decades, may have prompted writers to seek out new directions. "Sir Hugo's Prayer," for instance, seems to owe some of its inspiration to Wilde's "The Canterville Ghost," another tale in which the phantoms, all too aware of the demands that literary convention would exact from them, choose to rebel instead of following the script.

Taken together, these stories present Victorian ghosts in a wide variety of incarnations, from the grotesque to the pathetic to the irreverent, and they return for the holiday season to entertain modern readers just as they did more than a century ago.

SIMON STERN
October 2018

SIMON STERN received his Ph.D. in English literature from Berkeley and his J.D. from Yale and is an associate professor at the University of Toronto, where he is a member of the Faculty of Law and the Department of English.

NOTE ON THE TEXT

The texts of the stories in this volume are faithfully reprinted from the periodicals listed below, except for obvious printer's errors, which have been silently corrected. Because it was common practice during the Victorian period for a story to appear in one magazine or newspaper then subsequently to be reprinted in others, we are not able to say with certainty whether the dates and publications listed below represent the story's first appearance or a reprint.

"The Ghost of the Cross-Roads": *South London Press*, Dec. 23, 1893

"19, Great Hanover Street": *Sheffield Weekly Telegraph*, Dec. 24, 1889

"Sir Hugo's Prayer": *Hampshire Telegraph*, Dec. 25, 1897

"Walnut-Tree House": *The Illustrated London News*, Dec. 28, 1878

"Haunted Ashchurch": *The Argosy*, December 1893

"The Haunted Tree": *Every Week*, Jan. 1, 1871

"A Dead Man's Face": *Stonehaven Journal*, Dec. 25, 1884

"The Ghost's 'Double'": *Windsor Magazine*, December 1898

"The Haunted Manor": *The Guardian*, Dec. 26, 1885

"The Nameless Village": *Hampshire Telegraph and Sussex Chronicle* (Christmas Supplement), Dec. 19, 1896

"Old Simons' Ghost!": *The Bridgnorth Journal*, Dec. 26, 1896

"Miriam's Ghost": *Gloucestershire Chronicle*, Dec. 25, 1897

"The Vicar's Ghost": *Express and Advertiser*, Dec. 20 and 27, 1890

"The Ghost of the Hollow Field": *Newry Commercial Telegraph,* Dec. 25, 1867

"The Wicked Editor's Christmas Dream": *Tamworth Herald*, Dec. 23, 1893

"The Barber's Ghost": *The Glossop Record*, Dec. 25, 1869

"A Spirit Bride": *North Wales Times*, Dec. 26, 1896

"The Haunted Oven": *Leeds Times*, Dec. 15, 1877

"The Devil's Own": *Cardiff Times*, Nov. 30, 1895

"A Christmas Ghost Story": *Lincolnshire Echo*, Dec. 19, 1895

Frederick Manley

THE GHOST OF THE CROSS-ROADS

An Irish Christmas Night Story

NIGHT, AND ESPECIALLY CHRISTMAS NIGHT, is the best time
to listen to a ghost story. Throw on the logs! Draw the curtains! Move your chairs nearer the fire and hearken!

Not one among the little group that sat in the snug parlour
of Andy Sweeny's homestead, that wild Christmas of 1843, when
Mrs. Sweeny went to the window and drew the snow-white
curtains very close, remarking at the same time, "God shelter all
poor travellers!" but whose thoughts were as plainly expressed
in the general huddling-up which took place as though each one
had told his neighbour his particular idea of comfort; and when,
in answer to the good woman's prayer, they joined their voices
in one deep, fervent "Amen!" and huddled together in the brave
glow of the turf fire, the general sentiment of the party was published by a red-haired, dapper little fellow named "Reddy," who
said, in a rich voice:

"'Tis thanking God we should be for this comfort, not forgetting Mrs. Sweeny!"

Although the Sweenys were known the county over for
their hospitality, on this particular night they outdid all their
previous efforts at entertaining. The oak table in the middle of
the floor was covered from end to end with good things. We say
good things, and we mean it so. There were no wafer-like sandwiches on that table, nor cold liquids in colder bottles, nor frail
china-ware (no china-ware could stand food so substantial), not
fancy salads, nor any of those dainties which as good as say to a
hungry man, "Come and eat me; I'm too nice to be lying here,"
and which, when he has done them justice, spoil his evening's
enjoyment and cause life to be a burden to him.

No; there were no such insidious edibles on Mrs. Sweeny's table. To think of that supper is to be hungry. Hills of potatoes, all in their coats on account of the severe weather; lakes of soup, mountains of roast beef, with goose and turkey in the valleys between; pigeons, imprisoned in cells of crust, in which were little slits like loopholes, through which the inmates might peep—indeed, one brave bird that, we daresay, had become alarmed at the great number of diners, was attempting to escape, and actually succeeded in getting a leg through the bars, where he stuck and became discouraged; mounds of bread and butter; the whole Pie family, from plebeian Apple to rich Mrs. Mince, were there in their crusty suits. The table mumbled and groaned. But who cared for the table's sorrows? In truth, who could think of anything but gladness in that home of light and joy on that frozen night?

Outside, the storm raged. The country around, a bleak stretch of moorland, was buried deep in snow. The winds had been busy, and many were the quaint mansions they had built, and strange and weird were the changes they had wrought. The sign-post at the four cross-roads—a most commonplace affair in clear weather—was now a terrible monster with four hideous arms, that were thrust out to seize the belated traveller. All traces of the road were lost, and it would have gone hard with a stranger had he been caught in the storm that December night. Derry Goland, in King's County, Ireland, is so drear and wild that the destroying elements have made it their meeting-place. Here the winds gather and plan their courses. Here they start from, and to this place return. Any winter's night you may hear them. At first they whisper among themselves as they map out their ways. Then may be heard deep murmurs, angry murmurs, shaking the boughs, as though the Storm King had given out orders which they did not like.

How the Storm King hated Andy Sweeny's snug home and the cheerful light shining from the windows, throwing a golden pathway into the night!

More turf for the fire! Every one has a glass of steaming punch in his hand; every one's face is lighted with love and radiant with joy; every one toasts every one, sings merry songs, dances with his sweetheart, or makes love to her in some shady corner, while the aged every-ones make matches for their boys and girls; and the blind fiddler plays away for dear life. The flames grow brighter as the storm without increases in violence. The punch glows a deeper red and sparkles as with delight. The old clock in the corner has a drowsier tick, and is at peace with the world, for the jolly round face on its dial smiles on the scene; and even the table, forgetful of its complaints, has ceased to groan. In short, there never was a happier home; there never were such music and such punch as Mrs. Sweeny's, nor jollier souls to drink it.

The floor had just been cleared for dancing, and the fun was at its height, when out in the storm, seeming far away, there rose a cry—a terrible cry—a cry that spoke the anguish of a soul. Those within were silent, and listened with blanched faces to that cry without.

"God save us!" cried Andy. "What was that?"

"The Lord bethune us and all harm! It was the banshee's cry!"

At this name, so fearful to an Irish ear, the children ran to their mothers and buried their little heads. Wives clung to their husbands, sweethearts to their sturdy lovers, and all waited anxiously for a repetition of the cry. Then something happened which caused all hearts to stand still and sent the cold blood rushing down the back. It was a human voice calling aloud for help! Soon after, the crunch of flying feet was heard. They came nearer and nearer.

"Open the door! Fling it wide!" cried Andy.

Willing hands soon had a broad pathway of firelight streaming from the doorway. The storm rushed in and scattered the turf and tore pictures from their places and made sad havoc with everything. But no one cared; no one noticed it. All eyes were watching a man who came flying towards the house; for though it was a blustering night, the moon peeped at intervals through the storm-rift clouds, casting a ghostly light. And now it shone down upon this figure that sped to the door and cried, in a voice made weak by fear and running, "Save me!" then tottered across the threshold and fell prone upon the sanded floor.

Andy Sweeny turned quickly to the door, and, listening, peered long and searchingly into the darkness. At last he cried out:

"Who's there?"

The only answer was the soughing of the wind across the moor, and a gruesome answer it was.

"Who's there?" asked Andy again.

"Sure, no wan, avick," returned his wife. "Shut the door and be aisy."

Andy cast a rueful, backward glance at the door, as Mrs. Sweeny led him away from it.

"Look at the poor man foreninst ye!"

The poor man before the fire was unconscious. One motherly body was chafing his cold hands, another was bathing his forehead with punch she had seized in her hurry instead of water, and yet another forced the steaming liquor between his clenched teeth.

He was a young—a boy almost—whose age might have been guessed as twenty, and guessed correctly. That he was a stranger in Derry Goland was easily discovered, for the suit he wore was made of fine cloth and cut in the most approved style. Fashionable clothes were as common in Derry Goland as bears, and there wasn't a bear in the county. A silk-lined cloak, thrown back from his broad shoulders, disclosed a sparkling gem that winked and blinked at the firelight as though the sudden brilliancy was too much to stand. His features, although well formed and regular, had a suggestion of weakness in them, especially the chin and mouth, which lacked firmness, and wore a smiling expression of gentleness more fitted to a woman than a man. The people immediately divined that a gentleman, presumably an Englishman, judging from his dress, had fallen among them, and they went to work on him as though he were the dearest friend of each man who bent over him, or the husband, brother, or sweetheart of each good woman who carried pillows for the weary head and brought a glow of life into the pale face, so numerous were the little offices performed, so heartfelt and deep their solicitude. At length, to the great relief of all, the stranger slowly opened his eyes.

"Here ye are, sir, safe an' sound!" cried an old woman, cheeringly. "Look up, sir; 'tis wid fri'nds y' are."

The young man raised himself up, and asked Andy to assist

him to a seat. He trembled violently as he moved with livid face to the chair which Andy had placed near the fire for his use. They stood at a respectful distance from the young man, regarding him with looks of half fear, half wonder. As the moments passed, he seemed to grow stronger; and presently he raised his head from his breast, in which position he had been gazing intently at the fire, and asked whether any one believed in ghosts.

"Ghosts, your honour?"

"Ghosts."

"We do, your honour," chimed in an old woman. "'Tis me well knows we do. Wasn't there Mary Doolan's mother—Lord rest her!—dead and gone ten years come next Ash Wednesday—as fine a woman as iver put foot to leather, as I've often said, and always will say, please God, if I die for it—an' I don't care who knows it—a fine lump of a girl when I first knew her. I knew her mother before her—a dacent body, too, who married Mike Carlin after he'd buried his first wife, and then married Pat Doolan when Mike kicked the bucket—God forgive him for a rascal! Didn't Mary Doolan—rest her soul!—didn't she meet a ghost at the cross-roads? Didn't she?"

As no one contradicted, the old woman was preparing to give the story in its entirety, when the stranger interrupted.

"At the cross-roads, did you say?"

"Tin years come Ash Wednesday. She"——

"There is a milestone near by"—he appeared to be murmuring to himself, as he kicked the blazing turf with the toe of his riding-boot—"a flat milestone, like a gravestone?"

"The same place, sir. And Mary Doolan—rest her soul!—a dacent, thrifty"——

"Which of you is the landlord of this place?"

"There's no landlord here," said Andy Sweeny. "This is my home. These are my friends and neighbours."

"Will you give me a bed? I'll see that you are paid for it."

"You are welcome to my place, sir, without money. I don't want that," said Andy, rather sharply.

The young man noticed the touch of anger in Andy's voice.

"I beg your pardon. I did not mean to hurt you. I hardly know what I am saying."

He buried his face in his hands, leaning his elbows on his knees.

Andy's guests, who but lately had stood in fear of the young stranger, now looked at him with great pity stamped on their kindly faces; and even the garrulous old woman whom he had interrupted so persistently ventured close to him, saying, in a friendly way:

"Is it on Christmas, sir, ye'd be givin' way so?"

"Christmas!"

"Av course. What else? Here, Mrs. Sweeny, ma'am, if yez please, a glass o' punch for his honour!"

The young man had been stony-hearted, indeed, could he have refused the steaming glass which comely Mrs. Sweeny handed to him; hard as granite had he not melted before the expressions of homely sympathy that poured from all sides in a shy manner, as if they feared to offend; for only sufferers, brothers in sorrow, no matter what their station in life may be, know how to comfort sufferers.

The fiddler went to work once more, and played better than ever, too. The punch flowed again. The rough but sonorous voices joined in familiar airs that brought back many a half-forgotten holiday time. Hands were joined in reels and jigs, until it seemed that the storm had at last taken hold of Andy's cottage and was shaking it to pieces, so lively were the couples who "lathered the flure wid their heels," as Reddy remarked. The young people who had sought the terpsichorean honours of the evening, "by holding out to tire each other down," had at last tired themselves, and all sat round the fire, anxious for some other amusement than that which left them fatigued and short of breath. The old lady spoken of before, with the inherent instinct of a gossip—for gossips are born, not made—said to the stranger during a lull in the conversation:

"Did ye see a ghost to-night, sir?"

Andy Sweeny, imagining the old woman was annoying the gentleman, quickly interposed, and begged he would not mind her thoughtless questions.

"I am not offended," said he. "But I hardly know how to answer."

"Who was it that chased you when you came running here, screaming for help?"

"Something in black."

"How did it come to happen? You must pardon the question, sir, but as this is Christmas night, and knowing it is a time for great freedom, I thought you might be good enough to tell us all about it, sir—asking pardon once again, if I've offended you."

Andy Sweeny, like most men of ordinary intelligence and education among the Irish peasantry, had the reputation of being a "foine shpaker" and a "shmart man;" and when he had finished his tentative address, his guests winked and nodded among themselves to express their great admiration, and Reddy even went so far as to say, "There's for you."

"It's all very strange, to be sure," said the gentleman. Then he added, with a little forced laugh that would hardly come from a person whose nerves were in good condition, "I will tell you all that happened."

At these words, which promised the glorious entertainment always to be had from a ghost story, more especially when you sit in the midst of friends before a roaring, crackling fire, with a sparkling punch in your hand, listening to the storm that rattles the windows and doors, and hurls the snow down the broad chimney, hissing into the fire, as if it hated to see you so snug, and was determined to extinguish the cheerful blaze. It is then your mind wanders over dolorous, wind-swept moorland, trudges along the bleak path on the hillside, struggles with the storm on the highway, where every white-robed tree is a phantom and every rock a hiding-place of robbers and hideous somethings that await your approach and crouch in readiness to spring upon you.

Now every inoffensive oak is a terrible Briareus, stretching out its gaunt arms to seize you; now you feel certain a thing is dogging your footsteps while you fear to look behind, knowing that you would encounter its awful glance and be struck dead that instant, until the fancy becomes so strong that you break into a trot, from that to a run, and finally, with its footsteps but a few yards behind and gaining with every stride, coming so close you can feel its breath over your shoulder, your run quickens—faster—faster yet, till it ends in a wild flight, while you see nothing, think of nothing but it, and only stay the mad chase when the ruddy lights from some cottage window tell you that men, fellow-creatures, people of flesh and blood, are within hailing distance.

Now the fear, which up to this moment has paralyzed your tongue, comes forth in one scream that startles the quiet villager, and brings him, candle in hand, to his door, where he finds you stretched insensible upon the snow, and whence he carries you to his blazing turf fire, beside which you slowly regain your senses, thanking Providence you are saved. No wonder the cottagers huddled round the fire! So Andy's guests being Irishmen, and having adamantine faith in the existence of all manner of "uncanny" things, awaited the stranger's story with breathless interest.

"I may presume," he began, "that you all know Squire Good-fellow?"

"We do! Long life to his honour!"

"Well," he continued, "I was returning from his house to the inn at the village, where at present I am staying. What I had been doing there it is needless to say. The squire, who, as you all well know, is a downright good fel—gentleman, endeavoured to dissuade me from going home afoot in the storm, and invited me to sleep under his roof until morning. I, knowing he already had as many guests as his place could hold with comfort, thanked him for his kind offer, and started out for the inn—and bed, for I have been up—— Well, I have been travelling for the past few days. I need not remind you of the weather. Suffice it to say that the snow was blown into my eyes until it blinded me and I wandered from the road. My fingers were stiff and frozen, so that I found it impossible to hold my cloak about me. I could not see an arm's length before me, the snow fell so thick and fast, the night was so dark. My eyes were growing heavy. I felt sleepy. But, knowing to lie down in the treacherous snow meant death, I made one last, mighty effort and struggled on. At length I got so weak I could only stumble forward, and three or four, maybe ten times I fell. Then I cried out for help—cried, screamed, yelled as I never did before. I called. How lonely, how awfully gravelike the stillness was! My very voice seemed muffled. Then a feeling of rest, a sensation of great calm, came over me. I no longer felt the cold, nor heard the wind, nor knew fear, and I was about to sleep—it would have been my last—when some stories of travellers who had kept themselves awake by self-administered punishment came—most strange to tell—to my mind. The thought of death on that desolate moor, far from the hearts that loved me and awaited my homecoming, was so overpoweringly maddening, I tell you, that I tore my hair and shrieked out:

"I will not die! I will not!"

"I pulled open my coat and found my pocket-knife. That saved me. See where my coat is punctured. It's a mercy I didn't run it up to the handle into myself in my efforts to stimulate myself. In spite of all my efforts, I was slowly but surely—oh, so surely—sinking, till I cried again in desperation:

" 'Fool—fool! Why did you venture it? What wouldn't I give to be back at the squire's? All—everything! Anything to be saved—anything!'

" 'I'll save you!'

"My good friends, the voice that uttered these words was so close to my ear that it seemed a whisper from another land, and I thought I was already dead. How was I to reason otherwise? In that moment of death, on that distant moor, the words were like a supernatural answer to my prayer. I trembled. The sound of the winds, the falling snow, brought me to myself. Then the words were repeated:

" 'I'll save you!'

"I turned and looked at the speaker. His voice had sent a shiver—not like that produced by cold—through my frame, so that I was afraid to meet his gaze, which I know—I can't tell how—was fastened on me and pierced me through and through. Without venturing to meet his eye, I said:

" 'Who are you?'

"And he answered:

" 'One who will save you!'

" 'Are you a farmer hereabouts?' I inquired, at a loss what to say.

" 'Look and see,' he answered.

"As he said this, I fancied he chuckled quietly. Then, though I had no desire to do so, despite my efforts to do otherwise, I felt myself turning to meet him—I felt myself do this, I say, while I endeavoured most strenuously to keep my back to him. Shall I ever forget his eyes? Shall I ever forget the devilish leer on his face? Never, though I live to be a thousand years old. He was a very tall, thin, middle-aged man, dressed all in black, from the beaver, on which, I remarked, not a snowflake fell, to what I could see of his lower parts. I noticed his appearance in a second; and while I glanced at him, he stood grinning at me with the greatest good humour. I dared not speak. I could not speak. It was he who broke the silence, asking me in a very deep, musical voice, whether he resembled a farmer. I admitted that there wasn't the faintest anal-ogy—wishing deep down in my heart that there had been. You must not think I was frightened, for I wasn't. The place, the hour, the solitude, his sudden appearance, cast a sort of spell over me, and it was only by the putting forth of all my remaining strength that I had the heart to ask him to put me on the right path for home.

" 'I will do so with pleasure,' said he.

"I thanked him for his kindness, and off we started. He was so very affable, telling humorous stories to shorten our hard tramp; so extremely anxious regarding my comfort; so persistent in his efforts to please, and so polished and gentlemanly withal, that gradually I came to look upon him with less distaste, and before the cross-roads were reached, was actually exchanging addresses with him—verbally, of course. We had been speaking of the many ways which men have of amusing themselves, and I confessed that I was partial to card-playing as a pastime. He assured me it was his greatest pleasure. At length we came to the weird-looking post which stands at the cross-roads, pointing its long fingers in every direction in a most confusing manner. From that point my road was clear. 'Now,' said I to myself, 'to bid him good night.' And I proceeded to do so, holding out my hand and saying:

" 'A thousand thanks for your timely assistance—a safe jour-ney—and good-bye.'

"He did not seem to notice my outstretched hand, but looked into my face with a steady, fascinating stare, for all the world like a snake trying to fix its prey."

At this point the auditors gave vent to so many cries of surprise and fear that the narrator was forced to stop and wait until they became calm again.

"'We may never see each other again,' I returned, though why I spoke those words is a mystery. They invited conversation, and knowing this, I could have torn out my tongue with rage at my thoughtlessness.

"'Oh,' he said, 'we shall surely meet once more—where there shall be neither snow nor frost, wind nor rain.'

"I proffered my hand a second time, thinking he might not have seen it before—the night being so pitch-black—and I repeated my thanks and adieus.

"'Do you really wish to thank me for whatever small service I have been to you?' he asked.

"'If it be in my power to do so,' I said.

"'The simplest thing in the world,' he answered.

"'What is it?' I inquired.

"'Do you see this milestone?' said he, pointing towards a white mound.

"'I see something,' was my reply.

"'It is a milestone;' and as he spoke he brushed away the snow, disclosing the long, flat slab beneath.

"'Well?' said I.

"'You can thank me by sitting down facing me on that stone and appeasing a craving—a hunger—which tortures me.'

"By this time, as you may well suppose, I had grown very suspicious, and feeling certain that I had fallen in with a highwayman, whose dark purpose was to murder me for my money and jewellery, I determined to act with great circumspection—to humour his every whim, until a suitable opportunity of escape presented itself. Accordingly, I sat down on one end of the wet slab, and said to him in a voice which I endeavoured to make cheerful, 'Here I am!' His grim words, 'Appeasing a craving, a hunger,' kept me from being at all cheerful, for I anticipated being eaten alive. I put the best face I could on the matter, assuring myself that it was better and more manly to die fighting than to sit down and calmly consent to be metamorphosed into a midnight supper for the pleasure of the gentleman in black. And reasoning thus, I felt for my knife—my only means of defence—opened the largest blade, and waited for him. You must remember, my good people, that I thought of all these things in a second, while he advanced to the milestone, on which he presently seated his black self. I clenched my teeth and clutched my knife in readiness for the fight I thought must surely come. But to my surprise, he took from his back pocket a pack of cards, placed them between us on the slab, and said:

"'I will play you a few games of forty-fives, at a sovereign a game, before we part.'

"'Is this the craving you spoke of—this the hunger you must satisfy?' I asked him, almost too bewildered to articulate.

"'This,' he answered, slowly, 'is the first tool with which I worked my own ruin. Since I first had being, I have craved to win for myself all things which belong to others. The spirit of gaming was made part of me. It has grown with me, gained strength with years, until now it is all I live for. I began at an early age by wagering with another that the darker cloud of two which went sailing by in the heavens would disappear before the lighter one. He with whom I wagered won. Then, to regain what I had lost, I doubled the amount—I forget the subject of our bet. I lost again. I went on doubling and trebling, losing and winning alternately, until at last I found I was ruined. Then, indeed, I became desperate. Then was my whole mind given to the devising of schemes by which I was to recuperate my losses. I borrowed, I begged, I did everything to secure the necessary means wherewith to gamble. I have since gone on—sometimes living in luxury, sometimes in the most wretched penury; now sipping rich wine, again parching for a draught of clear water; to-day the guest of princes and lords, to-morrow the companion of filthy mendicants! But why waste time? Why tell you all this? Enough that last night I was lucky. I have money. On the way here you confessed a love of cards. Come; we will play!'

"These are his words as well as I can remember them. You may laugh at me when I tell you that, when he had finished speaking, I was seized with a desire to gamble and win the money he had mentioned. And there, on that wet milestone, in the dark night, with the storm raging round us, *that* and I began to play forty-fives for a sovereign a corner, with all the nonchalance and little amenities on his part which we observe when ladies and gentlemen play a rubber in the snug corner of a well-lighted parlour. I groped for the cards and cut them. He dealt. I picked up my five.

" 'Look here, sir. I can't tell what I'm holding. It's too dark,' I cried.

" 'Wait,' said he. With that his hand went down into the mysterious black pocket, and shortly afterwards, I heard a rattle as of iron."

"God bless us!" ejaculated the listeners.

"Then," continued the young man, "I heard a scratching, a light spluttered and hissed; and before I could make out what he was about, a lighted lantern was casting a broad glow of light on the slab and extending a few yards round it until it melted in the blackness beyond. My wonderment was momentary only. My nature seemed to have undergone some startling change, for I thought of nothing, forgot everything—my late suffering, the desolate place, the hour, the cold that had but lately been turning my fingers to stone, my mysterious companion—all save that there was a small heap of gold near the stranger—two golden coins in the middle of the slab—and that I was to gamble and win. The first game I won; the second, too. In the third I was successful. Luck continued to be with me, and I was quickly transferring the heap of gold to my corner of the slab. Up to this neither of us had spoken, but when I had taken all but a few pieces from him he remarked:

" 'You play a shrewd game.'

" 'Thank you, sir,' said I.

"After that we went on playing in silence. My luck was changing. I lost repeatedly, and when we had played several hands, he succeeded in getting the gold back to his end, with five pounds of mine along with it. This angered me, and I proposed that we should raise the stakes and play for two pounds a side. He was quite agreeable. I lost another five. Then I said we had better play for six pounds each hand. Still I was unsuccessful; still he drew my money to his end, until the last piece of gold having been swept into his pile, we played for half-crowns, then for shillings, then for sixpences, and at last I had only a few coppers at stake. The cards were given out. Eagerly I grasped mine, with the hope of holding the better hand. Alas, it was worthless! He won! Every farthing of two hundred pounds was gone, and I was constrained to tell him I could play no longer.

" 'Tut, man!' said he; 'the game is young.'

" 'Yes,' I answered, despondently; 'but my last penny is lost. There's nothing left.'

" 'Then I'll tell you what I'll do,' said he. 'I'm anything but a bad man, so I'll give you a chance of getting your money back.'

" 'You will?' cried I, delighted.

" 'I will,' he replied. 'What would you say if I were to wager all I have here'—he pushed the glittering pieces forward—'and all I have here'—taking a bag from his black pocket and emptying its golden contents on the slab—'that I will be victor in two games out of three?'

" 'You would be very magnanimous,' I returned, burning to hear the conditions. 'But I have absolutely nothing left.'

" 'You have your word.'

" 'What do you mean?' I cried.

" 'I mean that if you will pledge me your word to serve me hereafter at any time I may chance to call upon you, I will wager my gold against your word. If I lose, the gold is yours, all of it, every bright sovereign; and you may take back your vow, too.'

"As he spoke, he leaned forward, took the gold in his hand, letting it slip through his fingers in a sheeny, clinking stream. I did not hesitate to consider the import of his dreadful propositions. Gold I must have—not for its own sake, not because I am avaricious—simply because I hungered to gamble.

" 'It's a bargain,' I said.

" 'Then repeat these words after me,' he commanded.

" 'I swear'—he dictated, and I repeated word after word to the end—'I swear to be the servant of this man from this hour unto the end of time, to renounce all other masters, and to serve him faithfully and well in all that he may command.'

"I could hardly wait for him to finish, so eager was I to resume the play. Once more we seated ourselves on the milestone; again the cards were dealt out, and the strangest game that ever men played was begun. I won on the first hand. The cards came round a second time. He won. A game for each. Then I prepared myself for the last—the great struggle. Victory meant riches and freedom; defeat, I know not what. My brain was on fire; my hands trembled so that in picking up the cards he had placed near me—the cards which were to decide for or against me—they fell out of my shaking fingers and dropped on the snow at my feet." Here the speaker faltered and appeared reluctant to proceed. "My good people, when just as my fingers were about to fasten on the cards, my eye saw something that caused my blood to turn as cold as this snow on the ground—something that took from me the power to move, to speak, that petrified me and left me gazing at it like a statue. Think of being alone with that man out on the snow, away from all help, in a place seemingly deserted by its Maker, and shudder to dream of what I saw—of it!"

He shuddered even then—even as he sat in the midst of Andy's guests—in Andy's cheerful parlour. But surely he is not to be termed a coward, when we know that the cottagers at this point of the recital turned their heads and cast many uneasy glances towards the door, drawing closer to the fire as they did so.

"I was telling you I was rooted to my seat. No wonder! Before me, with the sickly light from the lantern shining right down upon it, was—a cloven hoof!"

"A cloven hoof! The divil!" cried everybody.

"I closed my eyes, thinking I was dreaming. But no; for when I opened them, there was the cursed hoof before me!"

"Lord save us!"

"Then the awfulness of the compact I had made came to my mind with terrible force. I was bartering my soul for gold. Now I see that Providence watched over me, for it was the thought of what I was doing that caused me to leap to my feet with a cry for help, and run with feet of wind—feet winged with fear—away from that thing! Every moment I expected to feel his hand on my shoulder, to be dragged back to that hellish game of cards at which my soul would be lost to it—to the thing in black. You must have heard my screams, for as I ran I saw—and how I thanked God for it!—I saw a stream of glorious light burst in the blackness! It gave new courage to my heart and new strength to my limbs. After that I remember nothing. I suppose I became unconscious. The rest you already know; and, believe me when I say it, I cannot easily forget your prompt assistance and heartfelt sympathy. I have finished."

With the stranger's adventure and all its hideous details fresh within the mind of every man, woman, and child present, the very idea of leaving that hospitable roof was thrilling in itself; so motherly Mrs. Sweeny found resting-places for the women and children, while the men slept on improvised beds of chairs, tables, &c., the greater part of them lying on the floor before the fire. The stranger retired shortly after he had concluded his story, and it was not long until the Sweeny household was asleep and snoring.

To the reader:

If you doubt any part of this narrative, you may visit Mrs. Sweeny and have it from her lips. Ask any one in Derry Goland, King's County, Ireland, the whereabouts of Andy Sweeny's house, and you will be sure to find it.

There were some cynics who said that the young man had been drinking freely at the squire's, had lost considerable money at playing cards, had wandered from the squire's in a maudlin state, had rested on the milestone and dreamed about the man in black, and that the only devil he saw was a creature of his drunken fancy, generally termed a "blue devil." But Mrs. Sweeny and most of her guests maintain that the gentleman could not have related his adventure, and described it so graphically, too, had he been intoxicated. I give no opinion in the matter. The readers may take what view of it they please.

Lillie Harris

19, GREAT HANOVER STREET

MY NAME IS ALAN FORSYTH, my age thirty-three. I stand six feet, one inch and a half in my stockinged feet. I am sound in wind and limb, I have splendid digestion, have not a grain of superstition in my nature, am a doctor by profession, and a bachelor, because I see too much of the so-called joys (?) of domestic life. "Domestic life," indeed, my experience of that gleaned from observations made while attending houses professionally is that it is a snare and a delusion. But it is not my purpose to speak on that subject. My task is to write out faithfully the extraordinary events that befell me while I occupied the house 19, Great Hanover street. Events that caused my hair to turn grey with horror in one single night, events that have seared themselves on my brain, events which can never be effaced from my memory while this life lasts. I say that I am strong and healthy because my narrative will sound like the delusions of some over-wrought brain, and yet I have always had the reputation of being a clear-headed, eminently practical man. I am not superstitious—but stay, I ought to say I *was* not, for I have been taught that "there are more things in heaven and earth than are dreamt of in our philosophy." In writing this history of facts I can offer no explanation of their extraordinary character. I shall give you the whole story of what occurred to me, and if you like to disbelieve it, go yourself and spend a month or two in that accursed house, and you will be convinced, but let the time of your tenancy be in *December*, and if you live through the horror of *what you will hear and what you will see*, you will be fortunate, but assuredly never, never will you laugh or jeer at the incomprehensible again. If, however, you take my advice, you will shun Great Hanover street, or, at least, number nineteen.

In 1884 I wished to commence practise for myself. I had been assistant to Doctor ——, and I daresay should have kept with him, but an old aunt of mine died, and left me some money, so I thought that I could not do better than utilise it by making a start on my own behalf. I advertised, and in due time I bought a practice, my predecessor selling it because of the ill-health of his wife, which compelled them to live in Cheltenham. Unfortunately I could not take their house, as they had had it on a lease, which was just up, and the landlord himself intended residing in it in future.

Now I had always had a house of my own, as when my poor mother died I had kept on the home, and Anne, my housekeeper (who had originally been my nurse, and so consequently petted and tyrannised over me, in the manner of old servants), kept it in a way which was alike the delight and envy of all my bachelor friends. Of course moving was a nuisance, but Slominster was only about 70 miles from London, where I was then living, and I knew that if I could get a suitable house Anne would speedily get it into comfortable order.

"Don't worry yourself," said Mrs. Price, the wife of the doctor whose practice I had bought, "you will soon get a house, and till then make this your home, if you don't mind us being in a state of confusion with packing, &c."

I thanked her; but still I resolved to get a house as soon as possible. I put myself in the hands of an agent, and for two days spent the best part of my time inspecting residences all more or less unsuitable. At length I got thoroughly wearied, I walked along mechanically, and somehow I found myself in a street that I had never been in before. It was an old-fashioned looking road, with quaint red brick houses on either side. I looked up to see the name of the place; there it was at the corner—"Great Hanover street." As my eye rested on the name, it also rested on a house. It was empty, and in the window was a card, "To Let." I crossed over. It was a corner house, well on to the pavement, but round the corner was a large square garden, and through the high iron railings mounted on a brick wall I could see a side door.

"The very house for me," I thought, triumphantly; "a quiet respectable neighbourhood; the door at the side would do excellently for the surgery; there's a nice garden. I think I will look over it." The "To Let" card informed me that keys and full particulars were to be obtained at Mr. Hunt's, Howard row, so I took out my pocket book and jotted down the address, and then looked at the number of the house. It was 19, GREAT HANOVER STREET.

As I strode along, I saw a hansom and hailed it, and was soon bowling off to Howard row. Mr. Hunt I found from the brass plate on the door was a land agent, and this was his office. On entering I saw that there were some half-a-dozen young fellows all busily engaged in writing. One of them got off his stool at my entrance.

"I have come for some particulars concerning a house," I said.

"Yes, sir," he answered courteously but indifferently. The office was very quiet; the pens of the five clerks went scratching over the paper, and I was conscious of a vague and insane desire that they would lift up their heads, and not be so aggravatingly industrious. "What house is it?"

"19, Great Hanover street," I answered.

There was a dead pause, my wish was gratified, the clerks had left off writing, and with one common accord had turned round to stare at me.

"19, Great Hanover street," I repeated impatiently.

The young fellow gazed at me, all indifference gone; he seemed amazed.

"I think," he commenced, in a quick, eager voice, strangely at variance with his former languid tone, when he was interrupted by the entrance of a small brisk-looking gentleman, who I rightly imagined was Mr. Hunt.

"What can we do for you, sir?" he asked.

"I want some information about the house 19, Great Hanover street," I replied.

Was it my fancy, or did the ruddy colour fade from his cheek? Anyhow he stared at me with the same blank look that I had noticed with the clerk.

"Certainly," he responded, recovering himself with an effort. "I take it that you are a stranger to the town?"

"Yes," I answered, "I am Doctor Forsyth. I have bought Doctor Price's practice."

"Ah, yes," he said, eyeing me curiously, "so you would like

particulars about number 19. It has been empty a long time, I might say a *very* long time, but the owners will be glad to do it up thoroughly for a good tenant," and then he gave me particulars as to accommodation, rent, &c.

The finish of it was that Hunt and I drove to see the house, but I was conscious that our departure in the hansom was watched with much interest by the clerks.

I was delighted with the house; the rooms were large and airy, the domestic arrangements splendid. On either side of the passage leading to the garden door was a good sized room, which would do capitally for surgery and consulting room; in short, it was a small mansion, and the only thing that surprised me was the ridiculously low rent, which Mr. Hunt informed me was owing to the house being empty for so long. Another thing that astonished me was the man's nervousness, for he was certainly the most nervous beggar I ever met. Once I let my stick fall on the tesselated hall, and when he heard the clatter he turned simply livid.

To cut the matter short, I took the house for three years, on the understanding that it was to be re-papered, whitewashed, and painted inside and out.

I was staying at the Price's, but they were both in Cheltenham, making final arrangements for their removal there, and I heard nothing about my house till nearly a fortnight after I had taken it. The work was being pushed on rapidly, but I had been so extremely busy professionally that I had only been down at number 19 twice, and I had been much tickled to see what an object of interest I was to all the neighbours, who eyed me from their windows with great curiosity.

The Prices returned in the evening, and at dinner I said to Mrs. Price, "I have got a house, and hope to be able to move in next week."

"I am awfully glad to hear that you are suited at last," she replied cordially, "where is it?"

"19, Great Hanover street," I answered.

There was a pause, and a smash, a glass that she held in her hand fell to the ground.

"Oh, Doctor, *not* that red brick corner house?" she said, "not the one with the corner garden?"

"Yes, that's the one," I laughed rather impatiently, "what is the matter with it, is it haunted?"

"*Yes*," she answered, "don't take it. I can't tell you how, or why it is haunted, but it is. Two people only have lived in it during the last 10 years, and one was found dead on the morning of the 22nd December, and the other, four years ago, on the same date, was found raving mad, and died a fortnight after without recovering his reason once, to say what he had seen or heard, in that fearful house."

I burst out laughing, and my merriment only ceased when I saw how thoroughly offended my hostess looked. "I beg your pardon," I said contritely, "but I really cannot help feeling amused. Imagine anyone in this prosaic materialistic age believing in ghosts. It is *too* funny. Why, I shall perfectly revel in Number 19. I have been pining all my life to live in a haunted house, to see a white-robed female carrying her head under her arm, and so on."

Mrs. Price looked offended, her husband changed the conversation, and the subject dropped, but directly after she left the room he said to me quite gravely, "Look here, Forsyth, don't live in that house, sneer at it as much as you please, but there is something uncanny about it. My wife mentioned two cases, but there are *five* authenticated cases of people who have resided at Number 19, and they have either been found dead or raving mad. No one knows what they have seen or heard, but the fact remains that strong, robust men of admirable physique have had their hair whitened and their reason destroyed with some unknown horror, and I beg of you not to rush into this mysterious danger."

The doctor's warning had no effect on me. I was an out and out sceptic, and the idea of a haunted house implicitly believed in, in this nineteenth century of ours filled me with delight.

The next morning, I went down to see Hunt. "So No. 19 is haunted," I remarked.

He turned ghastly. "Well yes, Doctor," he replied, recovering himself with an effort, "it has that reputation, and it has given us a lot of trouble. You know what it is, 'Give a dog a bad name, &c,' and as it has got about that the place is haunted folks are chary of taking it."

"Is it true," I asked, "that everyone who has lived there has either died or gone mad?"

He hesitated and fidgeted so, that I was quite convinced that Price's story was correct, but rash fool that I was nothing would warn me.

"To tell the truth, Doctor," said Hunt, in a burst of confidence, "the house *has* got a bad reputation. It was a splendid property till about twenty years ago. A doctor occupied it then. He was a foreigner—Doctor Caravini by name—and he had a very lovely young wife who disappeared mysteriously. It was believed that she had eloped, but anyhow she disappeared just before Christmas. Her husband, always a grave and reserved man, said nothing, and offered no explanation, and the following December he was found dead. I was only a young fellow at the time and I disliked the man most cordially for some unknown reason, but I shall never forget the awful expression of horror there was on his face when I saw him dead."

"What day in December did he die?" I asked curiously.

"*He was found dead on the morning of the 22nd of December*, and since then no one has passed a Christmas in the house," was the answer.

For a moment my heart beat faster, and I was stirred by a feeling of dread, then my common sense got the mastery of the idle superstition, and I said, "Well, I intend taking up my abode at Number 19, and shall certainly give any ghosts who feel inclined to play hanky-panky tricks with me a warm welcome."

"I can assure you, Doctor," cried the little house agent, seriously, "that if you show the people that these stories are mere nonsense you will be doing a public service."

After I left Hunt and went on my professional round I found that I was looked upon as quite a hero, and a very imprudent one, too. At nearly every house I was asked if it were true that I had taken Number 19, Great Hanover street, and when I replied in the affirmative I had a repetition of the solemn warning given me by the Prices. It amused me intensely. How the house was haunted, whether by sounds or spectres none could tell me. All they did was to shake their heads and repeat the stories of the deaths that had taken place there. I ventured to remark that it might only be a coincidence people dying there on the one date, but my remark was treated with derisive sniffs.

The time passed quickly, the house was finished, and as no expense had been spared over it, it looked splendid. So bright and cheerful, the sun gaily streamed into all the rooms, birds sang in the garden; in short, as I surveyed the place I thought what an idiot I should have been to have let any superstitious nonsense stand in my way of renting such a suitable residence. Anne had arrived with all my goods and chattels. The only thing that annoyed me was that not a Slominster girl would accept service in the house. It was an easy place. I offered high wages, but nothing would induce a local girl to come. They all said the same thing, "I'd come in the daytime, but I wouldn't sleep in Number 19 for wealth untold."

Fortunately for me Anne was an eminently practical woman. I had told her of the reputation that the house had, and she laughed with me at the idea of some people believing in such rubbish, so when she found that Slominster servants would not come she wrote to two of her cousins who wanted situations, and engaged them, and when they came they were as much amused as she and I were at the idea of ghosts.

Soon the house was put to rights, and it was the admiration of all my friends who called to see me. The plate-glass windows were veiled with the daintiest of lace curtains, flowers were scattered about. The street door, which stood hospitably open, showed a wide tesselated marble hall, littered with skin rugs and furnished in carved oak. Altogether it needed but one thing only—and that was a lady to preside over it and share it with me. My patients used the side door in the garden, and a red lamp was conspicuously placed over the gate, with the word "Surgery" on it.

As time passed on, I was more and more charmed with the house. The most timid person could not have detected even a suspicious sound. The wind never howled or moaned in the chimneys in an objectionable manner; doors never opened ghostily. In short, it was as quiet and as well regulated as a house could possibly be.

My practice was also growing apace. I had been fortunate

enough to perform a couple of very intricate operations successfully, and it had got my name well up with the local medical men.
My consulting hours at home were from 9 to 10 in the morning,
2 to 3 in the afternoon, and 6.30 to 8.30 in the evening. During the
latter two hours I was generally kept very busy. Sometimes I used
to go out for a stroll after 8.30, but if I were tired I stayed in my
consulting-room, and had a quiet rest and read.

I liked this room very much. It was large, had a southerly
aspect, and the outlook in the garden, was exceedingly pleasant.
My lady friends declared that it was the snuggest as well as the
best furnished room in the house. It had an oak suite uphol-
stered in crimson leather, and I had as well several very large
and delightfully cosy easy chairs scattered about. Heavy velvet
curtains draped the door, and successfully shut out all draughts;
one side of the wall was lined with book shelves, filled with the
works of my favourite authors, as well as the various scientific
books needed in my profession. In the alcoves by the handsome
black marble fireplace were carved oak cabinets, in which I blush
to confess was a small but choice collection of wines, spirits, and
cigars, comforts very dear to the heart of man. The long bay
window looked, as I have said before, into the garden, and altogether it was a most comfortable room.

Things went on very happily and smoothly, and I constantly
congratulated myself on my wisdom in not allowing superstition to have any influence over me. The winter of 1884 was an
unusually severe one in Slominster, and I was kept exceedingly
busy, so much so, that I had to decline all invitations for social
enjoyments, and was seriously thinking of the advisability of
taking a partner.

It wanted but a few days to Christmas. A patient of mine was
dangerously ill, and I went to see her at night about 10 o'clock.
When I returned home I let myself in with my latch key, for it
was one of the strict domestic rules that was rigidly adhered to,
that the servants, including Anne, went to bed punctually at 10. I
strolled into the consulting room, kicked off my boots, lit a cigar,
and sat down to have a good long read and rest, for I rarely if
ever retire till the small hours of morning. Nip, my fox-terrier,
a pure-bred dog, and my constant and most faithful companion

lay at my feet. I suppose that I must have dozed off, for suddenly I was awakened by the book dropping from my hand, and at that moment came a howl of terror from the dog. "Nip, old boy," I said, "it's all right," but to my astonishment I saw that he was standing upright, his hair positively bristling with fear, his ears thrown back, and every now and again he emitted the most blood curdling howls.

I looked round, there was absolutely nothing to see to account for the dog's terror. I went to my desk, took a revolver from the drawer, and called Nip to follow me, but he could only stand shaking an abject object of fear. I picked him up in my arms, and went into the passage. There his howls were fearful, and his eyes seemed starting out of their sockets, but still there was nothing to see. When I got to the front portion of the house he was quiet. I looked into all the rooms; everything was in its normal state, so I calmly went to bed, taking Nip up with me as usual. As I turned in, I looked at my watch—nearly half-past one.

I slept splendidly, and came down to breakfast with a flourishing appetite. Just as I was finishing my bacon, Anne came in.

"Good morning, sir," she said; "how are you?"

"All right, thanks," I answered.

"How is your patient?" she asked.

I stared at Anne curiously, faithful servant that she was, she had never hitherto displayed any such interest in my patients.

"Out of danger," I replied, "and I hope will pull through all right, now."

"It must have been a frightful case," she went on.

"Um, well, acute pluero-pneumonia is always rather dangerous," I answered, impatiently.

"Pluero-pneumonia," echoed the woman. "I don't mean that. I mean the fearful accident that was brought in last night. I wish, Mr. Alan, you had rung me up. I might have been of some assistance."

"Accident!" I repeated blankly, "what accident?"

"Last night, sir," she answered.

"There was no accident that *I* know of last night," I declared emphatically, "and I was in the consulting-room till past one."

"No accident," gasped Anne, and I saw that she was ghastly

white, and was trembling so that she had to hold on to the table for support. "Sir, there *must* have been, for both the surgery passage and consulting-room were *swimming with blood* this morning."

"Nonsense," I cried, "you have had a nightmare."

"I tell you, sir, it is a fact," she said. "When Jane went to clean the side door step this morning she came back saying that there must have been a bad accident last night, for the place was covered with blood. She had turned so faint that I went myself, and from the door right along the passage into the consulting-room, there it was, oh! a horrible, horrible sight."

"Is it all cleaned up, yet?" I asked.

"Not quite," answered Anne.

I left my breakfast, and as I strode along I nearly fell over Jane, who on her knees was busily engaged in wiping up *blood*. Yes, I saw it myself; from the garden door a horrible red rivulet ran, and here and there the wall was splashed as if someone had wantonly dabbled in and thrown up the liquid. Sick and dizzy I went into the consulting-room. There was a scarlet trail right along, and just by the fireplace there was a large hideous pool of blood soaking into the carpet, and leaving ghastly stains around.

I am not ashamed to confess that my brain reeled; the mysterious horror overcame me, and for a moment I thought that I was going to disgrace myself by fainting, then common sense asserted itself and I recovered.

"Someone has been playing a scandalous practical joke here," I said sternly, "and you may be sure that I shall spare no expense to bring the perpetrator to justice."

The servants looked but half convinced, and I even heard Anne mutter something about "a haunted house."

Although I affected to treat the matter lightly, yet I was sorely perplexed. I was quite convinced that it was a practical joke, but I was puzzled as to how the perpetrator or perpetrators could have got in to the house, then where did they get the blood from, and how silent they must have been? Suddenly I remembered Nip's terror, and a cold thrill went through me. Altogether I was not surprised when my patients told me how very ill I looked. Mind I had not the slightest belief in any supernatural agency, no thoughts of ghosts oppressed me, but I felt uncomfortable, as I could advance no reasonable theory to account for those ghastly marks.

When I got home for luncheon everything was as neat and trim as usual, excepting that my servants looked ill, and that a large skin rug had been placed over the stains on the carpet in the consulting-room. The marks from the wall had also been washed away, but I felt strangely upset and irritable, and my annoyance was culminated when I was told that Nip was dead. I had left him in my bedroom, and when the girls had gone in they had found the poor beast dead.

I was so thoroughly dispirited that when a friend of mine wired to me, and asked me to dine with him that evening, I gladly accepted the invitation as a means of ridding myself from my unpleasant thoughts.

It was a lovely night, clear, cold, and frosty. The moon was lighting up the star-spangled blue sky, the air was deliciously bracing and exhilarating, and as I walked along all my worries seemed to disappear. I spent a most enjoyable evening, and I wish you to bear in mind that the conversation never once touched upon the supernatural. I am an extremely abstemious man, and I drank only one glass of claret, and two glasses of champagne. You will soon understand why I am giving you these apparently unimportant details.

About half-past eleven, I said good-bye, and as I slipped into my fur-lined coat, my friend said laughingly, "What a big fellow you are, Forsyth." I glanced idly into the mirror, and thought how well I looked. The gas shone on my diamond studs, and my curly hair was as dark brown as it could possibly be, without being actually black; the next time I saw my reflection in a glass, it was the colour it is now, grey, bleached with horror!

I walked home, whistling blithely, and just as I neared my house I took out my bunch of keys preparatory to letting myself in through the surgery door. How bitterly cold it was. I had a feeling of pity for any unfortunate tramp that might be out; the wind had risen, and its icy blast penetrated even through my thick coat. When I got to the garden gate, judge of my astonishment when I saw crouching by the wall the figure of a woman. She rose when she heard my footsteps. I noticed that she wore a long black cloak, and a black hood covered her head.

She advanced to meet me, and the grace of her movements struck me with admiration.

"For the love of God," she said, in a low melodious voice, "will you help me?"

I put my hand in my pocket mechanically and drew out half-a-crown, which I handed to her.

She looked at it idly. "I don't want money," she said sadly, "it is of no use to me. I want shelter, for I am *so* cold."

"What do you require?" I queried impatiently. "I will give you another half-crown, and for five shillings you can get a bed anywhere."

She put out her hands, and laid them on my arm. How small and white they were. What an exquisite shape, the pretty rosy filbert nails, the slender tapering fingers, on which blazed some costly diamond rings. At their touch a thrill went through me. "I am *so* cold," she repeated, with infinite pathos. "Take me in with you and give me shelter."

"You must be mad to ask me such a thing," I said angrily; "go to an hotel."

"They will be all shut," she replied, "and I am *so* cold that I shall die." As she spoke the moon came out from a bank of cloud and lit up the unknown's face with a soft golden glory. Good heavens, what a face! Never could I have conceived anything earthly so lovely. Even now, waking or sleeping, I can see it before me. It was a purely oval face, with a delicate creamy complexion, absolutely colourless. The mouth was small and scarlet and the lips were tremulous and pouting like a child's. I felt a mad desire to kiss them into smiling content; the nose was perfect, but the eyes were the chief beauty. Large, liquid, violet eyes, shaded with long, black lashes—eyes that in their dreamy sensuousness were sufficient to make a man lose his soul, but for one glance of love from them. Rings of soft, yellow, curly hair escaped from the hood, and clustered over the low, white brow. I stood fascinated, and gazed upon this dream of female loveliness.

"Don't be vexed with me," she urged piteously, "but *he* has turned me out, turned me out to-night in this bitter cold, and I shall die if you will not give me shelter."

She came still nearer to me, her cloak touched me, I felt her warm fragrant breath on my cheek, her hands tightened on my arm, and I—well, I am only a man. The blood was coursing through my veins, and I was losing my head under the glamour of those wonderful eyes.

"Come in," I said hastily, "I will give you shelter for to-night. It would kill a wee frail thing like you to be exposed to the cold much longer."

She laughed gratefully, a low rippling laugh like the tinkle of bells. "You are good," she murmured.

She followed me up the path, I opened the door and as she came in I was vaguely struck by an impression that she knew her way about the house.

I took her into the consulting room, a bright fire was crackling in the grate, and she went to it at once. "I am *so* cold," she said again, and she held out her white hands to the blaze.

I turned up the gas, my brain was on fire; this was an adventure with a vengeance. But what would become of my reputation if it were to be known that a strange and lovely young woman had passed the night under my bachelor roof? As I looked at her, all my selfish doubts vanished. Laugh, sneer if you like, but I, Alan Forsyth, was madly in love, with a woman whose very name I did not know, and whose acquaintance I had made not a quarter of an hour back.

She had loosened her cloak, and stood in the bravery of her finery. She wore a gown of pale pink silk, made in a style that I had never seen before; the bodice was cut low in front, and showed a bosom perfectly modelled and as spotlessly white as marble; amongst the laces that fell and rose with every breath was a cluster of half-blown roses, and their faint sweet perfume seemed to madden me. They were fastened by a diamond brooch; the beautiful arms were bare to the shoulder, but diamond bracelets were clasped about them. Round the slender throat was a tight band of broad black watered ribbon, in the centre of which flashed a superb brooch of brilliants. This made the milky whiteness of the skin more vivid in contrast to the black. Her golden hair was piled up high on the queenly little head, and the coils were fastened by diamond pins.

How perfectly lovely she was. I rubbed my eyes to see if it were a dream, and if the vision would fade away; but no, she was still there, with the flames flickering on her marvellous beauty. Where had she come from? Who was she? I knew everyone in Slominster, by sight at least, and it was not likely that such a lovely creature could live in the town without being known; besides, her dress and jewels showed that she was wealthy.

"Are you warmer yet?" I asked smiling.

"No, I am *so* cold," she repeated wearily; "do you think I will *ever* be warm again."

I curbed the inclination to take the slender form in my arms, and warm it with the fervour of my embraces.

I put some brandy on the table, and mixed a little with water, which I handed to her. She took it with a grateful smile and sipped it, and I was relieved to see a tinge of pink come into the colourless cheeks.

"You must tell me who you are," I remarked gently, "so that I can communicate with your friends."

"My friends," she repeated vacantly; "I have no friends, *he* will not allow me to have any, *he* is so jealous, and to night *he* turned me out, out in the snow and rain, although *he* knows how I dread the cold."

"It was not snowing or raining to-night," I said, "but who is *he* that treats you so cruelly?"

"*My husband*, of course," she answered; "but don't let us talk of him, for I hate him, and oh! I am so afraid of him. Whenever his eyes are upon me I turn cold with dread, and when he attempts to kiss me I all but faint; and then he says that I have a lover, and that he will murder me, and I am so unhappy."

How can I convey any idea of the inexpressible mournfulness of her tone, of the piteous look in her eyes. Hazardous as her conduct was, I felt convinced of her goodness and purity, for who could doubt it after once looking into the exquisite, innocent face.

"Do not think of him," I said, "but rest here and get warm, and in the morning we will talk matters over, and if you will allow me I will assist you all in my power."

"How good you are to me," she murmured. "Yes; let us be happy to-night, for who knows where I shall be in the morning."

I drew one of the easy chairs close to the fire for her, and I bade her be seated. She nestled in its depths with a sigh of content. I had flung off my coat, and, kneeling on the rug, was endeavouring to rub some warmth into her small numbed hands. She bent forward to me and patted my face.

"How handsome you are," she said, "and how nice you look in evening dress."

I kissed her fingers passionately, but their dead coldness went to my heart with a chill.

"I am *so* cold," she again repeated. She stretched out her tiny feet, and as I saw the fine black silk stockings, and the thin kid shoes with their dainty bows and diamond buckle, I mentally execrated the man who had turned a woman out of doors clothed like this on such a night. I took off her shoes and rubbed her feet and made her swallow some more brandy. I added coals to the fire and wrapped my coat round her bare shoulders.

Every trivial event of that night is impressed on my memory, and will only be effaced with death. Once I asked her if she would like me to wake up the servants and let them take her to bed, but she refused with a gentle smile.

"Let me stay here," she entreated, "it is warm, and you know I am *so* cold."

She walked up and down the room, and once drew aside the curtains and blind from the window and looked out into the garden.

"I *always* hated that garden," she said.

"Why," cried I, astonished; "do you know it, then?"

She smiled inscrutably, and looked at me. She stretched out her arms, and I forgot everything, forgot that she was married, that being under my roof she should have been sacred. I say I forgot everything, but before you condemn me think of my temptation. I was only young, the blood of youth leaped through my veins, she held out her hands to me, and I rushed to her. I caught her in my arms, and I nearly crushed her slender form in the fervour of my embrace. I clasped her tightly to my throbbing, passionate heart, and rained hot kisses on her sweet face. I pressed my lips to hers, and tried to thaw their icy chill by the warmth of mine. I murmured endearing words to her, and swore that come what might she should never leave me. In those few blissful moments I felt the very ecstasy of love, my very soul went out of me, I was dizzy and blinded with emotion. I felt the supple form grow heavy in my arms, and she said faintly, "Let me rest."

I lifted her into the chair, and I was alarmed to see how ill she looked; her eyes were half closed, her whole figure dejected and helpless. "Forgive me, darling," I said, remorsefully, "I forgot myself."

She opened her eyes wearily. "I am *so* cold," she said, "and so faint; undo this band for the love of heaven, for I choke and die."

She half rose, with her hand to her throat, and then sank nervelessly back into the easy chair. I bent over her, and took the brooch from the band of black watered ribbon about her throat, and, great God, how can I write it, how can I steady my hand so as to pen the words; as I undid the ribbon, so did that *lovely head drop off*.

Oh, the horror of it, there where but one moment before was a beautiful breathing woman, was now a headless trunk, and at my feet was the head, hideous and bloody, the eyes open and glassy, and with an awful expression of terror in their depths, the teeth biting through the lips with a dumb agony. I looked round madly, *everywhere was blood*; the rug was soaked with it, it fell from the easy chair to the ground with a hollow splash, a trail of it went to the door, the curtains where *her* hands had touched were stained scarlet. I looked down again at the head. I was frozen with horror, it was there, but oh, terrible sight, no longer the head of a young and beautiful woman, but a hideous skull, one mass of vile corruption.

This was too much for me. I gave one yell of terror that rung through the quiet house, and just then my eye caught sight of the calendar. It was *the 21st of December*. I tried to move but the smell of blood sickened me. With a moan I fell to the ground senseless.

When again I recovered my senses it was June. For six months I had been raving mad. On the morning of the 22nd of December Anne had found me lying on the floor of the consulting room, the apartment looking precisely the same as usual, and for weeks and months I was insane, but, thanks to clever doctors, good nursing, and a strong constitution, I pulled round. Directly I was strong enough I went abroad, to endeavour to efface the memory of that awful night, but although some of the terror has gone I shall never forget it, and never shall I marry while the sight of that lovely face is still in my memory.

I can give no explanation of the mysterious occurrence, excepting that some six months after I had returned to my professional duties from my illness I attended an old lady, who had known Doctor and Mrs. Caravini, who had once lived at No. 19. I asked what she was like, and the answer was—*"A very beautiful girl, with an oval face and golden hair, and the most lovely violet eyes I ever saw. He was madly jealous of her, and, I believe, treated her very badly."*

I dare not ask anything more, but since then I have often wondered whether the doctor had murdered his fair young wife and buried her remains in the garden. This, however, is one of the mysteries that will never be revealed till the great day of judgment shall come, when the hidden secrets of all hearts shall be disclosed.

Needless to say I removed from the house without waiting for my three years' tenancy to expire, for I felt that another such night would kill me. As I drove past the other day I saw that the "to let" card was still up at 19, Great Hanover street.

G. B. Burgin

SIR HUGO'S PRAYER

For invisible to thee,
Spirits twain have crossed with me.
—UHLAND

I

"THERE'S NO REAL PLEASURE IN BEING A GHOST NOWADAYS, or nights either," grumbled the shadowy presentment of Sir Hugo Follett, as he clanked along the battlements of Dulverton Castle, his imperceptible sword slanting ruthlessly through Lady Follett's invisible legs.

Lady Follett apparently resented being amputated at her visionary knees in this unceremonious way. "Fie, Sir Hugo," she said, testily, "Marry, come up. Wilt thou remember that, although only a ghost, I can still feel."

Sir Hugo halted on the battlements with a shiver; for the night was cold and he lacked flesh wherewith to clothe his bones. "The truth is, my dear," he said irresolutely, "it is no use talking in this stilted and archaic fashion any longer. We must adapt ourselves to the times, and model our language accordingly. Although we have been the terror of this place for centuries, no one cares a button for us now. Only one consolation is that we are mentioned with pride in the advertisement when Follett wants to let the place for the season. I flatter myself, however, that we have always performed our purgatorial duties with punctuality and despatch."

"Quite so. Quite so."

"Well, what happens?"

"Ah, ah, nothing happens," sighed Lady Follett. "In fact, Hugo, we are becoming exceedingly dull; there's no doubt whatever about that."

"And the latest outrage—what d'you think's the latest outrage we have to put up with?" bitterly demanded Sir Hugo.

"There are so many," deplored his shadowy spouse, laying a ghostly mitten upon his phantom arm.

"Well the one consolation we had in our midnight promenade was that we could warm ourselves at the beacon cresset on the battlements here. Now, that economical old hunks, Follett, has cut off the beacon coals and substituted something which he calls electric light! It doesn't give any warmth at all and one needs warmth after dozing all day in the family vault. Shameful lack of consideration for us, I call it. I've a good mind to rub you all over with corpse-lights and plant you at the top of Follett's staircase, with blue snakes waggling about in your eye-sockets. That would give him a paralytic seizure if anything could."

Lady Follett, who had been the handsomest woman of her day, bitterly resented Sir Hugo's proposed additions to her toilette. "You never think of appearances," she said crossly. "The indelicacy of facing people in one's bones doesn't seem to have occurred to you. Besides, one would look so meagre."

"There would be quite enough of you to give him a scare," chuckled Sir Hugo. "It's about time you got over the fad of appearing in family costume only. When I look at Follett's guests, you seem quite out of fashion."

"At least I hide my bones; most of his guests don't," tartly retorted the lady. "They all wear as little as possible."

"It's their love of naked truth," airily suggested Sir Hugo.

"Naked fiddlesticks!" Lady Follett's mood suddenly changed; she began to weep. "And yet they are alive! Oh, to be alive again, to feel the warmth of the dear sun, to rise at cock-crow instead of going to bed at it in a badly ventilated vault! Oh, for the touch of a warm living hand, to feel baby lips upon my own, to live again upon the sweet earth." And ghostly tears fell from her sightless eyes.

"I—I—wouldn't if I were you," gruffly suggested Sir Hugo. "We had a good time of it when we were alive, and ruffled it with the best. Some day we'll get out of this purgatorial stage and give old Follett a turn, the unconscionable dog. It's ridiculous your wanting to be alive again. You'd have to go to school and learn to read and write."

"I don't think I should mind that much. If it came to sampler work I flat——"

Sir Hugo laid a phantom hand upon a phantom arm. "My dear, from what I gather when the young people come up here to flirt o'nights your sampler making would be as much out of date as my chain armour. One would be consigned to the lumber room, the other sold for scrap iron: and yet, with a little polishing, we should still be a fairly presentable couple." He ruffled along with a gallant air in the moonlight. "Gad, but I'd pledge you in a bumper of sack had I the wherewithal to hold it," he said mournfully. "Why so important a thing as a stomach should be left out of a ghost's anatomy I know not. Hush, here's someone coming."

Lady Follett adjusted her imaginary headgear. "It is the damsel they call Clare," she said, in a frigid whisper. "The minx has come up here to flirt."

Sir Hugo was interested. "She's devilish pret——"

"Hugo!"

"I beg your pardon."

"Oh, it's nothing." But Lady Follett's icy tone sent a shiver down Sir Hugo's spinal cord.

"I didn't say anything. My teeth merely chattered."

"Even a ghost has feelings," acidly declared Lady Follett. "To hear you admire mere flesh and blood, like that red and white forward chit of a child, is more than I can endure."

"A mistake I assure you. Take my arm. We will continue our promenade."

They strolled leisurely along the broad level walk, Sir Hugo endeavouring to restrain his curiosity as to what Clare Follett was doing up there in the moonlight. "Let us get up behind this chimney-stack and see what's going on," he suggested. "She appears to be dragging a kind of double wheel with her."

"She also appears to be dragging a young man after the wheel," suggested Lady Follett, cautiously peeping from behind the sheltering chimney-stack, and quite forgetting that she was invisible until the midnight hour chimed from the castle tower.

"There's another man with more wheels," said Sir Hugo. "They surely can't be going to start a carriage factory up here!"

"The things are called bicycles," said Lady Follett.

"What's a bicycle?" inquired Sir Hugo, resenting his wife's superior knowledge. "Sh-sh! Here they come."

II

Clare Follett was very pretty indeed; but what was she doing at the top of Dulverton Castle half-an-hour before midnight on Christmas Eve, accompanied by two young men, whose ill-concealed hatred of each other appeared to afford her a good deal of amusement. That this amusement was not wholly untinctured by anxiety was evident to Sir Hugo; for that ancient warrior, keenly versed in all matters pertaining to the sex, noticed that a tear glistened on her long lashes. At first, it seemed to him that this might be the result of the cold air; but when he saw Clare Follett furtively wipe away a tear from her other eye, and look appealingly round, his hand flew to his sword. He regretted bitterly that Lady Follett was there to check his chivalrous impulses, and that he could only look on inertly at this strange spectacle.

Miss Follett wore a very short cloth skirt and dainty little cap, whilst the young men were clad in knickerbockers. The lights of their bicycles twinkled like glow-worms, and their eyes glared malevolently at one another. As far as Sir Hugo could judge, the dark fellow looked like a hero; the fair man had a shifty expression, with cold, thin lips. His legs were enormous, his body thin and tough as an alligator's. He swung his arms to and fro in a leisurely manner as if utterly unconcerned. The other young man, whose legs were not nearly as big, appeared rather more anxious. He bit at his long moustache and swore softly under his breath in a way which gladdened the heart of that old reprobate, Sir Hugo. It was a long time since he had heard anyone swear.

"There's something up, my dear," Sir Hugo remarked to Lady Follett. "It looks to me as if these fellows are in love with the girl, and that there's going to be a row over it. I mean—ahem—that they will settle their differences with the sword."

"Oh, no, they won't," Lady Follett declared: "not they. No one knows how to use a sword nowadays. I rather like that fair young fellow."

"My dear! He looks like the biggest villain unhung. My sympathies are all with the dark man. He has such a frank, honest expression. In fact, he's rather like what I was at his age."

Lady Follett gave a little groan, which reached the group of bicyclists and made them stir uneasily. She was thinking of the time when young men had made their court to her. Of a verity it was dull work being a ghost. Oh, the dear earth and the joy of it!

"Beastly owls about somewhere," said the fair man. "Might-eh-get 'em to umpire doncherknow, Miss Follett, and we'd catch 'em some beastly mice for their Christmas dinner."

The girl looked at him fixedly, and not with favour. "I was made to consent to such a strange scheme," she said hesitatingly. "What made you propose it, Mr. Fairfax?"

The fair man grinned in a way which showed his white teeth right up to the gum.

"Well, you see, Miss Follett, Pennell is such a scorcher and he thinks he can do everything, so I lured him on to make the proposal. Now that you've agreed to it, I'll have him on toast."

"Cannibal!" said Sir Hugo. "In my day we killed a rival; we didn't eat him on toast."

"Hush-h! You misunderstand. Listen."

"Oh, shut up, Fairfax," said the dark man, who was kneeling by the side of his bicycle and pumping at the tire. "You haven't won yet."

"Not yet," said Fairfax, cheerfully. "Oh no, not yet. This little idea occurred to me several days ago, and I've been training hard every since. I'm fit to run for my life."

"Shouldn't think it's the first time either," said the other, wilfully misunderstanding him. "I'll ask some of the men of your regiment next time I'm in town."

Miss Follett gave an impetuous little stamp of her foot. "I've a great mind to go downstairs and end this nonsense at once."

"I don't think I would do it if I were you," suggested Fairfax, with a nasty sneer. "People would say you were afraid."

"Afraid of what?"

"Afraid of my winning."

"You haven't won yet," said Pennell, blowing his numbed fingers. "Now, Miss Follett, here's your bike all ready. You're to have thirty yards start round the battlements, and whoever catches you first is to win you for life."

Miss Follett looked anxiously at his legs and drew him aside.

"Do you feel up to it?" she asked. "He's evidently been training. You know how late you sat up with papa last night; that must have told on you."

"I wanted to win his heart, although I despaired about yours," said Pennell hastily. "Miss Follett—Clare—the brute can't see us—he's messing about with his lamp. Give me one kiss and I'll ride his head off or perish in the attempt."

"The little dear!" said Sir Hugo in rapture. "She's the love—"

"What's that?" acidly demanded Lady Follett.

"My dear, this girl's got your blood in her veins, and I'm da—— I mean may I materialise if I don't help her to marry the dark young fellow. You may remember," said the poor chivalrous old ghost, "I was dark once, my lady; and you were just like this girl, only lovelier, and with a statelier way. Gadzooks, I no more dared to kiss you—"

"Don't, don't, Hugo." wailed the other poor ghost. "What can we do to help her?"

III

"Are you ready?" asked Fairfax, with his customary sneer. "It's a mere matter of form, of course, unless Pennell would like to resign at——"

"Shut up," said Pennell. "Now, Miss Follett, let me hold your bike. Be careful of the turn where the wall has crumbled a bit. Good-bye."

"Let us say *au revoir*. Can you forgive me for being so utterly foolish?"

"Of course I can. If the beast should win, I'll never forget you."

"Don't let us be all night about a mere trifle of this kind," said Fairfax, with ironic emphasis.

"Now by the bones of my patron, St. Wencelaus," growled Sir Hugo, "I'll spit that churl through the midriff."

"It's no good," said Lady Follett, beginning to weep ghostly tears as big as beans. "If you do stick your sword in him it will only come out on the other side."

"They're off," said Sir Hugo, gnashing his fleshless gums together. "That girl will be over the battlements if she isn't careful."

"She sits on those little wheels and glides along like a bird," said Lady Follett. "Methinks a palfrey were more seemly."

"I'd like to see anyone get a horse up the turret stairs," snorted Sir Hugo. "Let us go to the gap and see how they're getting on. The girl daren't look round; she doesn't know which is the nearer."

Lady Follett began to breathe hoarsely as the wind rushed through her spectral ribs.

"Don't," said Sir Hugo, somewhat roughly. "Have you no sense of decorum?"

"I—I—ca-can't hel-ll-p it," sobbed Lady Follett. "That long-legged fair man is creeping in advance of the other. Look at his teeth in the moonlight."

"I don't want to look at his teeth," growled Sir Hugo; "I want to smash his skull in with a battle-axe."

"Hugo," said Lady Follett suddenly, as Miss Follett flew round, Fairfax fifteen yards behind her, "I can't help it. I can't help it. At the risk of being thought unladylike, I—I'm going to interfere."

"What's the good of interfering? We can't do anything. That dark fellow's getting pumped. No wonder, if he sat up half last night listening to old Follett's stories. It would put anyone at a disadvantage. It isn't fair, I say. Silly young ass! He'll lose the girl! Bravo! Bravo! He's spurting like one—I mean he's gaining a little."

Lady Follett groaned. "Oh, no, he's falling behind again. The girl is tired. Hugo, Hugo, at the risk of incurring your displeasure I—I'm going to interfere."

She waited until Fairfax rushed by, sprang lightly on the step of the bicycle, and began to blow with chilly emphasis right down his spine.

A deadly chill shot through Fairfax. He faltered, then continued to hold the bar of his bicycle with one hand, and turned up his coat-collar.

Lady Follett dropped off with a groan. "I've disgraced myself by catching hold of a strange man," she whispered. "And he's going faster than ever."

"Now it's my turn," growled Sir Hugo. "Another five seconds, and we shall be too late. Holy St. Wencelaus, I've always behaved myself as a ghost since you sent me to purgatory to expiate my sins. I know I was a tolerably bad lot when alive; but I've never done anything since. Think of the draughty, mouldy time I've had all these years! Let me materialise just for ten seconds. That's all I ask. Ten seconds."

Holy St. Wencelaus, the patron saint of all true lovers, was moved to pity by Sir Hugo's prayer. "So be it," a voice said softly, as Pennell plodded by, with aching calves and a desperate look in his dark eyes. "So be it; but it means an extra hundred years of this."

The knight groaned. "Oh, very well. I'm not going to see her marry that beast," he said. "My dear, do you consent? Another hundred years? Think of the misery of it, the dull, damp, mouldy misery of it! Quick, or I shall be too late. The girl's nearly pumped."

"I consent," said Lady Follett. "Rather than that dear girl should be sacrificed to this Fairfax man I'd—I'd marry him myself."

Sir Hugo pressed her fleshless hand. "Move on a bit, my dear, and give me room," he said tenderly.

Miss Follett dashed by, with a strained anxious look in her eyes. The victorious Fairfax was within ten yards of her, Pennell a long way behind.

Suddenly a giant grisly form, clad in a rusty armour, and holding a long two-handed sword, stepped from behind the chimney-stack as Miss Follett dashed round, put the two-handed sword between the wheels of Fairfax's bicycle, and heaved it over the battlements. Then it stepped back, and the victorious Pennell, panting up behind, laid his hand upon Clare Follett's shoulder.

An oath sounded a few feet below from the gnarled and clustering ivy which spread over the scanty tree tops. Then a head gradually appeared above the battlement, and Fairfax climbed up, grinning with rage. "You hired that brute to upset me," he shouted at Pennell. "I'll be even with you some day."

"What brute?" asked Pennell. "There's no one here."

"I distinctly saw a tall man in armour come from behind that chimney-stack and upset me with his infernal sword."

They rushed to the chimney-stack, but there was no one there.

Clare gave a little shriek of delight. "It must have been dear Sir Hugo's ghost. The battlements belong to him. Dear, dear Sir Hugo!"

Sir Hugo offered his arm to Lady Follett, and strutted round the battlements with a smile upon his grim lips. She said, "Dear Sir Hugo."

"Then it must have been his hag of a wife who blew down my throat and paralysed me," said Fairfax, with a scowl.

"If you must insult the memory of that lady, I'll throw you right over the battlements," said Pennell hotly. "So beautiful a woman as she was when alive must be exquisite, even as a ghost. Heaven rest the souls of both of them and give them peace."

"Hugo! Hugo! Where are you? I—I'm going," cried Lady Follett.

"I am with you," said a tender voice in her ear. "Holy St. Wencelaus has heard our prayer."

Mrs. J. H. Riddell

WALNUT-TREE HOUSE

A Ghost Story

CHAPTER I

THE NEW OWNER

MANY YEARS AGO there stood at the corner of a street leading out of Upper Kennington-lane a great red brick mansion, which one very wet evening, in an autumn the leaves of which have been long dead and gone, looked more than ordinarily desolate and deserted.

There was not a sign of life about it. For seven years no one had been found to live in it; for seven years it had remained empty, while its owner wore out existence in fits of moody dejection or of wild frenzy in the madhouse close at hand; and now that owner was dead and buried and forgotten, and the new owner was returning to take possession. This new owner had written to his lawyers, or rather he had written to the lawyers of his late relative, begging them to request the person in charge of the house to have rooms prepared for his arrival; and, when the train drew into the station, he was met by one of Messrs. Timpson and Co.'s clerks, who, picking out Mr. Stainton, delivered to that gentleman a letter from the firm, and said he would wait to hear if there were any message in reply.

Mr. Stainton read the letter—looked at the blank flyleaf—and then, turning back to the first words, read what his solicitors had to say all through once again.

"Humph," said the new owner, after he had finished. "I'll go and take a look at the place, anyhow. Is it far from here, do you know?" he asked, turning to the young man from Timpson's.

"No, Sir; not very far."

"Can you spare time to go over there with me?" inquired Mr. Stainton.

The young man believed that he could, adding, "If you want to go into the house we had better call for the key. It is at an estate agent's in the Westminster Bridge-road."

"I cannot say I have any great passion for hotels," remarked the new owner, as he took his seat in the cab.

"Indeed, Sir."

"No; either they don't suit me, or I don't suit them. I have led a wild sort of life; not much civilisation in the bush, or at the gold-fields, I can tell you. Then, I have not been well, and I can't stand noise and the trampling of feet. I had enough of that on board ship; and I used to lie awake at nights and think how pleasant it would be to have a big house all to myself, to do as I liked in."

"Yes, Sir," agreed the clerk.

"You see, I have been accustomed to roughing it, and I can get along very well for a night without servants."

"No doubt, Sir."

"I suppose the house is in substantial repair—roof tight, and all that sort of thing?"

"I can't say, I am sure, Sir."

"Well, if there is a dry corner where I can spread a rug, I shall sleep there to-night."

The clerk coughed. He looked out of the window, and then he looked at Messrs. Timpson's client.

"I do not think——" he began apologetically, and then stopped.

"You don't think what?" asked the other.

"You'll excuse me, Sir, but I don't think—I really do not think, if I were you, I'd stay in that house to-night."

"Why not?"

"Well, it has not been slept in for nearly seven years, and it must be blue mouldy with damp; and if you have been ill, that is all the more reason you should not run such a risk. And besides——"

"Besides——" suggested Mr. Stainton; "Out with it! No doubt, that 'besides' holds the marrow of the argument."

"The house has stood empty for years, Sir, because—there is no use in making any secret of it—the place has a bad name."

"What sort of a bad name—unhealthy?"

"Oh, no!"

"Haunted?"

The clerk inclined his head. "You have hit it, Sir," he said.

"And that is the reason no one has lived there?"

"We have been quite unable to let the house on that account."

"The sooner it gets unhaunted, then, the better," retorted Mr. Stainton. "I shall certainly stop there to-night. You are not disposed to stay and keep me company, I suppose?"

With a little gesture of dismay the clerk drew back. Certainly, this was one of the most unconventional of clients. The young man from Timpson's did not at all know what to make of him.

"A rough sort of fellow," he said afterwards, when describing the new owner; "boorish; never mixed with good society, that sort of thing."

He did not in the least understand this rich man, who treated him as an equal, who objected to hotels, who did not mind taking up his abode in a house where not even a drunken charwoman could be induced to stop, and who calmly asked a stranger on whom he had never set eyes before—a clerk in the respectable office of Timpson and Co., a young fellow anxious to rise in the world, careful as to his associates, particular about the whiteness of his shirts and the set of his collar and the cut of his coats—to "rough" things with him in that dreadful old dungeon, where perhaps he might even be expected to light a fire.

Still, he did not wish to offend the new owner. Messrs. Timpson anticipated he would be a profitable client; and to that impartial firm the money of a boor would, he knew, seem as good as the money of a Count.

"I am very sorry," he stammered; "should only have felt too much honoured; but the fact is—previous engagement——"

Mr. Stainton laughed.

"I understand," he said. "Adventures are quite as much out of your line as ghosts. And now tell me about this apparition. Does the 'old man' walk?"

"Not that I ever heard of," answered the other.

"Is it, then, the miserable beggar who tried to do for himself?"

"It is not the late Mr. Stainton, I believe," said the young man, in a tone which mildly suggested that reference to a client of Timpson's as a "miserable beggar" might be considered bad taste.

"Then who on earth is it?" persisted Mr. Stainton.

"If you must know, Sir, it is a child—a child who has driven every tenant in succession out of the house."

The new owner burst into a hearty laugh—a laugh which gave serious offence to Timpson's clerk.

"That is too good a joke," said Mr. Stainton. "I do not know when I heard anything so delicious."

"It is a fact, whether it be delicious or not," retorted the young man, driven out of all his former propriety of voice and demeanour by the contemptuous ridicule this "digger" thought fit to cast on his story; "and I, for one, would not, after all I have heard about your house, pass a night in it—no, not if anybody offered me fifty pounds down."

"Make your mind easy, my friend," said the new owner, quietly. "I am not going to bid for your company. The child and I can manage, I'll be bound, to get on very comfortably by ourselves."

CHAPTER II

THE CHILD

It was later on in the same evening; Mr. Stainton had an hour previously taken possession of Walnut-Tree House, bidden Timpson's clerk good-evening, and, having ordered in wood and coals from the nearest greengrocer, he now stood by the front gate waiting the coming of the goods purchased.

As he waited, he looked up at the house, which in the uncertain light of the street lamps appeared gloomier and darker than had been the case even in the gathering twilight.

"It has an 'uncanny' look, certainly," he considered; "but once I can get a good fire up I shall be all right. Now, I wonder when those coals are coming!"

As he turned once again towards the road, he beheld on its

way the sack of fuel with which the nearest greengrocer said he thought he could—indeed, said he would—"oblige" him. A ton—half a ton—quarter of a ton, the greengrocer affirmed would be impossible until the next day; but a sack—yes—he would promise that. Bill should bring it round; and Bill was told to put his burden on the truck, and twelve bundles of wood, "and we'll make up the rest to-morrow," added Bill's master, with the air of one who has conferred a favour.

In the distance Mr. Stainton descried a very grimy Bill, and a very small boy, coming along with the truck leisurely, as though the load had been Herculean.

Through the rain he watched the pair advancing, and greeted Bill with a glad voice of welcome.

"So you've come at last; that's right. Better late than never. Bring them this way, I'll have this small lot shot in the kitchen for the night."

"Begging your pardon, Sir," answered Bill, "I don't think you will—that is to say, not by me. As I told our governor, I'll take 'em to the house as you've sold 'em to the house, but I won't set a foot inside it."

"Do you mean to say you are going to leave them out on the pavement," asked Mr. Stainton.

"Well, Sir, I don't mind taking them to the front door if it'll be a convenience."

"That will do. You are a brave lot of people in these parts I must say."

"As for that," retorted Bill, with sack on back and head bent forward, "I dare say we're as brave about here as where you come from."

"It is not impossible," retorted Mr. Stainton; "there are plenty of cowards over there too."

After he had shot his coals on the margin of the steps, Bill retreated from the door, which stood partly open, and when the boy who brought up the wood was again out with the truck, said, putting his knuckles to his eyebrows—

"Beg pardon, Sir, but I suppose you wouldn't give me a drop of beer. Very wet night, Sir."

"No, I would not," answered Mr. Stainton, very decidedly. "I shall have to shovel these coals into the house myself; and as for the night, it is as wet for me as it is for you."

Nevertheless, as Bill shuffled along the short drive—shuffling wearily—like a man who, having nearly finished one day's hard work, was looking forward to beginning another hard day in the morning, the new owner relented.

"Here," he said, picking out a sixpence to give him, "it isn't your fault, I suppose, that you believe in old women's tales."

"Thank you kindly, Sir," Bill answered; "I am sure I am extremely obliged; but if I was in your shoes I wouldn't stop in that house—you'll excuse me, Sir, meaning no offence—but I wouldn't; indeed I wouldn't."

"It seems to have got a good name, at any rate," thought Mr. Stainton, while retracing his steps to the banned tenement. "Let us see what effect a fire will have in routing the shadows."

He entered the house, and, striking a match, lighted some candles he had brought in with him from a neighbouring oil-shop.

After an inspection of the ground-floor rooms he decided to take up his quarters for the night in one which had evidently served as a library.

In the centre of the apartment there was the table covered with leather. Around the walls were bookcases. In one corner stood a bureau, where the man who for so many years had been dead even while living kept his letters and papers.

He ate his frugal supper, and then, pushing aside the table on which the remains of his repast were spread, began walking slowly up and down the room, thinking over the past and forming plans for the future. Buried in reflection, the fire began to die down without his noticing the fact; but a feeling of chilliness at length causing him instinctively to look towards the hearth, he threw wood into the grate, and, while the flames went blazing up the wide chimney, piled on coals as though he desired to set the house alight.

While he was so engaged there came a knock at the door of the room—a feeble, hesitating knock, which was repeated more than once before it attracted Mr. Stainton's attention.

When it did, being still busy with the fire, and forgetting he was alone in the house, he called out, "Come in."

Along the panels there stole a rustling sort of touch, as if some-one were feeling uncertainly for the handle—a curious noise, as of a weak hand fumbling about the door in the dark; then, in similar manner, the person seeking admittance tried to turn the lock.

"Come in, can't you?" repeated Mr. Stainton; but even as he spoke he remembered he was, or ought to be, the sole occupant of the mansion. He was not alarmed, he was too much accustomed to solitude and danger for that; but he rose from his stooping position and instinctively seized his revolver, which he had chanced, while unpacking some of his effects, to place on the top of the bureau.

"Come in, whoever you are," he cried; but seeing the door still remained closed, though the intruder was evidently making futile efforts to open it, he strode half way across the room, and then stopped amazed.

For suddenly the door opened, and there entered, shyly and timidly a little child—a child with the saddest face mortal ever beheld; a child with wistful eyes and long, ill-kept hair; a child poorly dressed, wasted and worn, and with the mournfullest expression on its countenance that face of child ever wore.

"What a hungry-looking little beggar," thought Mr. Stainton. "Well, young one, and what do you want here?" he added aloud.

The boy never answered, never took the slightest notice of his questioner, but simply walked slowly round the room, peering into all the corners, as if looking for something. Searching the embrasures of the windows, examining the recesses beside the fire-place, pausing on the hearth to glance under the library table, and finally, when the doorway was reached once more, turning round to survey the contents of the apartment with an eager and yet hopeless scrutiny.

"What is it you want, my boy?" asked Mr. Stainton, glancing as he spoke at the child's poor thin legs, and short, shabby frock, and shoes wellnigh worn out, and arms bare and lean and unbeautiful. "Is it anything I can get for you?"

Not a word—not a whisper: only for reply a glance of the wistful brown eyes.

"Where do you come from, and whom do you belong to?" persisted Mr. Stainton.

The child turned slowly away.

"Come, you shall not get off so easily as you seem to imagine," persisted the new owner, advancing towards his visitor. "You have no business to be here at all; and before you go you must tell me how you chance to be in this house, and what you expected to find in this room."

He was close to the doorway by this time, and the child stood on the threshold, with its back towards him. Mr. Stainton could see every detail of the boy's attire—his little plaid frock, the hooks which fastened it; the pinafore, soiled and crumpled, tied behind with strings broken and knotted; in one place the skirt had given from the bodice, and a piece of thin poor flannel showed that the child's under habiliments matched in shabbiness his exterior garments.

"Poor little chap," thought Mr. Stainton. "I wonder if he would like something to eat. Are you hungry, my lad?"

The child turned and looked at him earnestly, but answered never a word.

"I wonder if he is dumb," marvelled Mr. Stainton; and, seeing he was moving away, put out a hand to detain him. But the child eluded his touch, and flitted into the hall and up the wide staircase with swift noiseless feet.

Only waiting to snatch a candle from one of the sconces, Mr. Stainton pursued as fast as he could follow. Up the easy steps he ran at the top of his speed; but, fast as he went, the child went faster. Higher and higher he beheld the tiny creature mounting, then, still keeping the same distance between them, it turned when it reached the top story and trotted along a narrow corridor with rooms opening off to right and left. At the extreme end of this passage a door stood ajar. Through this the child passed, Mr. Stainton still following.

"I have run you to earth at last," he said, entering and closing the door. "Why, where has the boy gone?" he added, holding the candle above his head and gazing round the dingy garret in which he found himself.

The room was quite empty. He examined it closely, but could find no possible outlet save the door, and a skylight which had evidently not been opened for years. There was no furniture in the apartment, except a truckle bedstead, a rush-bottomed chair, and a rickety washstand. No wardrobe, or box, or press, where even a kitten might have lain concealed.

"It is very strange," muttered Mr. Stainton, as he turned away baffled. "Very strange!" he repeated, while he walked along the corridor. "I don't understand it at all," he decided, proceeding slowly down the topmost flight of stairs; but there all at once he stopped.

"IT IS THE CHILD!" he exclaimed aloud, and the sound of his own voice woke strange echoes through the silence of that desolate house. "IT IS THE CHILD!" and he descended the principal staircase very slowly, with bowed head, and his grave, worn face graver and more thoughtful than ever.

CHAPTER III

SEARCHING FOR INFORMATION

It was enough to make any man look grave; and as time went on the new owner of Walnut-Tree House found himself pondering continually as to what the mystery could be which attached to the child he had found in possession of his property, and who had already driven tenant after tenant out of the premises. Inclined at first to regard the clerk's story as a joke, and his own experience on the night of his arrival a delusion, it was impossible for him to continue incredulous when he found, even in broad daylight, that terrible child stealing down the staircase and entering the rooms, looking, looking—for something it never found.

At bed and at board he had company, or the expectation of it. No apartment in the building was secure from intrusion. It did not matter where he lay, it did not matter where he ate; between sleeping and waking, between breakfast and dinner, whenever the notion seized it, the child came gliding in, looking, looking, looking, and never finding; not lingering longer than was necessary to be certain the object of its search was absent, but wandering hither and thither, from garret to kitchen, from parlour to bed-chamber, in that quest which still seemed fresh as when first begun.

Mr. Stainton went to his solicitors as the most likely persons from whom to obtain information on the subject, and plunged at once into the matter.

"Who is the child supposed to be, Mr. Timpson?" he asked, making no secret that he had seen it.

"Well, that is really very difficult to say," answered Mr. Timpson.

"There *was* a child once, I suppose?—a real child—flesh and blood?"

Mr. Timpson took off his spectacles and wiped them.

"There were two; yes, certainly, in the time of Mr. Felix Stainton—a boy and a girl."

"In that house?"

"In that house. They survived him."

"And what became of them?"

"The girl was adopted by a relation of her father's, and the—boy—died."

"Oh! the boy died, did he? Do you happen to know what he died of?"

"No; I really do not. There was nothing wrong about the affair, however, if that is what you are thinking of. There never was a hint of that sort."

Mr. Stainton sat silent for a minute; then he said,

"Mr. Timpson, I cannot shake off the idea that somehow there has been foul play with regard to those children. Who were they?"

"Felix Stainton's grandchildren. His daughter made a low marriage, and he cast her adrift. After her death the two children were received at Walnut-Tree House on sufferance—fed and clothed, I believe, that was all; and when the old man died the heir-at-law permitted them to remain."

"Alfred Stainton?"

"Yes; the unhappy man who became insane. His uncle died intestate, and he consequently succeeded to everything but the personalty, which was very small, and of which these children had a share."

"There never was any suspicion, you say, of foul play on the part of the late owner?"

"Dear, dear! no; quite the contrary."

"Then you cannot throw the least light on the mystery?"

"Not the least; I wish I could."

For all that, Mr. Stainton carried away an impression Mr. Timpson knew more of the matter than he cared to tell.

"There is a mystery behind it all," he considered. "I must learn more about these children. Perhaps some of the local trades-people may recollect them."

But the local tradespeople for the most part were new comers—or else had not supplied "the house."

"There is only one person I can think of, Sir," said one "family" butcher, "likely to be able to give you any information about the matter."

"And that is——"

"Mr. Hennings, at the Pedlar's Arms. He had some acquaint-ance with the old lady as was housekeeper both to Mr. Felix Stain-ton and the gentleman that went out of his mind." Following which advice, the new owner repaired to the Pedlar's Arms.

"Do I know Walnut-Tree House, Sir?" said Mr. Hennings, repeating his visitor's question. "Well, yes, rather. Why, you might as well ask me, do I know the Pedlar's Arms. As boy and man I can remember the old house for close on five-and-fifty years. I remember Mr. George Stainton; he used to wear a skull-cap and knee-breeches. There was an orchard then where Stainton-street is now, and his whole day was taken up in keeping the boys out of it. Many a time I have run from him."

"Did you ever see anything of the boy and girl who were there, after Mr. Alfred succeeded to the property—Felix Stainton's grandchildren, I mean?" asked the new owner, when a pause in Mr. Hennings' reminiscences enabled him to take his part in the conversation.

"Well, Sir, I may have seen the girl, but I can't bring it to my recollection: the boy I do remember, however. He came over here two or three times with Mrs. Toplis, who kept house for both Mr. Staintons, and I took notice of him, both because he looked so peaky and old-fashioned, and also on account of the talk about him."

"There was talk about him, then."

"Bless you, yes, Sir; as much talk while he was living as since he died. Everybody thought he ought to have been the heir. But if you want to hear all about him, Sir, Mrs. Toplis is the one to tell you. If you have a mind to give a shilling to a poor old lady who always did try to keep herself respectable, and who, I will say, paid her way honourable as long as she had a sixpence to pay it honourable with—you cannot do better than go and see Mrs. Toplis, who will talk to you for hours about the time she lived at Walnut-Tree House."

And, with this delicate hint that his minutes were more valuable than the days of Mrs. Toplis, Mr. Hennings would have closed the interview, but that his visitor asked where he should be able to find the housekeeper.

"A thousand pardons!" answered the publican, with an air; "forgetting the very cream and marrow of it, wasn't I? Mrs. Toplis, Sir, is to be found in Lambeth workhouse—and a pity, too."

Edgar Stainton turned away, heart-sick. Was this all wealth had done for his people and those connected with them?

CHAPTER IV

BROTHER AND SISTER

Mr. Stainton had expected to find Mrs. Toplis a decrepit crone, bowed with age and racked with rheumatism, and it was therefore like a gleam of sunshine streaming across his path to behold a woman, elderly, certainly, but carrying her years with ease, ruddy cheeked, clear eyed, upright as a dart, who welcomed him with respectful enthusiasm.

"And so you are Mr. Edgar, the son of the dear old Captain," she said, after the first greetings and explanations were over, after she had wiped her eyes and uttered many ejaculations of astonishment and expressions of delight. "Eh! I remember him coming to the house just after he was married, and telling me about the dear lady his wife. I never heard a gentleman speak so proud; he never seemed tired of saying the words, 'My wife.'"

"She was a dear lady," answered the new owner.

"And so the house has come to you, Sir? Well, I wish you joy. I hope you may have peace, and health, and happiness, and prosperity in it. And I don't see why you should not—no, indeed, Sir."

Edgar Stainton sat silent for a minute, thinking how he should best approach his subject.

"Mrs. Toplis," at last he began, plunging into the very middle of the difficulty, "I want you to tell me all about it. I have come here on purpose to ask you what it all means."

The old woman covered her face with her hands, and he could see that she trembled violently.

"You need not be afraid to speak openly to me," he went on. "I am quite satisfied there was some great wrong done in the house, and I want to put it right, if it lies in my power to do so. I am a rich man. I was rich when the news of this inheritance reached me, and I would gladly give up the property to-morrow if I could only undo whatever may have been done amiss."

Mrs. Toplis shook her head.

"Ah! Sir; you can't do that," she said. "Money can't bring back the dead to life; and, if it could, I doubt if even you would prove as good a friend to the poor child sleeping in the churchyard yonder as his Maker did when He took him out of this troublesome world. It was just soul-rending to see the boy the last few months of his life. I can't bear to think of it, Sir! Often at night I wake in a fright, fancying I still hear the patter, patter of his poor little feet upon the stair."

"Do you know, it is a curious thing, but he doesn't frighten me," said Mr. Stainton; "that is, when I am in the house; although when I am away from it the recollection seems to dog every step I take."

"What?" cried Mrs. Toplis; "*have you then seen him, too?* There! what am I talking about? I hope, Sir, you will forgive my foolishness."

"I see him constantly," was the calm reply.

"I wonder what it means!—I wonder what it can mean!" exclaimed the housekeeper, wringing her hands in dire perplexity and dismay.

"I do not know," answered the new owner, philosophically;

"but I want you to help me to find out. I suppose you remember the children coming there at first?"

"Well, Sir, well—They were poor Miss Mary's son and daughter. She ran away, you know, with a Mr. Fenton—made a very bad match; but I believe he was kind to her. When they were brought to us, a shivering little pair, my master was for sending them here. Ay, and he would have done it, too, if somebody had not said he could be made to pay for their keep. You never saw brother and sister so fond of one another—never. They were twins. But, Lor! he was more like a father to the little girl than aught else. He'd have kept an apple a month, rather than eat it unless she had half; and the same with all else. I think it was seeing that—watching the love they had, he for her and she for him, coming upon them unsuspected, with their little arms round one another's necks, made the old gentleman alter his mind about leaving the place to Mr. Alfred; for he said to me, one day, thoughtful like, pointing to them, 'Wonderful fond, Toplis!' and I answered, 'Yes, Sir; for all the world like the Babes in the Wood;' not thinking of how lonely that meant——

"Shortly afterwards he took to his bed; and while he was lying there, no doubt, better thoughts came to him, for he used to talk about his wife and Miss Mary, and the Captain, your father, Sir, and ask if the children were gone to bed, and such like—things he never used to mention before.

"So when he made the will Mr. Quinance drew out I was not surprised—no, not a bit. Though before that time he always spoke of Mr. Alfred as his heir, and treated him as such."

"That will never was found," suggested Mr. Stainton, anxious to get at another portion of the narrative.

"Never, Sir. We hunted for it high and low. Perhaps I wronged him, but I always thought Mr. Alfred knew what became of it. After the old gentleman's death the children were treated shameful—shameful. I don't mean beaten, or such like; but half-starved and neglected. He would not buy them proper clothes, and he would not suffer them to wear decent things if anybody else bought them. It was just the same with their food. I durstn't give them even a bit of bread-and-butter unless it was on the sly; and, indeed, there was not much to give in that house. He turned regular miser. Hoarding came into the family with Mrs. Lancelot Stainton, Mr. Alfred's great grandmother, and they went on from bad to worse, each one closer and nearer than the last, begging your pardon for saying so, Sir; but it is the truth."

"I fear so, Mrs. Toplis," agreed the man, who certainly was neither close nor near.

"Well, Sir, at last, when the little girl was about six years old, she fell sick, and we didn't think she would get over the illness. While she was about at her worst Mrs. May, her father's sister, chanced to be stopping up in London, and, as Mr. Alfred refused to let a doctor inside his doors, she made no more ado but wrapped the child up in blankets, sent for a cab, and carried her off to her own lodgings. Mr. Alfred made no objection to that. All he said as she went through the hall was,

" 'If you take her now, remember, you must keep her.'

" 'Very well,' she replied, 'I will keep her.' "

"And the boy? the boy?" cried Mr. Stainton, in an agony of impatience.

"I am coming to him, Sir, if you please. He just dwined away after his sister and he were parted, and died in December as she was taken in the July."

"What did he die of?"

"A broken heart, Sir. It seems a queer thing to say about a child; but if ever a heart was broken his was. At first he was always going about the house looking for her, but towards the end he used to go up to his room and stay there all by himself. At last I wrote to Mrs. May, but she was ill when the letter got to her, and when she did come up he was dead. My word, she talked to Mr. Alfred! I never heard any one person say so much to another. She declared he had first cheated the boy of his inheritance, and then starved him to death; but that was not true, the child broke his heart fretting after his sister."

"Yes; and when he was dead."

"Sir, I don't like to speak of it, but as true as I am sitting here, the night he was put in his coffin he came pattering down just as usual, looking, looking for his sister. I went straight up stairs, and, if I had not seen the little wasted body lying there still and quiet, I must have thought he had come back to life. We were never without him afterwards, never; that, and nothing else, drove Mr. Alfred mad. He used to think he was fighting the child and killing it. When the worst fits were on him he tried to trample it under foot or crush it up in a corner, and then he would sob and cry, and pray for it to be taken away. I have heard he recovered a little before he died, and said his uncle told him there was a will leaving all to the boy, but he never saw such a paper. Perhaps it was only talk, though, or that he was still raving."

CHAPTER V

THE NEXT AFTERNOON

Mr. Stainton was trying to work off some portion of his perplexities by pruning the grimy evergreens in front of Walnut-Tree House, and chopping away at the undergrowth of weeds and couch grass which had in the course of years matted together beneath the shrubs, when his attention was attracted to two ladies who stood outside the great iron gate looking up at the house.

"It seems to be occupied now," remarked the elder, turning to her companion. "I suppose the new owner is going to live here. It appears just as dingy as ever; but you do not remember it, Mary."

"I think I do," was the answer. "As I look the place grows familiar to me. I do recollect some of the rooms, I am sure, just like a dream, as I remember Georgie. What I would give to have a peep inside."

At this juncture the new owner emerged from amongst the bushes, and, opening the gate, asked if the ladies would like to look over the place.

The elder hesitated; whilst the younger whispered, "Oh, aunt, pray do!"

"Thank you," said Mrs. May to the stranger, whom she believed to be a gardener; "but perhaps Mr. Stainton might object."

"No. He wouldn't, I know," declared the new owner. "You can go through the house if you wish. There is no one in it. Nobody lives there except myself."

"Taking charge, I suppose?" suggested Mrs. May, blandly.

"Something of that sort," he answered.

"I do not think he is a caretaker," said the girl, as she and her relative passed into the old house together.

"What do you suppose he is, then?" asked her aunt.

"Mr. Stainton himself."

"Nonsense, child!" exclaimed Mrs. May, turning, nevertheless, to one of the windows, and casting a curious glance towards the new owner, who was now, his hands thrust deep in his pockets, walking idly up and down the drive.

After they had been all over the place, from hall to garret, with a peep into this room and a glance into that, Mrs. May found the man who puzzled her leaning against one of the pillars of the porch, waiting, apparently, for their reappearance.

"I am sure we are very much obliged to you," she began, with a certain hesitation in her manner.

"Pray do not mention it," he said.

"This young lady has sad associations connected with the house," Mrs. May proceeded, still doubtfully feeling her way.

He turned his eyes towards the girl for a moment, and, though her veil was down, saw she had been weeping.

"I surmised as much," he replied. "She is Miss Fenton, is she not?"

"Yes, certainly," was the answer; "and you are——"

"Edgar Stainton," said the new owner, holding out his hand.

"I am all alone here," he explained, after the first explanations were over. "But I can manage to give you a cup of tea. Pray do come in, and let me feel I am not entirely alone in England."

Only too well pleased, Mrs. May complied, and ten minutes later the three were sitting round a fire the blaze of which leapt and flickered upon the walls and over the ceiling, casting bright lights on the dingy mirrors and the dark oak shelves

"It is all coming back to me now," said the girl softly, addressing her aunt. "Many an hour Georgie and I have sat on that hearth seeing pictures in the fire."

But she did not see something which was even then standing close beside her, and which the new owner had witnessed approach with a feeling of terror that precluded speech.

It was the child! The child searching about no longer for something it failed to find, but standing at the girl's side still and motionless, with its eyes fixed upon her face, and its poor, wasted figure nestling amongst the folds of her dress.

"Thank Heaven, she does not see it!" he thought, and drew his breath, relieved.

No; she did not see it—though its wan cheek touched her shoulder, though its thin hand rested on her arm, though through the long conversation which followed, it never moved from her side, nor turned its wistful eyes from her face.

When she went away—when she took her fresh young beauty out of the house her presence seemed to gladden and light up— the child followed her to the threshold; and then in an instant it vanished, and Mr. Stainton watched for its flitting up the staircase all in vain.

But later on in the evening, when he was sitting alone beside the fire, with his eyes bent on the glowing coals, and perhaps seeing pictures there, as Mary said she and her brother had done in their lonely childhood, he felt conscious, even without looking round, that the boy was there once again.

And when he fell to thinking of the long, long years during which the dead child had kept faithful and weary watch for his sister, searching through the empty rooms for one who never came, and then bethought him of the sister to whom her dead brother had become but the vaguest of memories, of the sum- mers and winters during the course of which she had probably forgotten him altogether, he sighed deeply—he heard his sigh echoed behind him in the merest faintest whisper.

More, when he, thinking deeply about his newly found relative and trying to recall each feature in her face, each tone of her voice, found it impossible to dissociate the girl grown to womanhood from the child he had pictured to himself as wan- dering about the old house in company with her twin-brother, their arms twined together, their thoughts one, their sorrows one, their poor pleasures one—he felt a touch on his hand, and knew the boy was beside him, looking with wistful eyes into the firelight, too.

But when he turned he saw that sadness clouded those eyes no longer. She was found; the lost had come again to meet a living friend on the once desolate hearth, and up and down the wide desolate staircase those weary little feet pattered no more.

The quest was over, the search ended; into the darksome corners of that dreary house the child's glance peered no longer.

She was come! Through years he had kept faithful watch for her, but the waiting was ended now.

CHAPTER VI

THE MISSING WILL

Ere long there were changes in the old house. Once again Mrs. Toplis reigned there, but this time with servants under her—with maids she could scold and lads she could harass.

The larder was well plenished, the cellars sufficiently stocked; windows formerly closely shuttered now stood open to admit the air; and on the drive grass grew no longer—too many footsteps passed that way for weeds to flourish.

It was Christmas-time. The joints in the butchers' shops were gay with ribbons; the grocers' windows were tricked out to delight the eyes of the children, young and old, who passed along. In Mr. May's house up the Clapham-road all was excitement, for the whole of the family—father, mother, grown-up sons and daughters—girls still in short frocks and boys in round jackets —were going to spend Christmas Eve with their newly-found cousin, whom they had adopted as a relation with a unanimity as rare as charming.

Cousin Mary also was going—Cousin Mary had got a new dress for the occasion, and was having her hair done up in a specially effective manner by Crissie May, when the toilette proceedings were interrupted by half a dozen young voices announcing—

"A gentleman in the parlour wants to see you, Mary. Pa says you are to make haste and come down immediately."

Obediently Mary made haste as bidden and descended to the parlour, to find there the clerk from Timpson's, who met Mr. Stainton on his arrival in London.

His business was simple, but important. Once again he was the bearer of a letter from Timpson and Co., this time announcing to Miss Fenton that the will of Mr. Felix Stainton had been found, and that under it she was entitled to the interest of ten thousand pounds, secured upon the houses in Stainton-street.

"Oh! aunt, oh! uncle, how rich we shall be," cried the girl, running off to tell her cousins; but the uncle and aunt looked grave. They were wondering how this will might affect Edgar Stainton.

While they were still talking it over—after Timpson's young man had taken his departure, Mr. Edgar Stainton himself arrived.

"That is all right!" he said, in answer to their questions. "I found the will in the room where Felix Stainton died. Walnut-Tree House and all the freeholds were left to the poor little chap who died, chargeable with Mary's ten thousand pounds, five hundred to Mrs. Toplis, and a few other legacies. Failing George, the property was to come to me. I have been to Quinance's successor, and found out that the old man and Alfred had a grievous quarrel, and that in consequence he determined to cut him off altogether. Where is Mary? I want to wish her joy."

Mary was in the little conservatory, searching for a rose to put in her pretty brown hair.

He went straight to her, and said,

"Mary, dear, you have had one Christmas gift to-night, and I want you to take another with it."

"What is it, Cousin Edgar?" she asked; but when she looked in his face she must have guessed his meaning, for she drooped her head, and began pulling her sweet rose to pieces.

He took the flower, and with it her fingers.

"Will you have me, dear?" he asked. "I am but a rough fellow; but I am true, and I love you dearly."

Somehow, she answered him as he wished, and they all spent a very happy evening in the old house.

Once, when he was standing close beside her in the familiar room, hand clasped in hand, Edgar Stainton saw the child looking at them.

There was no sorrow or yearning in his eyes as he gazed—only a great peace, a calm which seemed to fill and light them up with an exquisite beauty.

Anonymous

HAUNTED ASHCHURCH

I T WAS A LONESOME LITTLE COUNTRY CHURCH, quite deserted and rapidly falling into decay. The nearest house was that of old Joe Salter, the blacksmith, and that was fully half-a-mile away. It could not be said that the little fabric possessed anything of architectural beauty or intent: a plain, oblong building, with a square, thick-set, squat tower. It had no chancel.

It was hard upon fifty years since regular services had been discontinued at Ashchurch, owing to the building and endowment of a handsome new church, nearer the centre of population and better adapted to the requirements of the parish.

For about the first half of these fifty years, the cracked old bell of Ashchurch still rang occasionally for the funerals of old residents of the parish; for the churchyard was not declared closed when the Sunday services ceased.

But the time came when the authorities decided that henceforward all burials must be in the new cemetery.

Up to that time, the aged church had been kept in some sort of repair, and had, at any rate, been water-tight. But, from that time, the efforts made to keep it so had been but spasmodic and inadequate, and, year by year, it became more and more dilapidated.

The ivy now grew in unchecked luxuriance, not only over the walls, but over the roof. As for the tower, it became a perfect bush of creepers under which the form of the masonry was concealed, like that of an esquimaux in his furs.

The once trim laurel hedge put forth greedy arms, and embraced within its unwieldy and irregular width many of the moss-grown gravestones. Grass grew coarse and rank on the churchyard paths. Here and there a headstone or mound of green turf showed signs of care and loving tendance; but, as a rule, the graves, like the church itself, looked neglected and desolate, and some were hidden by foxglove and nettles.

A stranger, accidentally detained in the parish by the effects of a fall from his horse, being convalescent, had strolled aimlessly down the narrow, winding lane, which led to the church, and, coming suddenly upon it, had been struck by its forlorn appearance.

Leaning over the rusty-hinged churchyard gate, he descried a woman and a sturdy girl hurriedly weeding one of the smallest of the green mounds of its rank growth of dock-leaves. His attention could not but be arrested by the headlong haste which characterised their performance of a task over which love usually lingers long.

As he was desirous of learning something of the history of the church, and of the causes of its present state of decay, he, with some difficulty, opened the crazy old gate and went towards them. But though he succeeded, by dint of questioning, in eliciting most of the facts, of which the reader is already in possession, he found the woman far from communicative and evidently anxious to be gone. Once only did her natural love of gossip prompt her to impart unsolicited information.

"Volks hereabout *du* say," she began, "ez how *she* had a hand—" But here, as though frightened at her own impulse, she broke off abruptly and, turning short round, ambled off at the top of her speed, closely followed by the girl, without shutting the gate behind her. The stranger heard the patter of their feet hurrying down the lane, and smiled the superior smile of an educated man.

"Some superstitious fancy!" he said to himself.

Choosing a flat tombstone, he lay down at full length thereon, and gave himself up to the full enjoyment of the lovely summer's evening. The pure physical pleasure of it, to one who had so lately been an invalid, was most grateful and soothing.

The intense quiet of the place, amid the sound sleepers beneath the sod, its touching air of desertion and its uncared-for aspect, the history of the abandonment of the church—all appealed strongly to his imagination, and he was soon lost in a dreamland of musings. At length, warned, by a cold gust of evening air, that he was hardly strong enough yet to risk being out in the dew, he rose to go.

He was amazed to find that he must have been there over two hours. It was getting dusk, and his watch told him it was half-past eight. He turned to take one last look at the lorn church, and, as he did so, caught a glimpse of the white drapery of a woman's skirts in the act of disappearing round the north-west corner of the tower.

He had a strong distaste for anything like intrusion on the privacy of one who was possibly visiting the grave of a relation, and he accordingly left the churchyard, without again turning his head.

But he was conscious that it cost him a strong effort to do so, owing to a most extraordinary craving, which he could not for the life of him explain, to look round the corner of the tower. On his emerging from the lane, he saw the cheerful glow of the blacksmith's forge some way ahead. Salter had done some work for him, and it might, he thought, be as well to ask the loan of a top-coat for the rest of his way home. In height and build they were much alike. So he turned in at the half-door of the forge.

"My sakes!" said the blacksmith, heartily, "why, it's Muster Cortram. Glad to see you, sir, out and aboot, though 'tis maist too sharp a evening, and you not quite set oop, as ye may say."

"True, Salter, and so I've come to ask you to lend me an overcoat."

"Right you are, sir, and welcome, too; but set ye down and have a warm first."

And the blacksmith, mindful of the duties of hospitality, drew his shirt-sleeves down over his mighty arms, and proceeded to light a pipe, by way of company to Mr. Cortram's cigar.

"'Tis a quaint spot this close by you," said the latter, as he struck a light and passed it over to Salter.

"Meaning——?" queried the smith, as he held the match over the bowl.

"Ashchurch."

Salter let the match drop.

"What! have you been there at this hour o' night?"

"Hour of night indeed! Why, it is barely dusk, and what is more, some lady or other is probably there still."

This time the blacksmith dropped his pipe, and it was smashed against the anvil in the fall. The man was pale as death.

"What ails you, Salter, my man? Here, have a cigar."

Salter took no notice of the proffered cigar-case. With an effort he drew himself up to his full height, and, in the deep shadows and strong lights of the forge he looked like a prophet of the olden time as he said, most earnestly and solemnly:

"Mr. Cortram, sir, go ye home, do ye now, and pray to-night when ye sez yer prayers, as in coorse ye do, that no harm may come this night to you or any av yer famuly."

Mr. Cortram respected the man's emotion, though quite at a loss to guess its cause, and, without bothering him further about the overcoat, walked briskly home.

Next day he sallied forth as usual in the evening for a stroll, but had not gone far when he met a mounted messenger from the telegraph office of the neighbouring town, who recognised him and handed him a telegram. It announced the sudden death of an uncle the previous evening at half-past eight o'clock. The recollection came to him like a sudden gust of icy wind, chilling his heart, that, at that very time, he had seen the mysterious white dress fluttering round the corner of Ashchurch tower. Why his instinct connected the two things together he could not divine. He was by no means a fanciful man, but was generally credited with a clear head and strong common-sense.

Having the responsibility for the arrangements of his uncle's funeral, he left the place that evening.

Some months went on, but, notwithstanding a great pressure of business, which came upon him in consequence of his uncle's death, the mystery of Ashchurch continually recurred to him. The strange behaviour of the peasant woman in the churchyard, the unexplained emotion of the blacksmith, his own strong and unaccountable yearning, that memorable evening, to look behind the tower, the odd coincidence of his uncle's death with his glimpse of the white dress, passed and repassed before his mind's eye over and over again.

One evening he had sat down to look over old papers and letters, with a view to destroying what was worthless. His uncle's correspondence had been extensive, and the task was a fatiguing one. He was on the point of giving it up for the night, when, out of one of the letters, there dropped a square piece of yellow-looking paper which fluttered down upon the carpet. He listlessly picked it up.

The inscription on it was so curiously in accord with the subject uppermost in his thoughts, that he was roused into strong interest. It ran thus:—

> "Her vesture, dimly seen afar,
> To him who sees, an evil star;
> Her self who sees, he shall be blest,
> And give her weary spirit rest."

His mind was so possessed with the conviction that the two first lines of the doggerel described what he had himself recently experienced, that he felt no surprise, at the time, on reading at the head of the letter in which the paper had been enclosed, the word "Ashchurch," over the date.

The letter turned out to be one written to his uncle by a former resident in the parish of Ashchurch, who had been many years dead.

It gave a long account of the Ashchurch ghost, quoting several cases of its white robes having been seen in the moment of their disappearance round a corner of the church—always the same corner, viz. the north west, and, in each case, some disaster was found to have befallen the person witnessing the spectral appearance at the very moment of the ghostly dress having been seen.

Strangely enough, Cortram had never heard his uncle mention the subject, and, up to the date of his accident some months before, he had never even heard the name of Ashchurch. On turning to his uncle's diary he found, within a week of the date of the letter, the following entry:—

"Went to Ashchurch ghost-hunting, to prove to poor Conner what fudge it all is."

The next entry was a fortnight later:—

"Not so sure about fudge. I certainly saw something; but it was probably a wreath of mist."

And three days further on:—

"George died the very night, and the very hour, in which I saw that something."

George was a cousin.

It appeared, from Mr. Conner's letter, that the rhymes on the bit of paper were a copy from an old parchment found in a chest in Ashchurch tower. Cortram carefully preserved both the letter and the copy of verses. His uncle had left him all his property, and he therefore wound up his own business, and settled down, as best he could, to the life of a country gentleman.

But he felt that the associations of Ashchurch had taken so powerful a hold of him that he could not shake it off. He had a feeling that, in some inexplicable way, against which his will seemed powerless to contend, he was being drawn to visit the place again. He long battled with the feeling as being morbid and childish. But finding that he was growing hippish and sleepless, he determined to try whether the actual sight of the place would not work a cure.

So about a twelvemonth after his first visit to it, he found himself once more in the Ashchurch lane, on an evening late in June.

He had been some days in the parish and had employed the interval in getting as much information as he could out of the oldest inhabitants; but this amounted to little beyond what he had already learned from Mr. Conner's letter to his uncle.

Of late years even the lane leading to the church had been religiously shunned by the parishioners; and a ghost, it is plain, cannot be seen without somebody to see it.

One additional piece of evidence, however, he had got at quite accidentally.

It happened that one day he had called upon the village doctor, whose acquaintance, in his professional capacity, he had made during his last stay in Ashchurch. The doctor was a squarely-built, weather-beaten man, as prosaic and matter-of-fact as a man could be. The conversation turned upon Mr. Conner.

"I knew him well," observed Dr. Cawson, "and attended him for some years before his death. He died at five minutes past four, on December 10th, twelve and a half years ago."

"Do you always remember so accurately the time of your patients' departure, Dr. Cawson?"

"Why—no! But there were peculiar circumstances——"

"Do tell me what they were."

"If you will promise not to laugh at me. It fell out, that afternoon, that I had been paying some professional visits, and was returning home by Ashchurch Lane on foot. I remembered that, in a corner of the churchyard, there grew a herb which I had often found useful, so I jumped over the gate to gather some. I was busy doing so, when I remembered I had another engagement later on and must make haste. Glancing at my watch I found it was five minutes past four. Just then, in the dim light, I saw the white train of a woman's dress disappearing round the corner of the church. It was so real, to my mind, that I felt sure I should have seen the whole figure if I had raised my head earlier. I had heard of the same sort of thing having been noticed before, and am not ashamed to say that I got back into the lane and home as fast as ever I could. When I reached my own door, I found that a messenger had been sent by Mrs. Conner, in my absence, to say I was urgently wanted, as Mr. Conner had been suddenly taken worse. I went immediately, but was too late. He had died at five minutes past four."

"And have you any theory about it, doctor—any explanation?" The doctor shrugged his shoulders, and the conversation changed.

Thinking of this, among other things, Cortram slowly proceeded towards the church. He felt a strong presentiment of some coming event approaching him with the slow steps of fate.

The gate had grown so rusty that it was some time before he could force it open. A hasty glance round the churchyard told him that neglect and decay were rapidly doing their work. The place was a greater picture of desolation than ever. He stationed himself where he could best watch the north-west corner of the building, leaning his arms on a headstone, and concentrating his whole attention on the spot where the apparition had before shown itself.

For a long time he so remained till his eyes began to ache with the fixity of their gaze.

At length there appeared on the surface of the ground, not more than two yards from the corner of the tower, a sort of wreath of vapour, as it seemed, gradually gathering consistency and moving very slowly along the ground towards the tower till at length it took the semblance of trailing garments.

It was in the act of disappearing as it had done before, when with a peculiar wavy motion of the drapery it suddenly seemed to halt, leaving still a portion distinctly visible, as though the mysterious wearer of the dress were standing just behind the ivy-covered corner.

Cortram felt his hair stand on end, and a cold dew seemed to break out on his forehead. Nevertheless he felt impelled to advance, as though some hidden agency within him, more powerful than his own will, were using his limbs for its own purpose.

And still, as he got more abreast of the tower, as well as nearer to it, more and more of the ghostly drapery became disclosed, till at length the tall figure of a woman, with a hood drawn over her face, stood close beside him.

Cortram, as though in a dream, heard a voice he did not recognise as his own, yet a voice using his tongue and his lips, say, in a hoarse whisper:

"In Heaven's name, what troubles you?"

Slowly the hood fell from the figure's face, a face unutterably sad and inexpressibly sweet, and its shadowy hand pointed to the wall of the tower. Then the lines of the shape grew indistinct and it melted away. Cortram staggered forward and marked the spot towards which the hand had pointed by tearing down a twig of ivy.

He then, with a shiver, hurried homewards, but a deadly faintness came over him, and ere he had gone many yards, he fell down in a swoon. When he came to himself, the moon was high in heaven, and it was close upon midnight.

As he crept home to his lodgings, stiff and cold, he determined to come next day alone and thoroughly examine the spot he had marked—having the profoundest conviction that he was on the verge of some discovery. Accordingly, after a good night's rest, feeling no ill effects from his adventure of the previous evening, he went once more to the little churchyard.

He found the branch of ivy hanging down with drooping leaves, and after some groping, he discovered a chink in the wall, into which he could thrust his hand, and out of which he drew a small wooden box, with clamps of iron at the corners, and tightly shut. With the help of a chisel which he had brought with him he burst it open.

Within there lay a paper folded and sealed. He opened and read it. In modern English it ran as follows:

"I, George Cord, killed my wife, Grace Mabel Cord, taking her unawares with a knife in the back, on the 3rd of August, 1742, when she was going round the corner of Ashchurch Tower, to visit our baby's grave, which was my pretext for getting her into a lonesome place, being firmly set to take her life. I buried her in a hole dug under the hornbeam on the north side. God help me! I have spilt the blood of the purest and sweetest wife ever man had, on foul and most unworthy suspicion, which drove me mad. I have this day found proof of her utter innocence. I leave this confession where the next comer will not fail to find it. In five minutes I shall swing dead from a limb of the hornbeam. And may God have mercy on my soul."

Cortram folded the paper carefully up, and having put it in his pocket, after replacing the box in the chink of the wall, went straight to the parish doctor's house. He caught him as he was starting off on his rounds.

"One word, doctor. Have you ever heard of one, George Cord, who committed suicide in Ashchurch some hundred years ago?"

"Yes, they say a rich young squire of that name hanged himself on a tree in the churchyard."

"Was any reason alleged?"

"The tale goes that his heart was broken by an unfaithful wife, who left him, and was never seen or heard of more."

"It was a lie, and I can prove it."

The doctor stared.

"Come to my room, after you have been your rounds, and I will tell you all about it."

The doctor and Cortram took such steps as were possible to clear the memory of George Cord's wife of the cloud which had so long rested upon it.

Her husband must have meant to place the little box in as conspicuous a position as possible, but it had dropped out of the trembling fingers, further into the chink than he had intended, and the ivy had grown over it. The poor bones under the horn-beam were given Christian burial in the husband's grave, and the dust of the murderer and the murdered commingle in peaceful rest.

It was the last funeral in the old churchyard. Nevermore were the ghostly trailing garments seen sweeping round the corner of Ashchurch Tower.

Anonymous

THE HAUNTED TREE

ABOUT FIFTY YEARS SINCE, upon one of the plains which over-spread large portions of the south-western part of Maine, certain mysterious things obtruded themselves upon the notice of the community. They startled the thoughtless, puzzled the philosophic, set the superstitious all agog, and made the timid tremble. Unaccountable sounds were heard there; unnatural signs were seen; and often without any visible cause, dogs, cattle, and horses were terribly affrighted.

A pine tree, which stood by the roadside, and which over-shadowed the way with its spreading branches, marked that spot which was noted for its wonders. It was tall, straight, and well proportioned—as fair to look upon as its neighbours—and still under its deep shadows all these unaccountable phantoms appeared. The surrounding forest was thickly studded with the same stately growth. In the light of day it was harmless. When the sun pressed its bright rays through that dark forest, when all natural objects were unmistakably distinct and visible, no fearful sight nor sound alarmed the passing man or beast.

But when the eve of day was closed, when deep night—doubly thick and heavy under those green, overshadowing tree-tops—wrapped all things in sable curtains, then these disturbing forces infested the place, and let loose these marvels.

It must be affirmed, however, that this tree did not stand in the most frightful spot traced by that lonesome highway. It was not in the middle of that gloomy forest. It stood nearer the side which bordered on the thickest settlement. Not far above it lay a dark, deep, chilly hollow—often entered with a shudder—which all would declare was the fit home of ghosts and hobgoblins, and where practical robbers would naturally select their ambush. Still, it soon became notorious that this apparently innocent and promising tree was a haunted tree—marked as such by all the surrounding inhabitants—heralded as such through all that region.

It must be added that this spot, which rose into such puzzling notoriety, was about two miles from a dull, unpretentious hamlet, where stores were kept, in which some useful merchandise could be found; but the great article of trade at that time, as it was everywhere, was ardent spirits. Many then regarded strong drink as the elixir of life; while it was surely gliding them into graver difficulties than frights and heart-beatings at the haunted tree. But business at the shops, at the post-office, and most of all at the stores licensed to keep and sell the fashionable, much-loved beverage, would draw the rustics thither after the toils of the day were ended, many of whom had to pass this haunted tree.

As a child could pass it harmless when the light of day guarded the place, they would start in season to pass it before the dusky and fearful hour of night licensed the appearance of these terrors. But if they went on foot, they would always have their dogs accompany them, and then not return alone if they could find company. But after taking a social glass, doing their business, listening to the gossip of the day, hearing the last-reported "scare" at the Tree, they would linger to discuss these mysterious appearances, *pro* and *con*, and avow their belief or disbelief in them.

Some who were constant attendants upon the preaching of the uneducated, unpolished, but deeply pious minister of the place, would take a still more serious view of these things. They would say:—"These mysterious sights and sounds mean something! They augur of crime—secret, dark, and heaven-daring. God is making inquisition for blood. Murder will out; and till the awful secret is divulged that spot will be haunted."

This would disturb the serenity of the man behind the counter. He prided himself as above belief in ghosts, witches, and phantoms; as too intelligent to swallow down such admissions of spiritual manifestations, or of supernatural appearances, and he would say, "Nonsense, nonsense! It is all imagination—all whims, all superstition!"

But at length his own turn came to try these troubles, and to see if it was all bosh and gammon. Returning home one evening upon that road, as he approached the haunted tree his horse stopped short, and stubbornly refused to pass it. It would no more go forward than the beast upon which Balaam rode, when the angel of the Lord, with a drawn sword in his hand, confronted him. This perplexed and disconcerted our merchant; but it was no place to be angry. Though he neither saw nor heard anything unusual himself, his noble horse was trembling with fear and unwilling to advance, as if the road was bristling with armed hobgoblins. He whipped and goaded him on till, with a desperate plunge, he dashed out into the thick, scraggy bushes, rushed by the obnoxious tree, and ran, at the top of his speed, until he brought up, panting and trembling, at his own stable door.

Another incident, which is hard to put aside as a mere phantasm. An elderly man, of a bold, defiant spirit, was passing that way in a partially intoxicated state. A son of six or eight years, and his faithful dog, were with him. As they drew near the tree, a light was seen, as if some invisible hand was holding a lantern. The old man cheered his dog to an attack. Bristling and barking, he bravely struck for the light, when it moved out into the forest. Our tippling friend, more daring than usual just then, attempted to follow it. Up to that point the courage of the boy held out (as he informed the writer), as he saw nothing but a light, and that retreating before the dog. But when the father turned into the bushes, he was thoroughly affrighted, and wished to hasten home if naught forbade it. But the light soon faded, the dog became composed, the father returned to the road, and another wonder was reported.

Sometimes these same persons would pass unmolested, silence reigning through the whole forest, and no unearthly sight disturb them. Some passed frequently in night's deepest darkness, and never saw or heard anything strange or supernatural. Such was the case with a young physician, whose practice often led him by that place. He was a man of integrity, every way reliable, generous, and kind in spirit. Keeping a clear conscience toward all men, he was fearless of both the dead and living; and often, in the still hours of night, rode by the tree, calling upon any one who had anything to make known, to come and tell it. But he had no vision of these things. Those who were molested by these unaccountable manifestations were usually struck dumb, passed it as best they could, and gave no challenge.

On a snowy winter day, two men, of good habits, sound judgment, and unquestionable veracity, were passing by that place with waggons heavily laden. The falling snow had become quite deep. They plodded slowly through it, beguiling their dreary way with occasional conversation. As one of them was observing that nobody ventured out, the storm was so severe, they both looked forward, and saw an old and peculiarly dressed man, footing it through the deep snow towards them. Both noticed him, saw that he was a stranger to them, but in all his appearances a veritable man.

The driver of the foremost waggon went forward to get his horses a little out of the road, and give the venerable stranger an easier passage by; and, behold, no one was to be seen! Looking around in every direction, and seeing no one, he asked his companion if he saw a man just before, approaching them? He replied that he did. What had become of him? He could not tell. They stopped their waggon, and made search; but could not discover any track in the snow, neither in the road where they thought they saw him, nor in any direction by which he might turn aside. Yet they both ever affirmed that they could not have been mistaken, and that the form, and dress, and motions of a veritable man surely appeared to them.

Thus several years passed on; the list of unnatural manifestations lengthened; the wonders of the haunted tree grew more and more wonderful, till they reached their climax in a face-to-face interview. The mystery was then solved; the curtain dropped; and no more troubles have been experienced.

Upon one of those fertile ridges which rise from the plain, there lived a young man, truthful in speech, industrious in his habits, of strong nerve, and not especially superstitious. Upon a bright moonlight night, in the month of September, he was returning from the store at an early hour, alone, but in a state of calm sobriety. Reaching the haunted tree, the horse upon which he rode came to a dead stand, and would not be urged further. Nothing unusual was there visible to the rider. He coolly dismounted, stepped before the horse, and led him, without any unwillingness, to follow his rider by that fearful place. Having passed the gulf safe and fearless, too, without premeditation—scarcely conscious of what he was doing, he spoke out in a firm voice, "If any one is here who wants anything of me, I would like to see him."

Immediately, a man, venerable in appearance, dressed in a gone-by style, with gray locks hanging below a broad-brimmed hat, stood directly before him. Surprised, dismayed, and nearly confounded, he felt that he was sent for, and the worst might as well come; so, in trembling tones, he asked, "What do you want of me?"

The spectre, in tones our dismayed friend could never forget, proceeded thus:—

"My name is Hiram White. Twenty-five years ago I was robbed of thirty silver dollars, and then murdered, under this tree. The names of two of the guilty perpetrators of that deed of blood will I give, as they are now living. They were Caleb Walsh and Franklin Orme: but some parts of that awful scene I cannot relate to you. Read the 9th Psalm, and you will apprehend them. I have long haunted this blood-stained spot, to make some one inquire for the terrible secret. You are the first person that has challenged me, and now I have divulged it, these things will no more appear. Follow me, and I will show you where they buried my body."

The spectre led the way into the forest, and our terrified friend followed, feeling that it was no time to oppose, or make excuses. Coming to a low, over-shadowed hollow, he affirmed, "Here is the place!" and instantly vanished. The young man, finding himself unharmed physically, and still alive—though the last dread summons could not have caused a greater mental anguish—made his way back to his horse, which, totally undisturbed, had not started from the place where he left him. He rode slowly home, deeply affected by what he had seen and heard. Upon reaching home, his sad and woful countenance betrayed him.

"What is the matter?" was the first inquiry of his wife.

He tried to evade a disclosure, but could not. Unbosoming himself freely, confidentially to her, it was too momentous, too sacred to be kept secret. Once let loose, it travelled with light-ning's speed and power through the community.

The place pointed out as that where the corpse had been buried, was dug open; and there, sure enough, human bones were found!

But did any other circumstances corroborate the young man's statement? The recollections of the aged were sounded; and some of them remembered that a man bearing the name of him who professed to be the victim, occasionally visited that place as an itinerant preacher about the time referred to in that disclosure; that his visits suddenly ceased, and he was not afterwards heard from. But as he came from a distant place in New Hampshire, and was somewhat eccentric, his non-appearance excited no surprise. His profession as a preacher may explain the peculiarity of his sending his auditor to an imprecatory psalm to find the supplement of his awful disclosure.

Another fact is well verified. About the same date of this alleged crime, a stray horse, with his saddle turned and bridle on, was found in the highway, about two miles from this noted tree; it was advertised; a green withe was kept upon his neck for several months, as the law required; but no owner ever claimed it; it remained with the person who picked it up.

The names given as the perpetrators of this revolting deed were not unknown—were not fictitious. They had lived and left families there, and these were sensitive and disturbed by these grave charges. They had died, too; and it was now remembered that the last trying scene with them was marked with long and intensified agonies. Beyond all precedent they rolled and struggled in the grasp of the grim monster, but seemed "forbid to die," till conscience was relieved by some death-bed confession.

With one of them it did come, but came to be locked up in the bosom of its recipient. After long and severe throes and awful moaning, he requested all present to leave the room save one aged, intimate neighbour. With a charge of perfect secrecy he entrusted to him the agonizing burden which no other ear must hear. This done, death completed his work. The waiting and anxious friends came in, but could learn only what they could read upon the troubled visage of him who possessed the dying secret of the departed. Evidently an awful disclosure had been made; but none could draw it from its appointed hiding-place.

Such were the firm impressions left upon the minds of the staid, honest-hearted, and more intelligent of that people. No one could convince them that these things were mystical or empty phantoms. They retained the recollection of these mysterious adventures, without attempting any other explanation than that which we have given.

Hugh Conway

A DEAD MAN'S FACE

I MAGINATIVE BEINGS WHO INVENT MARVELOUS TALES may take what license they please, but a simple narrator is nothing if not accurate; so, before beginning this, I looked up old correspondences and various memoranda made at the time when the following things occurred. The first paper upon which I put my hand was a letter. I may as well open with a copy of it:

"DEAR OLD BOY.—I have met her at last—my fate—the one woman in the world for me. Nothing is settled as yet; but I should not write this unless hope were a certainty. You must wish me joy, although she is a widow and an American—two qualifications which I know you will find fault with. No matter; when you see her you will recant and be envious. Yours ever,

"CLAUD MORTON."

The writer was my brother—I was going to say my only brother, but I had another once, although the less said about him the better. Nearly every family has its black sheep. Ours had been a peculiarly sable one. When he died, some years ago, I passed a sponge over his long list of delinquencies, and tried to think of him as kindly as possible. He died a disgraced man, far away from home.

I call this black sheep, Stephen, my brother, not Claud's, the fact being that Claud can scarcely be said to have known him. I stood in age midway between the two. Claud was sixteen years younger than Stephen, so that when the latter was shipped off as irreclaimable, the former was a little golden-haired fellow of seven.

The above letter made me feel both glad and sorry. I was glad that the boy—he was still the boy to me, although his age was seven-and-twenty—was going to be married; but I was sorry that his choice had not fallen on one of his own countrywomen, and one who could have given him her first love. Still, all this was his own peculiar business. No doubt he had made a suitable choice, and the only thing left for me to do was to write him a cheerful letter of congratulation, and hope that his love affairs would soon be happily settled.

A week went by; then came a long letter from him. He had proposed in orthodox form, and had been duly accepted. His letter lies before me at this moment, and I feel sad as I read again the two pages covered with the lover's usual raptures.

I am not a mercenary man, but I own I felt somewhat disappointed on learning that she was poor. Somehow one associates wealth with an American widow who is sojourning in England. But, so far as I could gather from Claud's letter, Mrs. Despard, or Judith, as he called her, was not well off. He spoke of her as being all alone in London, which fact, he added, would necessarily hasten his marriage. It would take place, he hoped, in a week or two. In conclusion he pressed me to run up to town in order to make the acquaintance of my future sister-in-law.

I was very busy at the time—I may say, in passing, that my business is to cure people's ailments, not to tell stories—nevertheless I managed to pay a flying visit to town, and was duly presented to Claud's betrothed.

Yes, she was handsome—strikingly handsome. Her whole appearance was much out of the common. She was tall, superbly built, on a large scale, perhaps, yet graceful as a panther in every movement. Her face gave evidence of much character, power, and determination, and of passion also, I decided. Her rich dark beauty was at that time in full bloom, and although I saw at a glance that she was some years older than my brother, I was not at all inclined to blame Claud for his rapturous expressions. So far as personal charms went, I could find no fault with Judith Despard. For the rest it was easy to see that she was passionately in love with Claud, and for the sake of this I gladly overlooked all my fanciful objections to his choice, and congratulated him heartily on having won so beautiful a creature.

Yet, strange to say, in the midst of his newfound happiness

my brother seemed any thing but his usual cheerful self. He, the merriest and most talkative of men, seemed taciturn, moody and preoccupied. The curious thing was that his changed manner struck me particularly while we were in Mrs. Despard's company. He spoke and behaved in the most affectionate and lover-like way, but there was in his general bearing something which puzzled me altogether. It seemed to me that he might perhaps be nervous as to what impression his fair friend might make upon the elder brother whom he so reverenced and respected.

This theory of mine was strengthened by the fact that when, at night, we found ourselves alone and I was able to freely express my admiration of Mrs. Despard's good looks, he brightened up considerably, and we sat until a very late hour, and talked over the past, the present and the future.

"When do you mean to be married?" I asked.

"In a fortnight or three weeks. There is nothing to wait for. Judith is living alone in lodgings. She has no friends to consult, so we shall just walk to church some morning and get it over."

"Well, let me walk with you. I should like to see the last of you."

"All right, old fellow. But you'll be the only one—unless Mary likes to honor us."

Mary was my wife; but as her time was just then fully occupied by a very young baby, I did not think it at all likely she would be able to make the long journey to town.

"I shall fix the earliest day I can," added Claud. "The fact is, I have been feeling rather queer lately. I want a change."

Thereupon I questioned him as to what ailed him. So far as I could ascertain, all that was the matter was his having worked too hard, and being a little below par. I prescribed a tonic, and quite agreed with him as to the benefit which he would derive from change of air.

When I reached home my wife scolded me for my stupidity. It seems that it was my duty to have found out all about Mrs. Despard's antecedents, relations, connections, circumstances, habits and disposition, whereas all I could say was that she was a beautiful widow with a small income and that she and Claud were devoted to each other.

"Yes," said Mrs. Morton, scornfully, "like all other men, the moment you see a pretty face you inquire no further. I quite tremble for Claud."

When I reflected how little I really knew about Mrs. Despard, I felt abashed and guilty. However, Claud was a full-grown man, and no fraternal counsel was likely to turn him aside from his desire.

In the course of a few days he wrote me that he was to be married on the 5th of the next month. I made arrangements which would enable me to go to the wedding; but three days before the date named I heard again from him. The wedding was postponed for a fortnight. He gave no reason for the delay; but he said he was anxious to see me, and to-morrow he should run down to my home.

He came as promised. I was aghast when I saw him. He looked worn, haggard, wretched. My first thought was that business had gone wrong with him. His looks might well be those of a man on the brink of ruin. After the first greeting I at once took him to my study in order to be put out of suspense. Just as I was about to begin my anxious questions he turned to me.

"Frank, old fellow," he said, imploringly, and with a faint attempt at a smile, "don't laugh at me."

Laugh! That was the last thing I was likely to do. I pressed his hand in silence.

"You won't believe me, I know," he continued. "I can't believe it myself. Frank, I am haunted."

"Haunted!" I was bound to smile, not from any disposition toward merriment, but in order to show the poor boy the absurdity of his idea.

"Yes, haunted. The word sounds ridiculous, but I can use no other. Haunted."

"What haunts you?"

He came close to me and grasped my arm. His voice sank to a hoarse whisper.

"A horrible, ghastly, grewsome thing. It is killing me. It comes between me and my happiness. I have fought and struggled against this phantom terror. I have reasoned calmly with myself. I have laughed my own folly to scorn. In vain—in vain. It goes, but it comes again."

"Overwork," I said, "insomnia, too many cigars, late hours; and had you been a drinking man I should add, too much stimulant, too little food, anxiety, perhaps. Have you any thing on your mind—any special worry?"

"Of course I have," he said, pettishly. "Did I not tell you it is killing me?"

"What is killing you?"

He rose and paced the room excitedly; then suddenly he stopped short, and once more clutched my arm.

"A face," he said, wildly—"a man's face; a fearful white face that comes to me; a horrible mask, with features drawn as in agony—ghastly, pale, hideous! Death or approaching death, violent death, written in every line. Every feature distorted. Eyes starting from the head. Every cord in the throat standing out, strained as by mortal struggle. Long dark hair lying flat and wet. Thin lips moving and working—lips that are cursing, although I hear no sound. Why should this come to me—why to me? Who is this dead man whose face wrecks my life? Frank, my brother, if this is disease or madness, cure me; if not, let me die."

His words, his gestures, sent a cold thrill through me. He was worse, far worse, than I had feared.

"Claud," I said, "you are talking nonsense. Cure you! of course I mean to cure you. Now sit down, collect yourself, and tell me how this hallucination comes."

"Comes! How does it come? It gathers in corners of the room; it forms and takes shape; it glares at me out of the wall; it looks up at me from the floor. Ever the same fearful white dying face, threatening, cursing, sometimes mocking. Why does it come?"

I had already told the poor fellow why it came, but it was no use repeating my words. "Tell me when you see it," I asked; "at night—in darkness?"

He hesitated, and seemed troubled. "No, never at night. In broad daylight only. That to me is the crowning terror, the ghastliness of it. At night I could call it a dream. Frank, believe me, I am no weak fool. For weeks I have borne with this. At last it has conquered me. Send it away, or I shall go mad!"

"I'll send it away, old boy, never fear. Tell me: can you see it now?"

"No; thank God, not now."

"Have you seen it to-day?"

"No; to-day I have been free from it."

"Well, you'll be free from it to-morrow, and the next day, and the next. It will be gone forever before you leave me. Now come and see Mary and the babies. I haven't even asked you how Mrs. Despard is."

A curious look crossed his face. "I think she grows more beautiful every day," he said. Then he seized my hand. "Oh, Frank," he exclaimed, "rid me of this horror, and I shall be the happiest man in the world."

"All right," I answered, perhaps with more confidence than I felt.

Although I made light of it to my patient, his state greatly alarmed me. I hastened to put him under the strictest and most approved treatment. I enforced the most rigid sumptuary laws, made him live on plain food, and docked his consumption of tobacco unmercifully. In a few days I was delighted to find that my diagnosis of the case was correct. Claud was rapidly recovering tone. In a week's time he seemed restored to health.

The days went by. As yet Claud had said nothing about leaving me; yet, unless the date was once more adjourned, he was to be married on the 19th. I did not counsel him to postpone the happy day. He was by now so well that I thought he could not do better than adhere to his arrangement. A month's holiday, spent in the society of the woman he loved, would, I felt certain, complete his cure, and banish forever that grisly intruder begotten of disorganized nerves.

From the monotonous regularity and voluminous nature of their correspondence it was evident, delay and separation notwithstanding, that matters were going on quite smoothly between Claud and Judith Despard. Every day he received and wrote a long letter. Nevertheless, it was not until the 16th of the month that I knew exactly what he meant to do about his marriage.

"Frank," he said, "you have been wonderfully kind to me. I believe you have saved my life, or at least my reason. Will you do something more for me?"

"Even unto half my kingdom," I answered.

"Look here: I am ashamed of the feeling, but I absolutely dread returning to town. At any rate I wish to stay there no longer than is needful. Thursday morning I must, of course, be there, to be married. You think me cured, Frank?" he added, abruptly.

"Honestly, yes. If you take care of yourself you will be troubled no more."

"Yet why do I dread London so? Well, never mind. I will go up by the night mail on Wednesday—then I need only be there for a few hours. Will you do this for me—go up on Wednesday morning, see Judith, and explain how it is that I shall not see her until we meet in the church?"

"Certainly, if you wish it. But you had better write as well."

"Yes, I shall do that. There are several other little things you must see to for me. The license I have, but you must let the clergyman know. You had better go and see my partners. They may think it strange if I marry and go away without a word."

Thinking it better that he should have his own way, I promised to do as he wished. Upon my arrival in town on Wednesday afternoon I went straight to Mrs. Despard's. I was not sorry to have this opportunity of seeing her alone. I wished to urge upon her the necessity of being careful that Claud did not again get into that highly wrought nervous state, from which my treatment had so happily extricated him.

She was not looking so well as when last I saw her. At times her manner was restless, and she seemed striving to suppress agitation. She made no adverse comments on her lover's strange whim of reaching town to-morrow only in time for the ceremony. Her inquiries as to his health were most solicitous, and when I told her that I no longer feared any thing on his account, her heartfelt sigh of relief told me how deeply she loved him.

Presently she looked me full in the face. Her eyes were half closed, but I could see an anxious, eager look in them. "He saw a face," she said. "Has it left him?"

"He told you of his queer hallucination, then?"

"No; but once or twice when sitting with me he sprang to his feet and muttered: 'Oh, that face! that ghastly, horrible face! I can bear it no longer!' Then he rushed wildly from the room. What face did he see, Dr. Morton?"

To set her mind at rest, I gave her a little scientific discourse, which explained to her how such mental phenomena were brought about. She listened attentively, and seemed satisfied. Then I bade her adieu until to-morrow.

The marriage was to be of the quiet kind. I found that Mrs. Despard had made no arrangement for any friend to accompany her; so, setting all rules of etiquette at defiance, I suggested that, although the bridegroom's brother, I should call for her in the morning and conduct her to the church. To this she readily consented.

Somehow that evening I did not carry away such a pleasing impression of my brother's bride as I did when first I met her. I can give no reason for this, except that I was not forgetful of my wife's accusation, that when first I met Judith Despard I had been carried away by the glamour of her beauty, and thought of nothing else. As I walked to Claud's rooms, which I occupied for the night, I almost regretted that he had been so hasty—certainly I wished that we knew more of his bride. But it was now too late for regrets or wishes.

I called for Mrs. Despard at the appointed hour, and found her quite ready to start. Her dress was plain and simple—I can not describe it; but I saw that in spite of her excessive pallor she looked very beautiful. In the carriage on our way to the church she was very silent, answering my remarks with monosyllables. I left her in peace, supposing that at such a moment every woman must be more or less agitated.

When the carriage drew up at the church door, the bride laid her hand upon my arm. I could feel that she was trembling. "Claud will be here?" she asked. "Nothing will stop him?"

"Nothing. But I may as well step out and see that he is waiting."

Yes, Claud was in the church waiting for us. We exchanged greetings. The old sexton summoned the curate; and Judith Despard, my brother, and myself walked up to the altar rails.

Claud looked very well that morning; a little fagged perhaps, but the long night journey would account for that. He certainly looked proud and happy as he stood on the altar step side by side with the woman who in a few minutes would be his wife.

But before the curate had finished reading the opening address a great change came over him. From where I was standing I could see only his side face, but that was enough to show me that he was suffering from some agitation—something far above the nervousness so often displayed by a bridegroom. A deadly pallor came over his face, small beads of perspiration sprang to his brow, and I noticed that those tell-tales of mental disturbance, the hands, were so tightly clenched that the knuckles grew white. It was evident that he was suffering anguish of some kind, and for a moment I thought of stopping the service. But the rite is but a short one, and from whatever cause Claud's agitation might proceed, it was perhaps better to trust to him to curb it for a few moments than to make a scene. Nevertheless I watched him intently and anxiously.

Then came the charge to declare any impediment. As the curate made the conventional pause, Claud, to my surprise, glanced round in a startled way, as if fearing that his marriage would at the last moment be forbidden. The look on his face was now one of actual terror.

Both bride and bridegroom said their "I wills" in such low tones that I could scarcely hear their voices. Then, in pursuance of my duty, I gave the woman to the priest. He joined the hands of Claud and Judith.

After having played my little part I had not moved back to my former station. I was now close to the bride, and as Claud turned to her, could see his face to advantage. It was positively distorted with suppressed emotion of some kind. His mouth was set, and I could see that his teeth were closed on his under lip. He did not look at his fair bride. His gaze passed over her shoulder. In fact, he seemed almost oblivious to her presence. I was dreadfully frightened.

The clergyman's voice rang out: "I, Claud, take thee, Judith, to my wedded wife." Then, hearing no echo of his words, he paused.

"Repeat after me," he prompted. Again he began, "I, Claud—"

But his voice was drowned in a louder one, which rang through the empty church. With a fierce cry, as of inexpressible rage, Claud had thrown the bride's hand from him, and was pointing and gesticulating toward the wall, upon which his eyes had been riveted.

"Here!—even here!" he almost shrieked. "That cursed, white, wicked, dying face! Whose is it! Why does it come between me and my love! Mad! Mad! I am going mad!"

I heeded not the clergyman's look of dismay, or the bride's cry of distress. I thought of nothing but my unfortunate brother. Here, at the moment which should be the happiest he had yet known, the grewsome hallucination had come back to him. I threw my arm round him and tried to calm him.

"It is fancy, dear boy," I said. "In a moment it will be gone."

"Gone! Why does it come? What have I to do with this dying man? Look, Frank, look! Something tells me if you look you will see it. There! there! Look there!"

His eyes were ever fixed on the same point. He grasped my arm convulsively. I am ashamed to say that I yielded, and looked in the direction of his gaze.

"There is nothing there," I said, soothingly.

"Look!" he exclaimed. "It will come to you as to me."

It may have been the hope of convincing Claud of the illusionary nature of the sight which tormented him, it may have been some strange fascination, wrought by his words and manner, which made me for some moments gaze with him. God of heaven! I saw gradually forming out of nothing, gathering on the blank wall in front of me, a face, or the semblance of a face, white, ghastly, horrible! Long, dank, wet-looking dark hair, eyes starting from their sockets, lips working—the whole appearance that of the face of a man who is struggling with death: in every detail as Claud had described it. And yet to me that face was more terrible than ever it could be to Claud.

I gazed in horror. I felt my eyes growing riveted to the sight as his own. I felt my whole frame trembling. I knew that in another moment I should be raving as wildly as he raved. Only his hoarse whisper recalled me to my senses.

"You see?" he asked, or rather asserted.

Horror forced the truth from me. "I see, or fancy I see," I answered.

With a wild laugh Claud broke from me. He rushed down the

church and disappeared. As he left me, the face, thank Heaven! faded from the wall, or from my imagination.

I turned to my companions. Judith Despard was lying in a dead swoon on the altar steps; the curate with trembling hands was loosening the throat of her dress. I called for water. The sexton brought it. I bathed the poor woman's temples, and in a few minutes she sighed, opened her eyes, and then shuddered. I took her in my arms and staggered to the church door. The curate removed his surplice and followed me. I placed my almost senseless burden in the carriage.

"For Heaven's sake, see her home," I said to the curate. "I must go and look after my brother. As soon as I have seen him I will come round to Mrs. Despard's. Get her home quickly. The coachman knows where to go."

The brougham drove off. I threw myself into a cab, and drove toward Claud's rooms. I hoped he might have gone straight there.

To my great relief, when I reached his house he was on the door-step. We entered his room together; he sank wearily into a chair, and buried his face in his hands. I was scarcely less agitated than himself, and my face, as I caught its reflection in the mirror, was as white as his own. I waited for him to speak.

Presently he raised his head. "Go to her," he said. "Ask her why that face comes between us. You saw it—even you. It can be no fancy of mine. Tell her we can meet no more."

"I will wait until you are calmer before I go."

"Calm! I am myself now. The thing has left me, as it always does. Frank, I have hidden from you one peculiarity of my state. That awful face never shows itself to me unless I am in her company. Even at the altar it came between us. Go to her; ask her why it comes."

I left him, but did not quit the house for some time. I went into an adjoining room and tried to collect my thoughts; for, as I said, my mind was more troubled than even Claud's could be.

I am ashamed to re-assert it; I am willing to own that excitement, my brother's impressive manner, superstition which I did not know I possessed—any thing that may bear a natural explanation—may have raised that vision. But why should that phantom, gathering and growing from nothing until it attained to form, or at least semblance, have been the face of one I had known? Why should the features distorted in deadly agony have been those of my brother Stephen? For his was the dreadful face which Claud's prompting or my own imagination had raised.

Almost like one in a dream I went to do Claud's bidding. I was thankful, upon reaching Mrs. Despard's, to find that she had gone to her room, and left word that she could see no one to-day. This gave me time to consider the position.

Acting on a sudden impulse, I went to the telegraph office, and sent instructions to my wife to forward to me, by passenger train, a small box in which I kept old letters and papers. Then I went back to Claud, and after some persuasion induced him to leave town at once. I told him I would arrange every thing on the morrow. He was better away.

In the morning my box arrived. In it I found what I wanted. After the calming effects of a night's rest I felt ashamed of my weakness as I drew from old letters a photograph of my brother Stephen—one taken about two years before the report of his death reached us. Nevertheless I put the portrait in my pocket, and about noon went to Mrs. Despard's.

I was at once admitted, and in a few minutes she came to me. She looked worn and haggard, as if sleep had not visited her for nights. Dark circles had formed round her fine eyes; lines seemed to have deepened round her firm, passionate mouth. She advanced eagerly toward me and held out her hand. I took it in silence. Indeed, I scarcely knew what to say or how to act.

"Where is Claud?" she asked, in a quick voice, but scarcely above a whisper.

"He has left town for a few days."

She pressed her hand to her heart. "Does that mean I shall see him no more?"

"I am afraid I must say it does. He thinks it better you should part."

She gave a sharp cry, and walked up and down the room wringing her hands. Her lips moved rapidly, and I knew she was muttering many words, but in so low a key that I could not catch their meaning. Suddenly she stopped, and turned upon me fiercely.

"Is this by your council and advice?" she demanded.

"No. It is his own unbiassed decision."

"Why?—tell me why? He loved me—I love him. Why does he leave me?"

The passionate entreaty of her voice is indescribable. What could I say to her? Words stuck in my throat. It seemed the height of absurdity for a sane man to give a sane woman the true reason for Claud's broken faith. I stammered out something about his bad state of health.

"If he is ill, I will nurse him," she cried. "I will wait for years if he will give me hope. Dr. Morton, I love Claud as I never before loved a man."

She clasped her hands and looked imploringly into my face. In a mechanical way I drew the portrait of my dead brother from my breast. She saw the action.

"His likeness!" she cried, joyfully. "He sends it to me! Ah, he loves me!"

I handed her the photograph. "Mrs. Despard," I asked, "do you know—"

I did not finish the question, yet it was fully answered. Never, I believe, save then did a human face undergo such a sudden, frightful change. The woman's very lips grew ashen, her eyes glared into mine, and I saw them full of dread. She staggered—all but fell.

"Why is it here—who is it?" she gasped out.

I was a prey to the wildest excitement. To what revelation was this tending? what awful thing had I to learn?

"Listen," I said, sternly. "Woman, it is for you to answer the question. It is the face of this man, his dying face, that comes between you and your lover."

"Tell me his name." I read rather than heard the words her dry lips formed.

"The name he was once known by was Stanley."

A quick, sharp shudder ran through her. For a moment I thought she was going to faint.

"He is dead," she said. "Why does he come between my love and me? Others have loved or said they loved me since then. They saw no dead faces. Had I loved them I might have married and been happy. Claud I love. Why does the dead man trouble him?"

"That man," I replied, "was my brother—Claud's brother."

She threw out her arms with a gesture of utter despair. "Your brother—Claud's brother!" she repeated. Then she fixed her eyes on mine as if she would read the secrets of my soul.

"You are lying," she said.

"I am not. He was our eldest brother. He left England years ago. He passed under a false name. He died. When and how did he die?"

She sank, a dead weight, into a chair; but still she looked at me like one under a spell. I seized her wrist.

"Tell me, woman," I cried—"tell me what this man was to you; why his dying face comes to us? The truth—speak the truth."

She seemed to cower beneath my words, but her eyes were still on my face. "Speak!" I cried, fiercely, and tightening my grasp upon her wrist. At last she found words.

"He was my husband; I killed him," she said in a strange voice, low yet perfectly distinct.

I recoiled in horror. This woman, the widow and self-confessed murderess of one brother, within an ace of being the wife of the other!

"You murdered him?" I said, turning to the woman.

"I murdered him. He made my life a hell upon earth. He beat me, cursed me, ruined me. He was the foulest-hearted fiend that ever lived. I killed him."

No remorse, no regret in her words. Quite overcome, I leaned against the chimney-piece. Bad as I knew Stephen Morton to have been, I could at that moment only think of him as a gay, light-hearted school-boy, my elder brother, and in those days a perfect hero in my eyes. No wonder my heart was full of vengeance.

Yet even in the first flush of my rage I knew that I could do nothing. No human justice could be meted out to this woman. There was nothing to prove the truth of her self-accusation. She would escape scot-free.

"Would that I could avenge his death!" I said, sullenly.

She sprang to her feet. Her dark eyes blazed. "Avenged!" she cried. "Is it not doubly, trebly avenged? Has he not taken all I care for in life from me? Has he not taken my love from my side? Coward in life, coward in death. When I killed him I knew he would try to come back to me. He has tried for years. Ah, I was too strong for him. I could banish the face with which he strove to haunt me. I could forget. I could love. I could have been happy. Yet he has conquered at last. Not me—he could not conquer me—but the one I love. Oh, the coward is avenged!"

In spite of my feeling of abhorrence, I gazed on the speaker in amazement. Her words were not those of one who had committed a black crime, but of one who had suffered wrong. The strange, fanciful idea that the dead man had been trying to haunt her, but had been kept at bay by her strong will, was in my experience unprecedented. As I saw the agony of mind under which she was labouring, the thought came to me that perhaps her words were true, that my brother's death was this day avenged. I resolved to leave her. I could gain no good by prolonging the painful scene.

She was still pacing the room in fierce passion. Suddenly she stopped short, and in thrilling accents began to speak. It seemed as if she had forgotten my presence.

"See," she cried, "the river-bank—the dark rushing stream. Ah, we are all alone, side by side, far away from every one. Fool! if you could read my heart, would you walk so near to the giddy brink? Do you think the memory of the old love will stay my hand when the chance comes? Old love is dead: you beat it, cursed it to death! How fast does the stream run? Can a strong man swim against it? Oh, if I could be sure—sure that one push would end it all and give me freedom! Once I longed for love—your love. Now I long for death—your death. Oh, brave, swift tide, are you strong enough to free me forever? Hark! I can hear the roar of the rapids in the distance. There is a deep fall from the river cliff; there are rocks. Fool! you stand at the very edge and look down. The moment is come. Ah!"

With her last exclamation she used a violent gesture, as if pushing something fiercely from her. She was, I knew, in her excitement, re-acting the tragedy.

"Free! free! free!" she cried, with a delirious, almost rapturous laugh, and clasped her hands. "Hold him, brave stream! Sweep him away. See! he swims; but he dare not swim with you. You are hurrying down to the rapids. He must face you, and wrestle with you for his life. Bear him down; keep him from me. If he masters you, he will land and kill me. Hold him fast, brave stream! Ha! his strength fails. He is swept away; he is under. No, I see him again. He turns his face to me. He knows I did it. With his last breath he is cursing me. His last breath! He is gone, gone forever! I am free!"

The changes in her voice, ranging from dread to tearful joy, her passionate words, her eloquent gestures, all these combined to bring the very scene before my eyes. I stood spell-bound, and even, as she described it, seemed to see the unfortunate man battling for dear life in the rushing stream, growing every moment weaker and weaker. As the woman's last wild exclamation—"Gone forever! I am free!"—rang through the room, I seemed to hear the cry of despair drowned as the waves closed over the wretched man's head. I knew every detail of my brother's fate.

I turned to leave the room. I longed to get away, and if possible to banish the events of the day from my mind. It was not given to me to be Stephen Morton's avenger.

My hand was on the door, when the woman sprang to my side. She grasped my arm and drew me back into the room.

"Look!" she whispered. "Do you see it! There! The face—that awful face! It has come at last to me. The dead man has conquered. There! look! His eyes glaring, his mouth mocking. Now it has once come, I shall see it always—always. Look!"

No, I was not doomed again to see or to fancy I saw that face. Its mission, so far as I was concerned, was at an end. But the look of concentrated horror which Judith Despard cast at the wall of the room beggars description. Then with a piteous cry she fell at my feet, and seemed to strive to make me shield her from something she dreaded. I raised her. She broke from my grasp, and again fell upon the floor, this time in paroxysms of madness.

My tale is ended. That night she was removed to a private lunatic asylum, where for three years she was kept at my expense. She died raving mad, and from inquiries I made I know that from the moment when it first appeared to her to the hour of her death the face of the man she had killed was ever with Judith Despard.

L. F. Austin

THE GHOST'S "DOUBLE"

"A SECOND FLOOR IN ST. JAMES'S STREET," according to Barty Josselin's biographer, should be a haunt of fashionable dissipation. For some years past I have found it a very decorous abode, "a gentlemanly residence, by Jove!" as Meredith's General Ople would say, but decidedly prosaic. There used to be a black cat which waited for me on the doorstep whenever I came home in the small hours; but even that emblem of dubious habits has disappeared. My second floor is so austere that a friend who always complained that the atmosphere, the furniture, the prints on the walls, filled him with suicidal depression, sent me last Christmas the bust of a Faun, a wicked old classic with vine-leaves in his hair, and his features contorted by a very disreputable wink. This piece of *vertu* stands on the sideboard, and keeps up the wink with singular tenacity, though his surroundings must have convinced him long ago that this superannuated gaiety is quite thrown away.

I was sitting by my fire very late one night at the beginning of autumn. A clock, four clocks, struck two in succession, and I was wondering whether it was happy chance or a polite understanding which prevented them from clashing, when suddenly there was a tremendous pealing of bells on the other side of the street. I looked out of the window; not a soul was to be seen; but at that instant there was a burst of laughter, a woman's laughter, behind me, and turning round, I was amazed to behold in a chair on the opposite side of the fireplace a lady in a curiously old-fashioned evening toilette. She was young, extremely good-looking, and wore her black hair in very full braids on either side of her face, reminding me of an old print of Byron's Gulnare.

A nice visitor at such an hour! I glanced involuntarily at the Faun, whose features seemed to be wrinkled with a fresh and most compromising grin. Following my eyes, the young woman laughed again, and tripping across the room, laid her cheek against his. The picture appealed to my artistic perceptions, but it was not to be tolerated for a moment.

"Really, madam," I said, "I must protest against this intrusion. A second floor in St. James's Street, though you may not think it, has a character to lose. You have mistaken the house, madam, and——"

"Hoity toity!" said she, in an oddly artificial voice, which sounded as if it came out of a phonograph; "I have known this room, sir, for a hundred years. But how you have changed it! Books!"—she made a wry face at the learned tomes which littered the table—"You are sad and scholastic, I fear, not one of the pretty fellows of my day. Still, that Faun——"

"Madam," I said, with dignity, "I must beg you not to jump to hasty conclusions about that—hem!—that object of *vertu*. I do not understand what you mean by a hundred years, and if you will have the goodness to retire——"

She laughed again. "Man alive, what a dull block you are! Did ye not hear the bells over the way?"

"The bells—yes, but——"

"I rang them! I am a ghost—such a very old ghost——"

She paused; evidently I was expected to pay a compliment.

"Time writes no wrinkles—hem!"

"On my azure brow! Very polite of you! So people still quote Byron! We died in the same year, he and I, and I have often wondered why I never met his ghost. We might have such games with the bells!"

"Surely you would not expect the ghost of Byron to engage in such an undignified romp?"

"Pooh! You don't know the ghostly world. We have left off all our classic airs, blood-curdling lamentations, and so forth, and taken to practical joking. It is so much more amusing than waking people in the night to tell them about buried treasure and hidden bones; that sort of melodrama went out of fashion years ago. When you have to be a ghost for ever, you cannot endure gloomy monotony. Now, ringing bells—yours, for instance——"

"Good heavens, madam! I hope you will do nothing of the

kind! The valet who sleeps in the basement will come up, and as he is a most particular man, the sight of you at this hour——"

It was too late. Every bell in the house rang with a startling peal. There were steps on the stairs, and, rushing out of the room, I met James, the valet, to whom I explained rather incoherently that I had become accidentally entangled with the bell-handle. At that moment his candle went out, and something rustled past me with the unmistakable sound of a giggle.

"Very good, sir," said the voice of James in the darkness with sarcastic emphasis.

She was gone, taking my reputation with her! . . . What did this mean? When I re-entered my room, there she sat in the same chair, but with a totally altered expression. The air of saucy mischief was succeeded by a grim stare from her black eyes. The face was much paler, and there was a small red mark on her right temple.

"Pardon me," I stammered, "I fear you are not well. If you will permit me to——" There was a little brandy in a cupboard, but I had a sudden doubt of its efficacy for a fainting spirit!

"What ails you, sir?" The voice was different too—much more phonographic.

"I—I was afraid you were not well. You were so cheerful a few moments ago, and now——"

"What do you mean, man? I never saw you before," she retorted.

"Really, madam, isn't this—hem—rather capricious? Just now you said you were fond of practical joking, and you rang all the bells. Then you passed me on the stairs and laughed. James heard you, and as he is a most particular man——"

She sprang up with a cry which sent a shiver through me—the first ghostlike sensation I had felt since the beginning of these singular proceedings.

"It is my double," she exclaimed; "my deceitful, hateful double! Look at me. Am I like a ghost who would play the fool by ringing bells?"

She was certainly not. Her eyes had a cavernous glare, and from the red mark on her temple a small crimson drop began to trickle.

"Seventy years ago this very night, the man I loved came to me and said he had been ruined by play at Crockford's——"

"Now the Devonshire Club," I remarked. "No gambling there now, I assure you. I am a member."

"Don't interrupt me!" she said fiercely. "He declared he was ruined. It was a lie! He told me he was going home to commit suicide. I asked him to do it here, but he refused."

"Quite right. What would James have said? I beg your pardon. Seventy years ago it was different, of course."

"He swore to me he would blow his brains out at three o'clock. I said I would not survive him. As the clock struck three I shot myself. But he, the monster, betrayed me, and continued his despicable life!"

"A very shabby trick!"

"Is not that enough to poison eternity for a ghost? And now I have a double, a wretched shade, who makes me ridiculous, whereas I used to be respected! This upstart race of spirit-doubles has destroyed the old aristocracy of the ghostly universe. We are driven from our haunts by buffoons! I shall never appear again—never!"

I was irresistibly moved to offer consolation, though I had no idea what I was saying.

"My dear madam, pray don't take it so much to heart. The other lady is certainly flighty. She made most injurious suggestions about that—that object of *vertu* you see on the sideboard——"

Something pinched my ear violently. At my elbow stood the "double," radiant, triumphant, laughing immoderately.

"Ladies!" I cried. "For pity's sake don't quarrel here! If James should come, what on earth should I say? One is bad enough, but two——"

A clock struck the first note of three. I saw a pistol barrel gleaming against the white temple where the red drop had trickled.

"Not here, I implore you. Think of the scandal——"

There was a loud explosion, then a shriek of laughter, and I was alone in the room.

Next day I remembered that I had read something about this theory of the spectre's spectre. Alas! poor old-fashioned ghost, how thy tradition is trampled on and derided by the Comic Spirit!

E. H. Rebton

THE HAUNTED MANOR

𝔄 𝔊𝔥𝔬𝔰𝔱 𝔖𝔱𝔬𝔯𝔶 for 𝔠𝔥𝔯𝔦𝔰𝔱𝔪𝔞𝔰

The Manor stood in a fair domain,
　　Old, in ruins, and grey,
And ivy grew on the broken walls,
　　And brightened its grand decay;
And the stately trees threw a sombre shade
　　The silent paths along
Inviting the owl to a nightly prowl,
　　And the thrush to a morning song.

It had had no tenant for many a year,
　　And its owners, now, were dead,
The last had died on a foreign shore,
　　With a curse upon his head—
The curse that follows a wicked man.
　　Tho' Peasant, or Prince, is he;
He died like a dog, and as a dog
　　They flung him into the sea.

So 'twas said, the manor was "haunted" now,
　　Whatever that may be—
I cannot tell, but I know the place
　　Was shunned to a great degree,
And sounds were heard which to mortal ears
　　Brought ever a shuddering sense,
And creatures came which could ne'er be seen,
　　And none could say from whence.

And bells rang out on the still night air,
    With a strange and jarring sound,
And feet went scampering through the house,
    From the attic to the ground,
And passers-by described the tread,
    As of a mighty host,
And so at last it was resolved,
    To call this legion "Ghost."

Then there arose in every mind,
    The thought it must be settled.
It had been tried before and failed,
    And folks were somewhat "nettled"
To think that what they could not see,
    Should set them at defiance—
And so the village one and all,
    Proposed a strong alliance.

All to the Manor boldly did repair,
    Of course in the "dead of night"—
For Ghosts, as they say "not liking the day,"
    Must be seen in a "different light"—
But when they got there down the dark kitchen stair
    Went rushing the common grey rat,
And up a flight higher near a broken bell-wire,
    Which she played with, was seated—a bat.

J. E. Thomas

THE NAMELESS VILLAGE

A Mystery of the Mendip Hills

Dead and forsaken, buried 'neath a ban,
Nameless, and lost to memory of man.

I HAD BEEN WALKING NEARLY ALL DAY over the Mendip Hills. Many a village and hamlet had I passed in my wanderings, but none so quaint as the one, half hidden in a rosy haze, which I was approaching.

It was nestled deep down in a hollow, and the setting sun tinged the little thatched roofs of the cottages, and the autumnal tinted foliage with touches of gold and crimson and purple.

A faint scent of sweetbriar seemed to pervade this tiny village. It formed altogether such a pretty old world picture, soft moss grew luxuriantly over the little porches, and the last roses of summer bloomed in their tender beauty from the cottage walls and covered like a fairy curtain the diamond-paned window.

Giant hollyhocks and prickly holly bushes, smothered already in scarlet berries, stood like enchanted sentinels at the rustic wooden gates. What, however, struck me as curious was the deathly silence which reigned over all. Not a soul could I see, not a sound greeted my ears. I felt as if I had walked into some spell-bound haunt, or a village buried in the dusty forgotten past of the middle ages.

Not far from the church stood the old manor house. I walked along the avenue of splendid chestnut trees which led to it, wondering how it was I had come across no mention of this queer out-of-the-way little place in my map. The house, built of grey stone, and mantled in ivy, was evidently of very ancient date. Over the stone portico an inscription was carved, but so discoloured by damp as to be impossible to decipher. The door itself, of massive oak and studded with nails, was black with age. My efforts to open it proving unavailing, I was about to retire, when I saw an old dame hobbling towards me. She was attired in a worn black velvet gown, and a white frilled muslin hood covered her head. I asked permission to look over the house; she was apparently dumb, for she vouchsafed me no answer, but silently produced from the reticule a heavy iron key, with which she began to fumble at the lock; it creaked ominously, opening with a harsh, grating sound to admit me. The old lady did not accompany me but left me to make my investigations alone.

The floors were thick with dust, and the furniture, which mainly consisted of oak, was worm-eaten, whilst some fine specimens of tapestry hanging limply on the walls were fretted by a relentless colony of moths.

In the long oak-panelled dining hall several family portraits were fitted into the wainscotting; one of these struck me forcibly, it was the picture of a thin-faced, dark-eyed man, wearing a ruff; but the expression was so life-like and peculiar that it repelled and fascinated me at the same time. Opposite hung the portrait of a girl, but the gloom surrounding the face was so deep that I could make out very little of the features.

A handsome silver sconce, the candles burnt almost to the sockets, and an iron inkhorn were standing on the table.

I passed through many rooms, but a sense of oppression weighed me down, and an indefinable musty odour clung to everything.

My footsteps resounded mournfully through the deserted corridors, and I glanced back more than once when I fancied I could detect the sound of hushed voices whispering behind me.

At last I entered a queer little chamber, more cheerful than the rest. On the deep window seat lay an old manuscript of music, and a mandolin, the chords of which were broken. I looked out of the lattice and saw what must once have been my lady's pleasance; now it was over-grown with weeds and brambles. Just in the middle of the lawn stood a curiously-shaped sundial.

The heavy perfume of a magnolia tree in full bloom, which climbed the wall outside, filled the chamber, while a breath of air came sighing in and stirred the tarnished hangings of the four-poster. At that moment I happened to glance once more at the sundial, and caught my breath suddenly. The transparent form of a girl was standing before it, gazing with bent head at the desolation around her. But the vision of illusion quickly faded and I was left contemplating only the dark shadows of the trees cast by the last flickering rays of the sun on the neglected garden.

After some little difficulty I managed to find my way out of the rambling old house, and on looking back I saw the heavy door slowly pushed from inside and close with a clang, while the key grated in the lock and turned with a hollow groan.

All sorts of odd fancies crowded through my brain as I walked in the direction of the Church, which I was determined to see; the lovers, joys, sorrows and tragedies of byegone days arranged themselves in fantastic groups in my imagination as I passed up the weed-grown pathway.

The church door was open, but it was so dark inside that at first I could make nothing out, but as my eyes grew accustomed to the gloom, I noticed that the air of mystery which enveloped both the mansion and village was not wanting here. The pews, black with age, were all very high and narrow. The large one at the chancel end of the church was even higher than the rest, and square in shape; it also boasted pillars richly carved at each corner, and all round hung velvet curtains spangled with silver cobwebs. Over the altar was a kind of alcove, ornamented with a fresco of cherubim adoring the Holy grail.

Suspended from the groined roof were some tattered flags, whilst long-robed and mail-clad effigies seemed from their shadowed recesses to fix me solemnly with stony, sightless eyes.

Feeling an unaccountable weariness creeping over me, I seated myself in the great square pew, leaving the door open.

Looking up I noticed that the wax tapers on the altar were burning, throwing a dim light over the scene.

Then—my heart stood still, for, gliding slowly up the aisle, came a strange procession.

First, the figure of a girl, covered with a long white veil, and by her side a tall, fair man, then followed a silent, gorgeous crowd. The bride and bridegroom approached the altar rails and knelt there. Three monks stood awaiting them, and one, a man with eyes like fierce gleaming jewels, stretched forth a trembling bony hand above their heads as if in benediction.

Spell-bound I waited—but the vision faded, passing away noiselessly as it had come, into the gathering night.

As I continued to gaze in the direction of the altar my eyes fell upon a coffin: it was draped with a purple pall, while a young, fair-haired man knelt, keeping lonely watch beside it. Then a monk appeared. I saw his face plainly. It was that of the man whose portrait I had seen in the old dining-hall. He stole stealthily up to the kneeling figure. My sight was next dazzled by an upward gleam of steel—something sinking in a dark, huddled heap on the floor—something darker still trickling down the steps—and—nothing more. It must have been a dream conjured up out of the hidden past. That night, when, rather late, I reached the Cheddar, I tried in vain to gain some information regarding the curious little hamlet through which I had passed. Neither my own touring map nor any of those scattered about on the parlour table could afford me the desired information. "Maybe old Sarah can tell you something," suggested mine host.

So next morning, being directed as to her whereabouts, to old Sarah I accordingly went.

She was sitting at the door of her tiny hut, superintending a buxom young lass in her efforts at gardening. She was chatting volubly, and held a long rake in her horny hand, with which she was apparently in the habit of enforcing her remarks at intervals on the rosy-cheeked maiden, thus obviating the trouble of following her about her small domain.

She was evidently not disposed to be communicative to me, the only answer she vouchsafed to my earnest inquiries was "Sae ye have seen the mist village, have ye? Aye, aye, be thankfu' ye cam' oot o' it sound o' limb, nae seek tae enter it again: 'tis dead—dead—I tell ye, sure 'twas a gruesome tale—now Nance, shut thy mouth, child, and tend the lavender yonder." And Nance only managed to elude the pointed exhortation of the rake by a nimble spring over the watering can.

I have often since pondered over my strange experience that day on the Mendip Hills.

Was it but a wraith after all—or "mist village," as old Sarah had called it?

I cannot tell, but next year I must search again for the village which seemed so suddenly and utterly to have vanished from human ken.

Anonymous

OLD SIMONS' GHOST!

O LD SIMONS WAS THE MEANEST and shabbiest old man alive, and living alone on the second floor, the general idea was he had heaps of money. He never showed any; he never spent any; he never paid what he owed until pressure was put upon him, and very frequently he did not pay even then. Earls Court was not at any time inclined to be dressy, but, at the sight of old Simons' squalor, the other tenants rose as one man and cried shame on him.

You who have travelled often up and down by Five Points in Bowery, may have noticed Earls Court,—a small collection of shabby little tenements, over which reigned a gentle melancholy few but the residents therein—for the turning leading to it led nowhere else—cared to disturb.

Sometimes a stray dog tempted by the promise of grateful shade, turned from the noonday sun, strolled in, and stretched himself out for a sleep. One of these wandering mongrels—who had seen better days, perhaps, and mixed with good company— took dire umbrage at Simons' rags one day, and shook them for him vigorously, until the keeper came to the old man's rescue, and forcibly expelled the breaker of the peace.

When he got his breath again, old Simons turned upon his benefactor.

"How came you to let the dog in?"

"I didn't, sir; he came in by himself."

"It was your place to see he didn't come in, then. What do you suppose I pay you for?"

"You don't pay me, sir."

"What do you suppose I owe it for you, then?"

"I don't know, sir; it puts me to a deal of inconvenience."

"You think that's smart, perhaps; but I shall make you pay for my coat."

"As long as you don't make me wear it, sir."

"Don't be impudent. It's my opinion you set the dog on to bite me."

"I'm sure I didn't do that, sir. For my part, I can't think however he could have made his mind up to do it."

With which remark the dialogue terminated rather abruptly, and old Simons retired to his rooms to think it over.

Except that old Simons lived upon the second floor, and kept a clerk, very little was known of him, except, again, that the clerk was a highly objectionable member of the Earls Court community.

The nature of Simons' business was anything but clear to those whose business it hardly was to inquire; and a misty vagueness enveloped his clerk's duties not easily fathomable by the outer world. Except that he sat on a stool, in a sort of little cage, under a skylight, as though he were some sort of choice but ugly plant in process of forcing, but little was known of him.

Except that he made lots of blots. And wondrous was the way in which he squirted ink upon surrounding objects, and carefully shut up blots in day-books and ledgers, and systematically entered smears of all shapes and sizes in various volumes under his care, indexing the same with smeared references to other pages full of scattered ink.

To rectify, to some extent, an obscurity naturally attendant upon this wholesome blotting, it was the habit of this clerk to use his "scratcher" with praiseworthy assiduity, so that a sort of nibbling sound, resembling the gnawing of a rat, frequently struck upon the ear of passers-by upon the stairs, when Simons' outer door stood ajar, and set them wondering what on earth could be the occupation of the Simons minion, partly visible by an artful side view through the keyhole of the inner door.

As may be presumed, from the fact of so slight a noise reaching the passers-by, a profound silence prevailed in Earls Court, even in the busiest hours of the day; but at midnight the stillness of the place had something almost awful in it.

Left alone by himself, the friendless old man must have had a dreary time of it,—and for that reason was it, perhaps, that he had engaged the services of the clerk to keep him company, under a pretence of business.

The clerk, called Bruff, and distinguishable by the fancy name of Artful, was by nature of a sociable and even rollicking turn, with much inmate playfulness of disposition, manifested in harmless pleasantries at the expense of other residents in the Court, though more especially the man in charge of the gate.

The relation of "them antics of that there Artful," formed no mean portion of the discourse of the laundress who had charge of the block to which Simons' set belonged; whilst the phrase of "Oh, that there's Simons' Artful," accounted fully for anything having gone wrong without the trouble of lengthy explanation.

To while away those of his business hours that hung heaviest on his hands, Artful would invoke undecided snatches of music from an instrument of his own invention, fashioned, with much cunning, out of broken nibs of steel pens imbedded in the wood of his desk. From this a little twanging sort of tune could be extracted with some labour, resembling in jerkiness the uncertain results deliverable from a musical toy-omnibus; and he also practised upon a tin whistle with a perseverance that would have been praise-worthy, had not the neighbours found it such a nuisance.

But even Artful's natural buoyancy of spirits was not proof against the dreariness of Simons' set, which became an irksome prison-house, wherein the bloom of Artful's youth seemed seriously threatened. Bottled up here in a horrible little box of an office, part of the roof of which was a skylight, and part the bottom of a cistern, Artful, when he had booked his daily blots, began sometimes to find his official life a burthen to him, and stole out upon the landing to commune with his kind, or into old Simons' room, next door, to gaze out from the window into the little court below, or take deadly aim at the gate-keeper with a catapult, which he kept for that purpose.

At other times, leaning back with his office stool at a dangerous angle, he would gaze drearily upwards at a forest of chimney-pots, the crookedness of which was exaggerated by the distorting properties of the skylight, its every other pane containing a flaw.

But the dreariness of these daylight hours was as nothing when compared to the solitude of night, should old Simons chance to go out, and leave him to his own resources. Upon such occasions he would steal out too, and if he had no money to spend in refreshment, walk the street until he was quite tired out, and hurry into bed, dragging the bed-clothes over his head for safety.

"I wonder how old Simons stood it all by himself before I came?" he used to think. "I wonder how the deuce I should stand it without old Simons?"

And then another reflection would presently occur to him.

"If I had Simons' money, I should precious soon cut this dead-and-alive old shop, and spend the rest of my life in a reasonable manner."

His notions with regard to a manner that was more reasonable might have appeared a little unreasonable to an unprejudiced third person. The summit of his ambition at this early period was to wear clothes "built proper," as he would have termed it, with all the newest "fakements," and he would have liked to have taken the chair at a "select harmonic," or been a regular in the lounge of a music hall, on "pally terms" with the comic "talent."

But these views of his underwent some slight change as time rolled on, and gradually a sort of idea crept into Artful's mind that the old set in Earls Court might be made endurable if he had Simons' money to spend in it. Where was Simons' money, though? Ah! that was a question to be answered only by Simons himself, and would he ever answer it? And would Artful ever have any of it? Who could say? Not Artful, certainly!

The way that Artful had come to live with old Simons was this:—

Simons had said one day, suddenly entering the office for the purpose of asking the question, and surprising Artful tilted at an amazing angle, with his gaze fixed on the chimney-pots,—

"Is the money I give you enough to keep you!"

"It keeps me alive," responded Artful.

"You don't have enough to eat?"

"Not nearly."

"How much does your lodging cost you?"

"One dollar a week."

"You can save that, if you like, by sleeping here. I've got a bedstead in the loft that you can have."

Half an hour later old Simons appeared again, with equal suddenness, to ask another question.

"Stop a bit, though: you're an orphan, aren't you?"

"Yes."

"You've no relations living, have you?"

"No."

"No more have I," said old Simons; "but perhaps you won't be able to sleep on a straw mattress."

When old Simons had spoken about a bedstead, he had said a bedstead, but had made no mention of bedding beyond the mattress particularized.

The mattress in question proved to be of the thinnest, so that after the first night Artful arose severely scored by the wooden framework, from the sharp edges of which it afforded no material protection, while the one thin blanket Simons had given him could hardly be called a sufficient provision against the chilliness of a November night. It was not, indeed, until more than a month had elapsed, that Artful slept with anything like comfort.

But he got accustomed to the hardness of his bed as he grew used to the dreariness of the old Court, and as years crept slowly past, and he still occupied the stool beneath the skylight, one fixed idea took possession of his mind, which, put into words, meant something very like this:—

"Here am I, young and active, worth double my wages, and yet wasting my life away in the service of a selfish old wretch, who will some day kick me out into the street, when he takes a fancy to do so, and I shall have nothing to show for all the long years I have lost working for him. On the other hand, there is a selfish old wretch, whose life is a burthen to himself, and a drawback to the comfort to others, who has money that is no good to him, and who hasn't a soul in the world to leave it to. Why doesn't he give a little of it to me while he lives? He'd never miss it. Or, if he won't do that, why doesn't he die and leave it me, which would be much the best thing he could do?"

One night, when the clerk was thus reflecting seated at a table opposite to the old man, who, bending over a book of accounts, rested his head upon his hand, and shaded his eyes from the light, old Simons leant back and fixed him with a steadfast gaze.

"I don't suppose," said he, "that I shall last much longer."

The colour faded suddenly from his companion's cheeks, and his eyes drooped beneath the other's eyes.

"Who says you are going to die?" he asked, with a nervous twitching of the lips. "Who wants you to die, I'd like to know? What do you mean?"

"I don't know who should wish me dead," said old Simons, after a few moments' silence. "Not any one that I owe money to, I should think; and no one can have any expectations from me, for no one has any claim on my consideration."

"No one," thought the clerk to himself. "Not even me, who have wasted my life for him."

But he said nothing. Only waited and watched, and cudgelled his brains. "Did any one exist who could lay claim to the old man's money when he was gone? Was he likely to go soon? Where was the money?"

To have found an answer to any one of these three questions was no easy task. To answer them all, a seeming impossibility. But one answered itself the very next night.

They sat alone again, master and clerk. The clerk was eating a frugal supper of bread and butter. Old Simons, with the same account-book he had been studying the previous evening spread open before him, sat in much the same attitude, his head resting on his hand.

He sat in such a way that his upraised hand shaded his face, and the clerk more than once stole a stealthy glance at him, to see that old Simons was not watching him covertly.

"What's he thinking of, I wonder?" the younger man thought. "Is he counting up those figures? No, he's too long about that. There's something on his mind, and he's not well. Why shouldn't I put it to him? He's a bit shaken just now, and can be managed all the easier, with a little care."

And so he presently spoke aloud, drooping his own eyes though, as he did so, for he felt that old Simons was looking at him fixedly.

"I've been thinking over what you said, sir, last night, and I hope you won't take it as a liberty if I say a few words."

Here he paused, but Simons made no reply, and he continued:

"Of course, sir, I hope you had no reason for saying what you did say about not lasting long, for I don't think I ever saw you look heartier."

He paused again here, but still there was no answer.

"However, sir, as you put it that way, and as you know the best of us are only mortal, as it were, I thought I would make so bold as to ask if you would at any time, when most convenient to you, give me a few instructions I might act up to, in case—of—in case of anything——"

He felt that he was turning the phrase awkwardly, and stammered and stopped, expecting that Simons at last must make some rejoinder.

But he was still silent. Was he offended? Was he thinking what reply to make? He was slow enough sometimes in making a response. A minute passed—two minutes, and yet he had not spoken.

"Mr. Simons!"

No answer.

"Mr. Simons!"

Was he asleep?

The clerk, with a strange terror creeping over him, raised the candle, and threw its rays upon his master's face. The eyes, as he had thought, were fixed upon him, but with a meaningless stare.

For he was dead!

One of the three questions thus settled in favour of Artful Bruff, there yet remained two others for which he looked for an answer. Would any one put in a claim for the old man's money? and where was the money?

The latter question seemed to the cold-hearted knave the foremost for consideration, as, after the first frantic rush of wild terror, he had run out upon the stairs, calling for help. As it occurred to him, he came to a sudden standstill, and ceased his cry.

No one had heard him. Yes, a window was thrown open

upon the opposite side of the court, and a head appearing there, seemed to listen for a while. Then the window was shut to again. All else was silent.

He paused to collect his thoughts and regain his lost courage.

Should he venture back again, and have a look round, before any one came? Yes, he would creep noiselessly back, and when he had made all safe, raise the alarm.

He paused again, however, upon the threshold of the room, and peered in with a sort of sickening dread that something might have changed its place while he had been away.

But nothing had stirred; and drooping over one side of the arm-chair, where he had left it, he found the body still, with the breast-pocket of the coat he had torn open a while ago invitingly agape.

With the conviction strong upon him that possession was nine points of the law, Artful Bruff waited for nobody's permission, but buried the old man in the cheapest possible manner, and seized upon his goods and chattels. These he found, for the most part, of very little value, though good enough for use. There were also a couple of sacks of coal in the cellar, and them, as it was bitter December weather, he found a very pleasant acquisition.

But as to money, when the funeral expenses were paid, there remained little over twenty shillings in hard cash. What had become of it all?

Many long hours Artful Bruff sat alone, cudgelling his brains, much as he had done during the old man's life, for a solution to this difficult problem. Where was the money locked up? How was it to be got at?

There must be papers and documents somewhere that would throw some light upon the subject. Was there no banker's book? No. And the book of accounts that the old man studied so frequently? Incomprehensible. And the books that Artful Bruff himself had kept so zealously during his clerkship in the box?

He turned these pages over and over, now that he had, as he considered, acquired a sort of hereditary right to their contents, and searched for a happy result among the multitudinous blots and smears he found there. But if the truth must be told, this fellow was, at best, but a shallow rogue and thief, and, like most rogues and thieves, a great fool withal, at anything outside the small trade of petty larceny.

He had floundered for years among these pages of figures without being able to understand their principle; and now, when it was all in all to him to solve the mystery of their meaning, he could make nothing of it.

Yet how was this? Was there any intended mystery? Not at all. The mystification arose out of Artful Bruff's stupidity. He had entertained a vague idea that old Simons was carrying on a large business of some sort or other, with the exact whereabouts of which he was unacquainted, but which he supposed it would be easy enough, whenever he thought fit to take the trouble, to obtain all particulars. Now, however, when the time had come, he failed.

Here, sure enough, were payments and receipts in plenty; but where was the business, and of what nature?

Who were the Harringtons and Robinsons referred to? How was it something was left over, and what was the nature of the "old account?"

During his life, old Simons' behaviour had always been very mysterious. No one had, at any time, to Artful's knowledge, called on the old man. His own duties as a clerk, dispassionately considered, were, to a great extent, vague and unsatisfactory, and, at the beginning of his servitude, he had more than once wondered to himself why Simons kept a clerk at all.

Except the entry and endorsing in his ledgers of such mysterious items as those enumerated from old Simons' private notebook, Artful did no other kind of work, never, on any occasion, was sent on an errand, and never accompanied old Simons when he went abroad, which he did daily for an indefinite number of hours.

What on earth was his business? During the old man's life, in the early period of his clerkship, he had never sought to know, and had not cared to do so. It had been enough for him that he was sure of his food and shelter, and such wages as old Simons chose to give him. Later on, when he was anxious to know all he could, the old man had been even closer about his affairs than ever. Artful had, therefore, bided his time, making certain that at his death, his private papers would reveal all.

Now that he was dead, and the private papers carefully searched, the secret remained as dark as ever. The papers revealed nothing.

There was no evidence of any kind of property existing—no banker's book, no receipts, no business address—in short, not one tittle of evidence to show that old Simons had ever had anything to do out of doors.

Artful Bruff, the search at an end, felt that affairs were looking anything but promising.

What was he to do when his little store of cash was exhausted, and when he had realized what money he could upon the furniture contained in the room? Well, he could go on for a week or two, and then something might turn up, perhaps. In the meanwhile, he would make inquiries.

To begin with, what did the court-keeper know? The court-keeper had always understood old Simons had some money.

"Did he ever talk to you about his business?"

"He was always precious close about it to me."

"He never said where it was?"

"Where what was?"

"Where he went to, I mean, when he went down the City."

"Never knew for certain that he went down the City."

"He never sent you with any message?"

"Never, all the eighteen years I've been here."

"He came before your time?"

"A matter of ten years before."

"Do you think the landlord knows anything of him?"

"The present landlord, I think, knows nothing. The one that Mr. Simons took the chambers of is dead."

This information obtained from the court-keeper was, in substance, the information obtained in all other quarters where Artful Bruff made inquiries, and he lost no opportunity of asking questions.

The night of old Simons' death was the fourteenth of December. On the night of the twenty-fourth, his self-constituted legatee sat by the fireside, warming himself with his last scuttle of coals, and turning over in his mind the momentous question of what he should do with his last dollar.

It was a bitterly cold night, and the Court seemed more lonely and silent than usual. In the distance, as he sat listening, he thought he could now and then detect the sound of Trinity bells. It was Christmas Eve, and most people were merry-making after their own fashion.

Artful Bruff stabbed the coal in the stove savagely with the poker as this reflection occurred to him. He had not grown over-sociable of late years, and he did not care particularly for merry-makings, but he would have liked to have felt more certain than he did of a Christmas dinner.

There was left of a little store Simons had treasured up a solitary bottle of Bourbon. He brought it out from the cupboard, and half filled a tumbler, then lit a pipe, and drew his chair nearer to the stove.

"I'll get through to-morrow the best way I can," said he, "and next day I'd better realize on the chairs and tables—what's that?"

He was making this reflection when a loud noise upon the stairs caused him for a moment to suspend the progress of the Bourbon from the table to his lips. He put the glass down and listened. Something had bumped loudly against the wall. And now the sound was audible again, nearer the room door. Artful Bruff arose and went to see what was the matter, and saw a large black trunk coming up the stairs.

A second glance showed him that a man accompanied it, but the trunk came up first upon his shoulders. When they reached the landing on which Bruff stood, the man paused for breath, and put the trunk down.

"For Mr. Bruff," the man said.

"For me?"

"For Mr. Bruff, Earls Court."

"All right."

The man carried the box into the room, and took off his cap to wipe the perspiration from his face.

"It's a heavy one, sir, this is. If it had had on the other corner, I don't think I could have carted it at all."

"The other corner?"

"There's only three on 'em as it is, sir, you see."

It was, as the man had intimated, a three-cornered trunk, and altogether of a curious build. Was it meant for him? Artful Bruff thought. Most likely not. There was another Bruff in the Court. But if the man persisted in leaving it, that was his look-out, and the other Bruff's, who ought to have looked out sharper.

"What are you waiting for?"

"Waiting for? I thought you might have the price of a drink, boss, that's all. It's a toughish job, all the way from the street across the yard and up these stairs. Shouldn't like to have to carry such weights often."

"Don't the people who employ you pay your wages?"

"Eh? Oh, yes, they pay me."

"That's all right, then," said Artful. "Good evening to you."

The carter put on his cap again, without waiting until he had left the room.

"I'm much obliged to you," said he, "and I wish you a merry Christmas, and many on 'em!"

"Thank you," said Artful, drily.

Then, having listened until the echo of the carter's steps had died away in the distance, he closed and locked the door, and sat down in front of this peculiarly made trunk.

To take a survey at his ease of his newly-acquired property, Artful seated himself upon a sort of locker, which was a fixture in one corner of the room between the window and the fireplace, close to the spot where the trunk had been put down by the carter.

"It's very certain," he said to himself, "that the thing is not meant for me. This is, without doubt, a Christmas present for the other Bruff, and how awfully sold he will be if he expected it particularly!"

There was an inscription on a piece of paper, pasted on the lid, and he leant forward and read the words with some little difficulty, for the ink seemed curiously old and faded.

"The fools have left it out in the rain. There's hardly any making it out, but sure enough there's no Christian name given.

It's Bruff only—Mr. Bruff. Why shouldn't that be me? No harm can come of opening it."

It was easy to say open it, but the operation promised to be rather a difficult one. As well as he could make out, the lid seemed to be screwed down on all sides. Luckily, he had got a small chisel, to find which, however, occupied a good half-hour. In a fury of impatience at this delay, he then set about the work with great violence, and broke the frail implement in two at almost the first wrench he give to the lid.

The court-keeper would be pretty certain to have a proper screw-driver. Should he ask for it? Why not? What o'clock was it? At the moment he asked himself the question, a neighbouring clock chimed a half-hour. It was half-past twelve.

Rather late for the keeper, who was in the habit of pulling the wire for the gate from his bed, and Artful was on anything but friendly terms with him. Still, it was worth trying.

He went to the keeper's room, and found that worthy just turning in for the night. He had not got a screw-driver, and didn't know who had. He was very certain he could not borrow one at that time of night.

Artful Bruff retraced his steps disconsolately to his rooms, and set to work again with the broken chisel, only to break it again, in a few minutes, without causing any noticeable change in the fastenings.

To search the rooms, and prise and wrench at the obstinate lid with every likely and unlikely tool and implement, even to the old man's razors, which he desperately jagged into the semblance of a saw, was the occupation upon which Bruff employed the next three-quarters of an hour. But yet the lid of the trunk remained firm as a rock.

Artful Bruff sat down quite exhausted, and, in a dreamy sort of way, read through the address once more.

"Mr. Bruff, Earls Court."

But there was something written below that he had not previously noticed,—"NOT TO BE OPENED TILL CHRISTMAS DAY."

"Why not?" Artful asked aloud. "But, whoever it was who said so, they seem very likely to have their way, for there's no saying for certain when I shall loosen these beastly screws. The confounded thing is fastened up as tight as if it were a coffin."

As if it were a coffin! What an unpleasant idea to occur to him all at once, and just at the moment, too, when the candle—the last candle he had got—began to flicker in its socket!

But, after all, the idea was very ridiculous, for who ever heard of a three-cornered coffin? though, for that matter, who ever heard of a three-cornered trunk? And a box shaped like that was, surely no other box had ever been shaped before like it—unless it were—good heavens!

Why, that locker fixed into the wall, between the window and the fireplace, was exactly similar to it! Bruff measured it hastily with his pocket handkerchief. Yes, it was the fellow locker to the one already in the room; and that over there was the corner where it ought to have been fixed in—where, perhaps, it had been fixed, at some remote period, before Artful Bruff made acquaintance with the chambers.

But then came the question, Who had sent it? The rascal's heart beat faster as a dreadful thought occurred to him, and, catching up the expiring light, he took another more careful look at the address upon the lid.

This time he made a discovery that he wondered he had not made before. This time, however, he was certain of the truth. There could, indeed, be no doubt about the matter.

The writing on the trunk was that of the dead man—old Simons.

One moment after he had arrived at this horrible conclusion, the expiring candle, with a last faint flicker, went out, and he was left in utter darkness.

Artful Bruff stood for a moment uncertain how to act, the perspiration breaking out upon his face. Then, guided by an instinctive sense of self-preservation, he groped his way hastily to the bedroom door, and pulled off his clothes and scrambled into bed.

"After all, though," he thought, when he had lain there with his head covered up by the bedclothes for some twenty minutes or so, "there's nothing wonderful in it. He must have directed the trunk to me some time ago. He meant it for a Christmas present. He was always so eccentric, and the weight of the box is easily accounted for, it's full of money; worse luck, I can't touch it till the morning, so I'll go to sleep."

Creak!

"The wind must have sprung up, and is at work with that crazy old shutter at the back. What a nuisance, if it's going on like that all night."

Creak!

"The noise isn't at the back. I hope I haven't left the outer door open."

Creak!

"If I have, I ought to get up and shut it."

Creak!

"What is there to be afraid of?"

Creak!

"But it isn't the door. It's something in the next room! It's the trunk!" It *was* the trunk. THE TRUNK WAS OPENING BY ITSELF!

Artful Bruff strained his neck and eyes in the direction from which the sound proceeded. He had left the sitting-room door open behind him when he beat a retreat, and as he lay in bed he could plainly see the mysterious black trunk, standing out from surrounding darkness in a sort of dim grey light.

As he watched, the lid, with a series of creaks, slowly opened, and, to his unutterable horror, a something in the shape of old Simons undoubled itself, as it were, creaking also at its rusty joints, and creeping out with a painful effort, as it seemed, sat down upon the edge of the trunk to get breath.

The hair of his head bristly with terror, Artful Bruff regarded this awful visitor with distended eyes, and wondered what on earth was going to happen next.

The ghost, meanwhile, was yawning, and stretching itself, and presently began very slowly to draw off its clothes, and then, taking up the empty candlestick in his hand, came towards the bed. Artful Bruff's flesh crept at the sight. His first impulse was to dive under the clothes, but the horror of being fished for by those long, lean, fleshless hands was more terrible for him than to face the phantom which now was standing by his side, and staring in seeming wonder upon him.

"Hallo!" said old Simons' ghost, "what are you doing in my bed?"

"I beg your pardon, sir," said Artful Bruff, "I didn't think you would want it again."

"Where are my coals and candles?" asked the ghost.

"I thought you'd done with them, sir," replied Bruff.

"What have you been doing with my razors?"

"If I'd had any idea I was disturbing you, sir," said Bruff, "I'd never have dreamt of doing it."

The ghost smiled at this, and scraped its chin with its hand in a way old Simons had of scraping his during his lifetime. Artful Bruff could not help thinking, even through his terror, how well the ghost took old Simons off.

"You've jagged the edges dreadfully," said the ghost; "but I dare say they will do well enough for what I want, even now. I shall go and fetch one, and cut your throat. Then your ghost and I will have a glass or two of Bourbon together until sunrise."

The phantom glided back into the parlour, having said this, and Artful Bruff fainted.

When he came to his senses again, the first thing he did was to feel his throat, and finding it pretty well in the same condition he had left it over night when he went to bed, except that it was inwardly rather hot and parched, he arose cautiously, and looked around.

Old Simons' representative was not present. It was past sunrise then, and he had returned to the box.

"He's shut the bedroom door after him," thought Bruff; "I recollect leaving it open."

He peeped cautiously into the next room when he had turned the door-handle, and uttered a loud exclamation of surprise.

Old Simons must have taken away the box—it was nowhere to be seen.

Just then a footstep was audible upon the stairs. It was the court-keeper.

"What time is it, do you know?" asked Artful.

"About noon."

"Noon! How soundly I have slept."

"Very sound, I should think, not to hear the noise that man made."

"What—Simons?"

"Simons! What do you mean?"

"Oh, nothing. What man were you speaking of?"

"The one that came for the box."

"A man came for the box—when?"

"This morning, about seven."

"And you let him take it?"

"He left it here in a mistake, he said."

"A mistake?" asked Artful Bruff; "who said it was a mistake? Where's he taken it to?—to the other Bruff?"

"No; he took it away altogether."

"And you let him do it?"

"I didn't know he had no right to do so. He told me you'd told him he could, and I saw that it was he who brought it last night."

"Was he an Adams' Express man? What sort of wagon had he?"

"He had a private wagon, both last night and this morning."

"Have you no idea where he came from?"

"No. Haven't you?"

"No," said Artful; "get out."

And so the court-keeper got out; and here this mystery ends.

The mystery of the trunk was never cleared up, nor was that of Artful Bruff's sudden disappearance, which occurred a few days after this strange event.

Whether or not the likeness between the address on the box and old Simons' handwriting was only the result of Artful Bruff's fevered imagination, or the Bourbon, is an open question.

J. W. Hollingsworth

MIRIAM'S GHOST

A Christmas Story

C APTAIN DESMOND LEANED BACK in the open carriage with
an unusual sense of enjoyment and relief, as his gaze took
in spots of peculiar interest in the changing views of the country
road, along which he was being rapidly whirled to his destina-
tion. The close atmosphere of a first-class carriage of an express
train from which he had emerged, after a four hours journey not
half-an-hour since, had left its usually cramped depression upon
an active man used to open-air exposure, and he felt the rush of
the wintry breeze upon his face with keen pleasure.

After the conclusion of the Afghan War, in which Hugh Desmond had gained both honour and distinction for the great ability
he had displayed, in the execution of several difficult and arduous
commissions, in which untiring watchfulness and marked bravery had placed his name in the forefront of those valued at the
War Office, he had now arrived in England on leave of absence,
after an unusually long period of service in India.

The Desmonds were an old and extremely aristocratic family,
who traced their origin back to a time previous to the period
of the Norman Conquest, and to whom the part of the country towards which he was being rapidly driven, had formerly
belonged up to the reign of Henry VIII, when the main portion
of the Desmond family became open adherents of the Protes-
tant cause and the Reformation. But during the conflict of the
two succeeding reigns the vast estates were lost to his family, and
had been repeatedly bought and re-sold; the present owner, an
extremely wealthy banker, being the grandson of the freeholder.
The Maitland family had been bosom friends of Desmond's
father, and so, very soon after his return to England, he was a

Christmas guest at Gurthford Manor, which was now visible from the acclivity he had reached on the road, and about a mile distant. A few minutes later the road commenced to descend gradually, leading through a wooded district on both sides of the way, terminating at Gurthford Park, upon entering the gates of which disclosed an avenue in a splendid forest of pine trees, which shortly after opened upon pasture land with the ancient Manor and Priory in full view in the sunshine of the wintry afternoon. On Desmond's arrival at the mansion a welcome reception awaited him, and he was soon engaged in rapid conversation with his host and family.

It wanted but three days to Christmas, and several guests were yet to arrive on a Christmas visit, and a large house party was arranged for the coming festival. The shadows deepened, and soon after the well-lighted and curtained room enhanced the comfort of the ruddy firelight, and the cheerful conversation was brought to a temporary close by his being compelled to retire to his room to dress for dinner. Less than an hour later the family were seated to dinner. The head of the family, Mr. Maitland, was a well preserved and handsome man rather under sixty. He himself had been an only son, and, with the exception of the private fortunes of his two sisters, had inherited the Manor and the adjoining estates, together with an immense fortune and successive interest in the large banking firm which his great grandfather had founded. Thus born heir to a very large inheritance, he was a rich man and had long since withdrawn from any active part in financial business of the banking firm. He married early and had in family two sons, Horace and Gilbert, now aged twenty-two and seventeen, and three daughters, Frances, Emily, and Lucy. The elder sister was about twenty-five years of age, her second sister was about three years younger though rather fairer and not quite so tall, yet bore a remarkable likeness to her. Lucy was a girl of fifteen. Mrs. Maitland was nearly ten years younger than her husband.

All without exception who have travelled for long in any far distant country, especially for years, realize in a most extraordinary manner the peculiarly happy sensation experienced upon returning to their native home. Hugh Desmond loved his country with a wonderful devotion, and his enjoyment at this moment was of that transcendent character which baffles description. He was a brave, generous, and devoted man in disposition, whose only personal regard was his honour, and at thirty years of age he was a singularly handsome man and a perfect type of an English gentleman. A sudden and new life was dawning upon him unconsciously this winter's afternoon, and illuminating his soul with an intoxicating rosy light, and uniting him with that abode in the realms of happiness which is perhaps the most blissful. He was seated next to the mother of Frances Maitland, but his gaze unavoidably rested again upon Frances, who was in truth a very beautiful woman. Tall and lithe of stature, the exquisite proportions of her form and figures were enhanced by a deep blue velvet winter dress, the rich folds affording a vivid contrast to the creamy whiteness of her arms. Her rich dark-brown hair fell in a profusion of natural ringlets over her temples and massing away from them over her head and drooping to the back of her neck. Her forehead was low and broad, her eyes deep, soft clear brown, with delicately arched eyebrows and long drooping lashes which looked almost black in their depth. Her nose was straight, with that finely chiselled arching at the nostrils which is called spiritual. Her lips were exquisitely formed with that upward turn at the corners called "Cupids bow," and denoting sweetness and amiability of temper, and which always indicates a noble self-sacrificing character. The expression which lent its peculiar charm to her very intelligent face was that of patient innocence. It was the happiest evening of his life, and later, when she sang for him, the sweet penetrating tones of her voice thrilled the depths of his soul, and, as it were, filled him with its melody. When a girl of little more than sixteen he had loved her, and after an absence of nearly ten years, that love awakened with a tenfold force. Her beauty had matured and developed into not only a glorious womanhood, but a powerful and exalted soul, the influence of which once thoroughly established, was not to be forgotten, and especially by such a highly appreciative man as Hugh Desmond, whose heart throbbed faster at the kind pressure of her hand, ere he retired for the night.

Christmas Eve brought with it not only a full house party for whom accommodation was arranged, but an unexpected lady guest as the last moment, whose comfort was a matter of consideration at a time when the family were alone.

"I should not like to let her share a room or to go into an unused one," observed Mrs. Maitland to her husband.

"Might I suggest," said Hugh, "that it would give me a great pleasure if the lady could have my room which is so very comfortable, and I should be quite safe and at home in an unoccupied one, for I have been used for many years to far greater exposures, to frequent inclemency, as regards my surroundings, to have any fear of a damp room."

"The difficulty is of another nature, Captain," replied Mr. Maitland, "though one of the best rooms in the house, it has been seldom used for years, for more than a night at a time; it has a bad reputation," and a smile crossed his face as he uttered the words—"it is called the Haunted Room."

Hugh's face lit up at the words. "The very adventure I have longed for as an experience for years. Pray gratify my wish now you have the chance; lest such an one might not occur again during my life-time," and he added "but I have no belief in apparitions, and I shall be disappointed if I do not go. Please let me have my own way."

All, especially Frances Maitland, endeavoured to deter him, for a look of apprehension crossed her face, but he persisted the more in his wish and broke into a merry peal of laughter.

"Let me tell you," said Mr. Maitland, "that it will be difficult to induce the servants to go there, and none of us ever do; it is kept locked, Captain."

Remonstrance was in vain, Desmond's merriment was infectious, and amidst the laughter he had provoked he enquired if there was any legend attached to the Haunted Room, and who was the ghost.

"It is said to be the ghost of the Miriam Desmond, who was one of the last of your known ancestors in England," was the reply. "She became a nun, and her two brothers went away no one knew whither; she is called by the country folks, 'the White Lady,' and that she is at times seen is a firmly rooted superstition."

"That clinches the matter," returned Hugh, "as long as I stay, please let me be there. I have a right to be with my ancestors who could not possibly harm me; yet I may not hope for a visit from one of them."

The bell was rung and when the aged butler received his instructions to convey to the housekeeper, with orders to assist her as rapidly as possible, for the Captain's occupation, his pale scared face told its own story. But he was a trusted servant and did not express his opinion. Fires were ordered to be lighted and kept going with the windows open for occupation on the succeeding night, as the lady visitor would not arrive till the morning of Christmas Day. That Christmas morn dawned as the happiest Hugh Desmond had ever known; his very eyelids enclosed with a great wonderment and half self-questioning of its reality. But it was all real and true, and breakfast would again bring him into the presence of Frances Maitland. It was a brilliant winter's day, clear and sunshiny, and free from snow. The large house party gave the family the full complement of guests, and at the evening party were assembled a number of neighbouring friends and children, which filled the spacious rooms, lighted and garlanded for the season's festivities; and as the evening wore on, the happy enjoyment seemed to deepen and gather greater happiness, as singing and dancing gave place to story-telling, and blind man's buff, and forfeits. The elderly lady visitor at the latter was the judge, and, alike with others, the lips of Frances Maitland met those of Hugh beneath the mistletoe, and his heart bounded with rapture, and a rosy haze blinded his vision for the moment. Now and again the guests would seek the cool of the conservatory, and amidst the soft glow of the Chinese lanterns Hugh and Frances stood by the rippling fountain, and, drawing her to him, he kissed her head, saying, "I love you; you cannot tell how much I love you," and again their lips met in a long, loving kiss, and then, arm in arm, they sauntered back and joined again in the waltz and country dance till a late hour, and the younger guests began to depart. It was approaching the midnight hour before the family and friends separated for the night, and Hugh, in a whirl of happiness and joy, took his way to his apartment.

As he entered the haunted room for the first time, and set his candle upon the table, and then closed the door after him, he then remembered his conversation regarding it with Mr. Maitland. It was a much larger apartment than the one he had vacated, being nearly or quite square with high, and, in places, carved and panelled oak wainscotting, polished, and black with age. A cheerful fire blazed upon the hearth and wide and heavy curtains overhung the window which appeared so large that he was impelled to draw aside the folds, when he found that the extensive window, which attracted his notice, was really three gothic-shaped windows, the centre one being the largest, with the curious diamond-shaped panes of glass, with leaden glazing, and latticed, opening outwards.

Hugh glanced at the fastenings of the windows; they were all secure, and then re-placed the curtains; then walking to the fire-place seated himself in the comfortable easy chair, and glanced round at the antique chamber with mingled wonder and admiration, for he could not but feel impressed with the solemn grandeur of the room; but equally he wondered at himself, for yet in a few moments his sensations had unaccountably passed from the most joyous hilarity to a feeling of sad and sorrowful regret, tempered with anxiety. The room was quite warm, perceptibly so, for the fire had been well kept up since the previous day; he felt no sign of chill or cold, yet the sudden transition was so great that an instant after he strove to ridicule himself for letting the remembrance of the legend weigh upon his spirits.

Hugh shook himself, stooped down, took off his boots, and put on his slippers; then, walking to the door, opened it, and put the boots outside; as he did so a rush of joyous warmth seemed to pervade his being, and instinctively he stepped out with his slippered feet and stood alone in the silent dark corridor. The change was remarkable beyond description, his whole being thrilled with a great comfort; then he turned, and re-entering the room closed the door, and turning the handle of the key in the lock felt the handle of the door. It was fast.

Once more he felt as though he had entered a tomb. He glanced at the very large, old, and handsome four-post bedstead, and ejaculated mentally, "I shall soon get spoiled at this rate; soft and easy quarters seem to be enervating, this is a proof of it."

Rapidly preparing himself, he undressed, extinguished the

light, and went to bed, feeling tired, partly, but longing most for sleep till morning. He lay watching the flickering shadows cast by the slowly declining firelight. He closed his eyes and sought repose, and tried to think of Frances, but it was with a sad anxious feeling that he longed for the morning, and now and again he dozed. Then he fell asleep. He awoke with a slight start as though some noise had awakened him, and turning, listened, but the most profound silence reigned, and then thinking he must have started in his sleep, drowsiness was again stealing over him, when the distant Church bell began to strike. Arousing himself for the moment, he listened attentively, for the bell was tolling the warning for the hour, then with the few seconds pause came the solemn deep-toned single stroke of one o'clock.

"Only one," he mused, as he closed his eyes again, "I could have slept only a few minutes; I thought it later," and soon he slept profoundly once more. How long he slept he could not tell, but again his slumber was broken in the same manner; he started awake, and feeling intense weariness listened. Perfect, stilly silence reigned, and longing for sleep he strove to quiet himself. Soon he fell in a half-sleep, and was again disturbed by a strange hollow and distant booming sound. Conjecturing that it might be an unclosed door jarring with the draught, he nearly slept again, when the same sound was repeated, and notwithstanding his every effort to compose himself, for the desire for sleep became almost hungry with its intensity, he repeatedly awoke with the same sound occurring at intervals of two or three minutes.

He asked himself what it could be, and whether in the house or far distant; or whether it was really a sound, or noise, or a deception of his senses. But the noise kept on. At the same short intervals of about two minutes came the weird boom, seeming to come from the depths of space, and to strike upon the centre of his being. And now a new feeling came over him more prominent than the distant weird disturbance, an awful thirst for sleep, and he knew that he was fighting, and as it were almost struggling, for repose. But strive as he might, there was no intermission. Then he ceased to feel it, and a feeling of relief, mingled with dread, came over him lest it should disturb him again. Once more he slept, but with his senses acutely strained even in sleep, when a new and shocking sound struck upon his ear—the awful sound to a true man of a woman's sob of intense suffering and sorrow; the deep drawn quivering sob of a woman in the extremity of anguish, weird, unearthly, distant, but yet still seeming to be within a few feet of Desmond.

A sensitive chord of his soul had been aroused, and from its depths mingled sympathy, grief, and compassion welled up, and with it regret, for he could think of no distant female friend who might be imagined to be in danger or suffering. But the desire for sleep became an agony, and closing his eyes again he strove to drown his senses, and almost succeeded when the same detonation already described, commenced again; it kept on in the same way, at the same intervals, and though prostrate with weariness, repose eluded him, and with each repetition his blood seemed to collide in its course, and he gasped for breath; it kept on, it grew insufferable, he could bear no more. Turning upon his back he swept the hair from his heated forehead with his hand, and with his arms flung wide gave up all hope of rest, and resolved to keep awake the rest of the night.

Now that Desmond was fully awake, intense silence prevailed. His senses were undisturbed. Yet he dreaded to sleep again. Then he remembered the strange reputation of the chamber in which he was, and he thought the coincidence remarkable, but resolved to make no mention of his impression on the morrow.

A new impulse came over him to get up and dress himself, and give up all prospect of sleep that night. He arose, struck a match, and lit his candle and looked at his watch. It was twenty minutes past two o'clock.

He dressed himself completely, put on his slippers, and seated himself in the easy chair, and leant back, gazing at the last expiring glow of the hollows left of the dying fire, and though his limbs almost ached with weariness, and he longed for rest, he yet felt glad he had risen and the reflection struck him that in an hour at most the candle would be burnt out, and he would be in the dark. He got up, walked softly to the window and drew aside one of the curtains. It was a brilliant moonlight. He flung all the curtains wide till the three large windows were bare, and the room was flooded with moonlight. Then he walked to the table and extinguished the candle, and the room seemed lighter than before, and he re-seated himself, and as he leant back in his chair, he grew more composed, pacified almost, but for the feeling of compassionate regret at the memory of the sound of that sob.

Perhaps half an hour passed, it seemed so long, and he grew chilly; he resolved to lie down again; at least, it would be warmer. His large, fur-lined railway and driving rug hung over a chair back, and he lay down, spread it wide over him, drew it beneath his feet by raising them, and in a few moments he was quite warm.

He rested, looking at the moonlight; then he dozed and opened his eyes again, looking at the window; then he dozed again; then he slept.

How long he slept he knew not, but he was aroused by something very gently touching his wrist. He opened his eyes, at first drowsily; then his orbits expanded to their fullest limit, and his blood seemed to grow cold. He could not utter a sound; his tongue became as rigid as his fixed gaze and motionless limbs. He was no longer alone.

Close to his bedside and in the full flood of the clear moonlight, with her hand outstretched to him in an attitude of supplication, was the figure of a small lady, clad in white from head to foot. Captain Hugh Desmond was a very brave man, an admirable soldier, regarding his utter fearlessness of death, added to his love of danger and perilous adventure, but never throughout his military career had he experienced the sensations of appalling dread which for the first few moments overcame him at this meeting between the earthly and the unearthly. But the spasm of horror was only for a few moments, the wraith was not only that of a small and delicate woman, but of a supplicant, compassion rose within him, and determination to aid her to the best of his ability gave him back the use of his limbs. He rose upon his elbow, slowly at first, disengaged his limbs from the folds of the rug, and regaining his feet, stood before her.

Her face, raised as it was appealingly, scarcely reached the level of his breast as he stood by her side awaiting her will and wish.

She stretched out her hand to him, her left hand which he took gently in his right. The touch was perceptibly hard, the bones of the tiny hand were fleshless and the slender finger joints were rigidly straight and drawn together as in the attitude of death, and as he gently took that fleshless hand in his, he noticed that the finely pointed bones of the fore and middle fingers were broken and absent.

With that touch all was changed. No need was there for words or human language. Desmond knew all from moment to moment, her will, wish, motive, and the longing to transmit her memory's records of the past.

Holding her by her fleshless hand, he walked by her side to the door which he unlocked, and threw open for her to pass. She guided him out into the dark corridor by that hand he constantly held, along through the black darkness, dark no longer now, for with them went a new and strange light, more like the light of day than the moonlight they had left.

Onward she led him, across the corridor, down a short corridor to the right, then a little way down a parallel corridor to the left, and across it to the heavy, black, oak-panelled woodwork. She paused at one of the dark alcoves, by her wish, and he knew what to do. He pressed a mound of heavy carving at the side, and the back of the recess gave way on its hinges, and they passed through the secret doorway—the same light going with them as they passed on noiselessly, but for the almost inaudible sound of Desmond's slippered feet, to the head of some wooden stairs, by means of which they descended to a stone passage with a window in it, similar in the diamond-glazing to the one in the chamber he had left, but that the recess of several feet in depth, was enclosed by a grating of iron bars of vast strength let into the solid stonework.

Crossing the vault they approached a partition of heavy wooden planks resembling the corner of a store-room. A wooden door was ajar. Desmond put forth his hand and drew it open. It was a double partition door, and the corner angle swung open at the touch, and as its double hinges revolved, they entered the vault through the wide corner opening. It was filled with the same light that seemed to form part of them, and they stood still contemplating a weird and awful sight which met his view.

There were large, rough wooden shelves in front, and to the right, and on these shelves, sideways, in the repose of death or sleep, lay two human skeletons, where, to all appearance, they had been for centuries. Long he gazed in pain and sorrow at the awful spectacle, as he still held her by her hand. Then he turned and looked upon her upturned face in its silent appeal, with deep sorrowful compassion and regret; he felt so sorry for her and her awful life, suffering, and death. The same transmitted power of memory revealed all, as she stood by him, the garments of the white nun alone concealing the fleshless form which was beneath, and the white hood concealing all but the wide, vacant orbits of the face of death, upturned to him in appeal. He understood all, then; the record of an awful crime, an unknown murder, through which she, the innocent one, suffered, and that which was buried beneath his feet, which belonged by right of birth to her and to the heirs of Desmond, and now to him, last of the race of the line direct. He felt all the gratitude he owed to his wronged ancestress through all the centuries of the past, but, above all, he felt that deep unfathomable sorrow and regret that is helpless and utterly unavailing.

Desmond turned away; gently and slowly he led his ghostly companion back the way they came. They re-ascended the wooden staircase. At his touch the great oak slab resumed its place, and she led him to his chamber door, and once more, with that awful face upturned to his in the appeal for compassion. She slowly withdrew her hand from his in silent farewell, and gave the adieu that would be only broken in the vista of eternity, when all see us as they are seen.

The visitor passed away, and with her faded the guiding light. Desmond turned, and entering the room, closed the door, and, lighting his candle, threw himself upon his knees by the bed-side and prayed as he had never prayed before for the peace and rest of the unhappy soul he had bidden farewell to. Then he threw himself upon the bed, and he, the strong man, burst into an agony of weeping, and sobbed like a child till his pillow was wet with tears.

With this paroxysm of grief came relief; he was calmer, but exhausted, and he closed his eyes to avoid seeing the great wheel rays caused by the candle light upon his humid eyes. Greater quietude stole over him till his thoughts wandered, and he forgot all in a deep slumber, which lasted till the butler knocking at his door awoke him at eight o'clock, and he sat up and called out, "Thank you."

Desmond's head ached slightly, but he felt refreshed, and thought that he must have slept for three hours at least, as the memory of that terrible night's adventure crowded in upon his waking thoughts, for his pillow was still damp.

"The candle must have burnt out," he said to himself, as he got upon his feet and approached the table; but he looked in blank astonishment when he perceived the extinguisher upon the candle as he left it when he lay down for the second time, for when the "White Nun" parted from him, he had only closed, but not locked, the door. With three or four hasty strides he crossed to the door and turned the handle; it was locked as he had left it, when he placed his boots outside the night before. "By Jove," he exclaimed aloud in bewilderment, "it must have been, it actually was a dream after all. But what a vision; I thought it real till this moment." His toilet was completed before the breakfast bell sounded, and he went down to the breakfast-room as it ceased ringing.

Frances and Mr. Maitland were in the dining-room when he entered, and their warm greeting was accompanied by Mr. Maitland exclaiming, "Why, Desmond, you look as though you had seen a ghost."

"I certainly had a wonderful dream of a White Nun," replied Hugh, relating the substance of what has been recorded. The recital formed the topic of conversation, till its minutest details were ended.

"There are several people living who describe the 'White Lady' exactly as you do," observed Mr. Maitland. "But your account of the night walk with her has something truly new and extraordinary about it, and if you like, presently, we will visit the place you speak of. You will be able to guide us."

Hugh acquiesced, and soon after the table was cleared. All but Mrs. Maitland accompanied him up-stairs to his room, from the door of which he led them into the next corridor to the right, which, unlike his story, terminated at the end in a solid wall, which he at once observed.

"But where," questioned Mr. Maitland, "was the parallel corridor you speak of?"

"Right here," replied Hugh, placing his hand upon the solid wall, "but there is no corridor, nor even woodwork here."

"Well, this is the marvellous part of your vision, Desmond; behind this wall is a corridor strongly resembling what you describe," rejoined his host, "and some twenty-five years ago, owing to the dampness of the old unused building, at the same time that improvements were being carried out, I had a complete separating wall built up from the basement to the roof at this juncture at great expense, but if you like we can enter it from the Priory ground."

With keenly excited interest all at once agreed, and in a few minutes were dressed for the short walk round to the old Priory Garden. Horace procured a lighted lantern from the head gardener, which he carried with him, together with the keys, and in a few moments were not only inside the ancient building but ascending to that upper part which brought them back to the Manor side, and in a few minutes they entered the gallery.

As they did so Hugh Desmond uttered an exclamation of amazement. "This is the corridor," he cried out, "wait a minute." Then when they had nearly reached the other end on the right hand side where all along the massive black oak woodwork was intact, he said, "This is the place," laying his hand upon a raised goblin face in one of the broad buttress posts of the alcoves, "I know it from the distance from the window, but it is solid, it will not yield."

"This is wonderful," mused Mr. Maitland, "and you were never here nor heard of it before?"

"Never!" returned Captain Desmond.

Meanwhile Horace had taken out his pocket knife, and, opening the blade, stooped down to the floor and probed with the point all along the recess, with Hugh at his side, but the point struck solid wood. Then he tried the one indicated by Hugh, on which he uttered a cry of alarm. The blade repeatedly penetrated like under a door. Then he worked away till it passed from post to post.

"See, it will go in under like a door," he said; and then he tried the next. It was solid, like the first, and so were all the others. Yet on close examination, the recess seemed as solid as all the rest. The goblin head was pressed with force, but without result.

"Wait, and I will get a hammer," cried Horace, and he went off to the gardener's house.

In a few minutes he returned with a large hammer, a branch log about eighteen inches long, and a sack. The sack was folded and laid against the curved goblin face, the billet was held with both hands, while Mr. Maitland struck careful heavy blows upon the reverse end, using it as a ram.

"It is giving," exclaimed Gilbert as he felt it, and examination proved the truth of this, the prominent circle surrounding the face was going in. Several more heavy blows sent it further, and then, at four more, it went in suddenly, giving way with a crash and a clinking rattle at the back of the woodwork, which quivered at the side. The goblin face was driven into the hole and the shock had apparently loosened the seemingly solid background. Then Hugh and Horace pressed carefully against this, and, by degrees, it yielded with a groaning, rasping noise, as at last the massive, rusted iron hinges gave way, and the secret door stood wide open, revealing to Captain Desmond's unutterable astonishment the landing and wooden staircase of his dream of last night, and he recoiled as he trod on something snake-like buried in the accumulated dust of centuries. On examination, it proved to be a loose piece of rope, but so old and decayed that it fell apart in pieces when lifted up with the hand. At the side of the stairway lay a large loose beam, as by the aid of the lantern they carefully descended the stairs, a dank and noisome odour from the vaults smelling of damp and decay, assailed their nostrils, and Hugh Desmond instinctively held out his hand for the lantern, which in the black darkness for caution he held near the ground. The dust of centuries, cobwebs, and decay were visible at every step; twenty yards further, the wide passage terminated in several divided cellars, as they afterwards found. But Hugh crossed this first vault in the direction of some woodwork, and then exclaimed, "Here are some bars." "And exactly such as you described except the window," said Horace.

"The recess is identical with the description," said Mr. Maitland, "and the window is likely to be at the end, though perhaps buried."

They commenced to examine the woodwork which formed

an angle with the next vault. Hugh passed the lantern up and down each right angle, and they found the only perceptible aperture near the first corner, but it would not yield to the hand.

Gilbert went back and brought the hammer and log of wood. They first used the hammer handle, and then inserted the log, a few blows widened the opening sufficiently for two to get double hold and force it open. The heavy planking jarred and vibrated with their effort, and gave way with a crash. Mr. Maitland stepped hurriedly on one side as the whole corner fell over with a great noise. It was a double awing door which had broken off the hinges, which were rusted away, and as they all perceived the wonderful coincidence, they shrank away from the wide entrance, and conversed in low, hushed tones, whilst the girls kept close to their father.

"Let us view the inside," said Mr. Maitland.

Thus admonished, Captain Desmond, holding the lantern before him, led the way. The interior appeared like a long unused spare vault, with wide shelves at right angles at the side and back, and all, with Hugh Desmond, at one and the same time, uttered a cry of horror, for on the raised shelves, encrusted and black with decay and mildew, and the dust of centuries, lay unmistakably the remains of bones, falling apart and separated in places, but all that was left of what had certainly once been two human beings.

At last Captain Desmond spoke, and addressing Mr. Maitland in a broken voice, articulated the words, "It is all true, the legend," and glancing at their pale faces, added, "I have without doubt seen the ghost of Miriam Desmond."

"A real vision, Hugh, without a doubt, but what of that which is buried, where is that? That which was once hers, and is now yours."

"I cannot recall," replied Hugh, but advancing and touching the ground with his foot, "This is the place."

"But what are these?" again asked Mr. Maitland, indicating the human remains.

"I cannot recall," at length said Hugh, "but I believe they are the evidences of, or connected with, some unknown crime, and I fear she was the victim. I am sorry, for last night I felt I knew all."

"Hugh, my dear boy," said Mr. Maitland, "listen to me. I firmly believe this is the hand of Providence. I do not doubt that treasure lies buried here, and I tell you now, I am certain it belongs to you and you alone by right, and that these are the remains of the lost Desmonds. Whatever lies buried here shall be yours. I will see the Vicar of Gurthford this afternoon, and so search all the records we can find."

"Thank you, sir," returned Hugh Desmond absently. "I cannot describe the grief I feel for my ill-fated kinswoman of past ages, and possibly her brothers. May Heaven give rest to her soul."

"Amen," said Mr. Maitland.

* * * * *

After having seen that the building was closed, Mr. Maitland took the keys back with him to his study, and directed the members of his family to make no further mention of the incidents of the morning, as the account would cause vulgar excitement, and do no good.

The Vicar returned to lunch with Mr. Maitland, visited the remains with him, and decided they had better be reverently enclosed and interred in the old burial ground of the Priory, and an order was sent to the neighbouring town for a suitable casket of the requisite dimensions, and in a few days this was carried out, and the Vicar and Dr. Thornhurst, who obtained special aid from London, compiled careful records of all the circumstantial evidences. The next day, after the interment, in company with Hugh Desmond and Dr. Thornhurst, Mr. Maitland returned to the secret vault, where a man sent for for the occasion, commenced to dig. At the depth of a few feet beneath the brickwork they came upon stones carefully laid in order, beneath which, buried in dry sand and enclosed in stones beneath, and all around as above, in wonderful preservation, a strong heavy oak chest, and nothing more; it was heavy and was conveyed to Hugh's room, the haunted chamber, where he still preferred to sleep, for since Christmas night his rest had been peaceful and unbroken. The ground was filled in, the secret door was repaired with new hinges and a lock, for on forcing it open the ancient mechanism was broken, being rusty and decayed. The whole being carried out under the supervision of an expert from London, skilled in investigation.

The oak chest was forced open by Hugh in the presence of Mr. Maitland and his sons the next day. It was found to contain an iron box. This in turn had to be forced, and contained, wrapped in a piece of worked tapestry about three yards square, which had been used as a wrapper, and, when carefully unwound, disclosed a large carved ebony casket with ring handles of the same wood in almost perfect preservation. To one of the handles a key was attached by strong worsted thread, and upon being cut off and used, after several attempts with the aid of oil, at last turned the lock and the lid opened readily. Upon the top of its contents lay three folded parchments. The first bearing the date September 29th, 1553, and written in the quaint old English of the time, but quite legible ran as follows:—

I, Miriam Desmond, being about to take the veil and forsake the world, give and bequeath to my dear brothers, John and Henry Desmond, and to their heirs for ever as a family inheritance, my necklace and bracelets, jewels, and tiara of diamonds, which I inherited at the death of my dear mother, to keep or use and dispose of as they may deem fit, for their own welfare, they being in peril, and may heaven preserve them.

MIRIAM DESMOND.

The next.
The last Will and Testament of John and Henry Desmond:—

Gurthford Manor, Nov. 17th, 1553.

I, John Desmond, being of sound and disposing mind, and in the first place sole heir of the Desmond estates, together with and in mutual agreement with, my own brother, Henry Desmond; in the second place, we the said John Desmond and Henry Desmond, have agreed for purposes of security, to secrete and bury the Desmond coronet and jewels, and the tiara and jewels of our only sister, Miriam, together with the deed of her gift to us, also, herewith, in addition, the title deed of the Desmond Estates; the motive being that we deem our lives and property in peril of forfeiture from religious and political enemies, we being Protestants. For this reason, we have decided to leave our native country for safety. But, as sons of the race of Desmond, we cannot be dishonest to our trust, or wrong our posterity of this inheritance by sale or disposal, and so have mutually buried the casket containing these jewels here, where they may be preserved by secrecy, for the possession of our true heirs in the future, and in safety. The secret of this hiding place will remain with me alone to be handed down even from father to son hereafter.

Signed by each in each other's presence.

JOHN DESMOND.
HENRY DESMOND.

The third parchment was an exceedingly ancient title deed in Latin and Old English of the Desmond lands, and property of the Tenth Century.

These were carefully laid aside, and the coronet, tiara, bracelets, necklace, rings, and orders, which were packed with extraordinary care in pieces of parchment and woven linen, were next opened to view by Hugh Desmond, amidst expressions of wonder and admiration, mingled with regret, at their beauty and enormous value; diamonds, sapphires, rubies, and emeralds glittered in rival brilliancy, and many of these precious stones were of great size. After some conversation had passed, Mr. Maitland at length asked Hugh, "What he should do with the great fortune he had thus possessed?"

"Strictly carry out the intentions of the testators," replied Hugh.

"A resolution worthy of a Desmond," returned Mr. Maitland, "and may this great fortune bring you equal happiness."

When valued, the contents of the ebony casket were estimated by experts to be worth nearly two hundred thousand pounds.

Hugh Desmond's visit to Gurthford was greatly prolonged, during which careful investigations were made, and the specialist from the investigations department arrived at the conclusion that the remains of the two human beings found, were those of the Desmond brothers, one of whom was married and left three children. These two brothers were supposed to have been murdered as they were never heard of after the year 1554. From the examination it was deemed likely that the mechanism of the secret door, which was evidently moved in order to open the secret panel from the inside by the aid of a rope hanging from above, and which had probably given way and imprisoned them alive, and the vast strength of the oak door had resisted every effort to escape. The beam found on the stairs was thought to have been used in an attempt to break it open, but in vain.

The fate of Miriam Desmond is unknown.

The wife of Henry Desmond had taken refuge in Holland or Germany with her children, and the descendants returned to England in 1593, during the reign of Queen Elizabeth.

One sunshiny autumn day, in the succeeding year, Captain Hugh Desmond stood at the Communion rails with Frances Maitland in Garthford Church, where they were united in marriage, and for many years enjoyed great happiness. They were blessed with a family of both sons and daughters. Under the dispensations made during his lifetime, subject to the discharge of certain conditions, which were fulfilled after his death, the whole of the Desmond estates, together with the freehold, for ever reverted to Captain Hugh Desmond, and his children inherited their rights.

The story of "The Haunted Chamber" is to this day a family legend, but "Miriam's Ghost" was never seen or heard of from that Christmas night of Hugh Desmond's vision.

Lucy Farmer

THE VICAR'S GHOST

or, The Secret of Penlyon Parsonage

CHAPTER I

A Mysterious Visitor.

IT WAS A HALF PROMISE TO MY AUNT, Mrs. Jacka, of Porth-muree, that I wouldn't relate the incidents of the scare we had at The Vicarage until the trouble had blown over; but as the whole business is now settled and done with, I feel released from my engagement, and may explain the awful mystery.

Folks down Porthmuree way tried to laugh us out of coun-tenance; but Aunt Martha, whose married name is Jacka—a terribly suggestive name of donkeys—and how they never had any children is easy to account for. Aunt Jacka told me the whole story, and it came true almost in my very face.

Andrew Jacka—I nearly put two more letters on his name—was, when alive, the gardener at The Vicarage where I spent last Christmas-tide with little Charley, our eldest, in Cornwall. The place is very pretty, in a valley, near the sea. The church is quite a show building, and the tower is built "perpendicular," as they call it there; and, of course, any one can see that. It's no wonder! If it was *horizontal*, now, there would be something remarkable in it.

We reached the lodge which Mrs. Jacka, my aunt, still inhabits, and found a hearty welcome; a Christmas welcome, I may call it, and truly so. There were all kinds of hollies and ivys and red berries galore; a delicious smell of mince meat and apples—quite appetising—and a tea table spread out in a way which made me imagine that my late uncle was not so deserving of those two extra letters as I had fancied. He couldn't have been that kind, and have left his widow so comfortable—and not even in black for him!

We were early at tea after our journey, and were just gossiping, when a knock came to the door, and little Charley ran to open it. He ran back quick enough, looking scared a bit, and saying,

"Mammy, it's a man at the door—a clergyman."

"Well, he won't eat you, child," cried my aunt, quick-like. "Don't be a goose."

I didn't quite like her manner of speaking to the boy; though, having no children of her own, I could excuse her. But she rose up and went to the door in the dusk. She hadn't gone long when she came back with a red face ruffling like a turkey-cock—making all allowances for genders—and without a word catches little Charley a slap on the shoulder-blade.

"Here, Aunt Martha, what's this?" I cried. "What's Charley done? I won't have him beat by anyone except his father—so there!"

"A bit of a brat to invent such untruths!" she exclaimed. "If he was my child I'd pound him!"

"Well, he isn't your child, aunt: and as you never had one you can't be expected to understand. Wasn't there anyone there, dear?" I said to him as he ran to my side.

"Yes, mammy," he whispered; "I saw him."

"A man, Charley?"

"Yes: a clergyman—a tall man with a red face like hers! It's the truth."

He pointed to Mrs. Jacka, who didn't much relish the reference.

"I am sure the child did see the man, aunt," said I. "He wouldn't tell a falsehood—would you, Charley?"

"I saw him," said the lad firmly. "He had a whip in his hand and spurs—golden spurs—on his boots."

"Mercy on us!" screamed my Aunt Martha; "he's come. Oh dear, oh dear, oh dear!"

She began to rock herself backwards and forwards like a see-saw, her apron thrown over her head, and groaning all the time as if in pain; a "hee-haw" kind of complaint, which came from her husband's side, perhaps—most likely.

I didn't heed her greatly, for, after her behaviour to the boy, I didn't care very much about her fright; though, I will not deny it, curious to find out the cause.

Mind, it *was* rather fearsome. We two lone women in the lodge beside the wood, of a darkening winter evening well on towards Christmas—the 19th of December it was. No one nearer than The Vicarage up the long avenue, and a ghostly, creepy feeling in the rustling trees. Ugh! it was creepy!

After awhile as the fire burned up more cheerful and I had made little Charley shut the door, Aunt Martha took her apron off her head, and looked round.

"Come here," she said, looking at Charley.

He wouldn't stir. She called him again.

"I won't hurt you, little silly," continued my aunt. "Come here, I want you."

"Go, Charley; auntie won't hit you again, I'll be bound," says I, firm-like.

She looked at me steadily as if scenting the battle afar off, but there was no fight.

"I didn't mean to hurt you, child," said she, patting Charley's cheek in quite a motherly way, for her. "Here's sixpence for a Christmas box in advance. It wasn't your fault, child. I am sorry I touched you."

"Kiss auntie, Charley; she has made you a nice present. There's a boy. Well, aunt, what's happened?" said I.

"Don't ask me, Lucy; I can't tell you; it's too dreadful any way," she whispered.

Of course I knew quite well that this was only "put off." A little pressing only was wanted, but I wasn't going to press her, so changed the subject to something else. To my great surprise she went on quietly along the new track, and never breathed a syllable about the queer visitor, as long as Charley sat up.

It was a clear, cold moonlight night. As I tucked Charley up in the little bed in my room I could see the moon shining, and when I put the candle out the room was quite light. Charley promised to go to sleep, and so I left him; just closing the door so that we might hear him if he called out.

I found Aunt Martha in the sitting-room, knitting. As I came in she put her needles down in her lap, and looked at me steadily over her tortoise-shell spectacles.

"Well, Lucy?"

"Well, aunt. What's the matter?"

"Isn't it terrible? Ain't you afraid?"

"Afraid of what, aunt?" I cried in surprise. "What's terrible?"

"Why, that—that *man!*"

"Why? Who is he? Does he live here?"

"*Live* here! Lucy, listen. I am counted a sensible woman; isn't it so?"

I said I had heard as much from her before. What then?

"Lucy Farmer, mark my words—ponder and digest them. That was no living man whom your Charley saw, and who *we couldn't* see—it was a spirit!"

I flopped down into a chair all of a heap as aunt took up her needles, and, after a look round the room, began working again, with her face turned to the door, and glancing up now and then as if she expected something or somebody.

"A spirit! A ghost! You don't mean it! Say you are only playing Christmas on me, Aunt Martha," I said at last.

"I wish I could, Lucy. But I am sure, from your child's description of the man, that it's the old Vicar."

"What! the *dead* Vicar?"

"Yes; the one what was drownded. He can't rest in his grave; or, I should say, he can't rest in the sea, because he wasn't buried."

"Did he fall into the sea, then?" I asked.

"He jumped in," whispered my aunt as she glanced fearful-like around the room. "He was riding out from here one winter's day—it was the nineteenth of December, eight-and-eighty years ago to-day, in the afternoon!"

"Well?" said I, as she paused.

"He was going over to the Nunnery yonder," continued my aunt, putting down her needles again, "and wanted to go by way of the beach. He was mounted on his black horse, Neff, a fine sensible beast, and the Red Vicar rode him at the cliff."

"Mercy on us! Go on, aunt."

"But the horse wouldn't jump the cliff, and the Vicar—Heaven forgive him—swore he'd go no other way. He whipped and spurred the animal, but it wouldn't budge. At last the Vicar got in a towering passion. He dismounted, gave his horse a cut with the whip, took off his gilt spurs, put them in his tail-pocket; and, swearing he would go his own way, leaped down from the cliff."

"Was he killed?"

"Dead as mutton," replied Aunt Martha. "He sometimes appears spurs in hand, sometimes booted and spurred ready to mount his horse again. Many have seen him, and something always happens after he has been seen. We ought to tell the Vicar, for something will surely happen before Christmas, Lucy."

I was silent. The idea of walking up the avenue at that time of the evening, while a ghost was haunting the place, was awful. Besides, Charley couldn't be left alone in the lodge, and I said so. Aunt Martha made no reply.

"Has the ghost ever appeared before?" I asked, after a pause of silence which was almost more dreadful than anything.

"Yes," she replied in a low voice. "He has come three times; and every time something has happened! Once the church was robbed—and there never had been a sacrilege here afore nor since. The next time young Fillian—a brave lad of eleven—was killed in the lane yonder by some most mysterious means in the storm—for a tempest always accompanies the appearance. And the last time the Manor House was 'burgled,' as Captain French called it. Robbed, he meant."

"Well, aunt, we can't go up to The Vicarage to-night," I said. "If the storm should come on we might be drenched, and I am sure I would die if we met the ghost!"

"Hush!" said my aunt, suddenly. "Listen! Don't you hear something?"

I listened with all my ears, and after a minute I fancied I could distinguish a moaning sound, which rose and fell in a curious, dull roar; but in the quieter intervals we could distinctly hear the clatter of a horse's feet. The sound came nearer and nearer—the animal was galloping like mad. No one could have ridden at such a pace, I should say, on such a night along the country road.

My aunt made a dart at me and caught me by the arm.

"Lucy, we're dead to a certainty! This is Neff, the galloping horse—the Red Vicar's horse. Listen!"

We stood up, close together, trembling like aspens. The noise came nearer and nearer, and passed in a few seconds. As it died away in the distance, I went to the casement and threw it open. The murmuring sound was quite audible.

"It is the sea," whispered my aunt. "The storm is brewing. Shut the window, Lucy, I bid you."

I shut it, and sat down. Then, after a spell of thinking, I said:

"Aunt Martha, I don't believe that horses have ghosts, and even so they wouldn't make that clatter. Perhaps we have been mistaken after all!"

"Rubbish!" she replied. "I must say, Lucy, I am surprised. I thought you had more sense."

With this remark, the clock was striking nine—being a full half-hour slow—my aunt took up a candlestick from the little sideboard, and walked away without even bidding me goodnight.

"Cornish manners, perhaps," I muttered to myself. "But Cornish or not, no one shall make me believe in the phantoms of dead horses rushing about country roads—before twelve o'clock at night, any way!"

But we hadn't done with the ghosts yet.

CHAPTER II

The Man on Horseback.

In the morning the wind was blowing like mad, the trees were all bending in the direction away from the sea, and the roar of the wind in the branches, added to the loud murmur of the waves on the beach, made up a most alarming noise to one not accustomed to ghostly storms.

There wasn't much rain—not heavy rain but it made up in thickness, and drifted in like smoke and steam, wetting everything in a second, and tasted of salt. But, notwithstanding the weather, aunt and I determined to go up to The Vicarage, and warn the Vicar about the ghost of his fore-runner.

"There's something going to happen," my aunt kept saying, until at last I began to wish that something would happen to her tongue for a while.

We struggled through the avenue facing the sea-way against the wind, and in about ten minutes we came in sight of the house amongst the bare trees, which were bending and tossing and complaining about the way in which the wind was treating them.

We went boldly up to the side-door, round the laurel and hydrangea bushes, and enquired for the Vicar. The young girl who came to the door told us we couldn't see him. He was very busy packing up and would be off to London in the afternoon!

"Going to London!" exclaimed my aunt. "Never! Why, who's to christen Mary Hadwen's child the day after to-morrow? and all arranged special!"

"I'm sure I don't know," replied the girl. "He told me this morning that he wasn't to be disturbed when I knocked at his door. Mrs. Mumbles has a holiday and George (the groom) is off after the mare. Master goes at four o'clock."

"A nice time to go riding about Cornish roads," I thought. "Which way is he going up to London?" I asked.

But bless ye, that girl didn't know. Why, if it had been me, I would have found out all about it in no time. She hadn't been long at The Vicarage, I supposed. She was pert enough, anyway, but prettier than any widower should have in his house in my opinion.

"Rubbish!" said my aunt, afterwards, "and him an old man of over sixty, and a real old gentleman too. Rubbish, Lucy!"

Rubbish or not, I didn't like that girl, and said so. But as we couldn't see the Vicar, and weren't likely to, he being engaged in packing up, we had to go home again, driven up the avenue by the wind, and continually having to turn round and face it because of its interference with our skirts—a regular bother on a windy day—and lucky we were private.

"What did that pert young woman say about the groom, and the mare, aunt?" says I, as we turned away home.

"George has gone after it somewhere. I wonder where! What

will the Vicar do without it? He has only the one animal."

"Aunt," said I, stopping and turning round to the wind, "listen to me. Don't you remember that we heard a runaway animal last night, pounding down the road in a terrible way. Perhaps the Vicar's mare was frightened, and ran away when the ghost of the other horse came into the stable."

My aunt shook her head, and then settled her bonnet and hair, being flustered.

"Lucy, my dear, mark my words, there's a great danger hanging over this place. A magpie darted out of our copse this morning, and the chimney smoked, which is sure signs. Mercy on us! listen to the wind; there will be wrecks to-night, and a spring tide, too. Come home."

We struggled on, and didn't dare to put our noses outside the cottage all day. You never saw anything like that storm. The wind tore up the trees and smashed branches; birds were dashed to pieces on the perpendicular tower of the church—aye, jackdaws were killed in the very roof—found dead in the gutters on the next Sunday. The swish of the rain, and the clouds of spray which were swept over the cliff, you'll hardly believe. Great masses of white stuff come up the hill, like birds, people told me; and next day, when we were all on the run because of the Vicar, I myself saw lumps of foam lying in the fields.

Little Charley was afraid of the roaring in the chimney, and we were glad enough, I can tell you, when one of the keepers came in about six o'clock to see how we were. He trembled a bit when we told him about the ghost.

"We'll keep a look-out to-night," he said, as he went away up to the village, buffeted by the wind, and regularly blown round the corner.

"Why will they keep a look-out, aunt?" I asked.

"Because of the Vicar's ghost," she replied. "It is sure to appear in the church to-night—at least it is *said* to come there and walk. A dim light, like a corpse candle, is to be seen by those who have the courage to go out. You'll hear the people presently."

"I've never seen a ghost," I began.

"You don't mean that you think of going out to look for it?" shouted aunt, staring at me as if I had seven heads.

"Well, if others go, why shouldn't I? Nothing from the next world can harm us," I said.

"Can't it?" she retorted, with a sniff. "An appearance killed poor young Fillian, and he eleven years old——"

"He was out in the storm, aunt, wasn't he?"

"Well, suppose he was! Would the storm crush his skull in, and lay him by the roadside—a tangled corpse? No wind as ever blew could punch in people's skulls! Don't tell me! There's true, real danger out to-night. It's terrible, so it is!"

Of course I said no more. The storm seemed abating, and about ten o'clock we were both thinking of going to bed when a quick knocking was heard at the door.

We sat still as mice, and looked at each other. My aunt's face was the colour of tallow, and I daresay mine wasn't much better. I couldn't stir an inch to save my life. The ghost had come again!

"It's there!" gasped my aunt. "Mercy on us! Pray, Lucy!"

If you'll credit me, I couldn't! I could no more repeat a prayer that minute, though were half-a-dozen at my finger-ends, and all the Creed on the tip of my tongue. No use. I couldn't speak, and the knocking continued.

Suddenly my aunt whispered, "Send the boy; it won't hurt *him!*"

Send Charley—in his nightdress too—to meet a wandering ghost of a suicided parson! Not I! You wouldn't catch me sacrificing an innocent lamb like him to the Evil One. I rose up then myself, and, with a quaking at my heart and a quaver in my voice, called out, "Who's there?"

"It's me—Robinson," replied the keeper. "I've heard a rumour as there's somethin' up at The Vicarage, and I've come down to see after it."

My aunt by this time was behind me, and opened the door, without a blush, saying:

"Come in, Mr. Robinson. Whatever is it? The ghost? We thought it *must* be you."

"No, ma'am, not the ghost. Phyllis, our neighbour's lass, has come down with the cream, and a story as there's no one in the house, and there's a light in the church moving about."

"Robbers!" I exclaimed.

"Ghosts!" cried my aunt. "I knew it."

"Well, it's a queer thing, and we're goin' to see about it. The girl's gone with master, they do say."

"What girl?" shrieked Aunt Martha.

"Not the pert hussy up at the house, surely?" said I.

"That's it," he said, nodding. "Susan has bolted, and someone has reported she was seen with master on the coast-road this afternoon."

"The old goose!" I cried. "What did I tell you, Aunt Martha? I took that girl's measure pretty quick!"

"Well, nothin' will persuade me that Vicar has gone with her outside the paths of duty. No, Lucy Farmer, Vicar's a clergyman, and ghosts from the churchyard wouldn't persuade me other-ways. Besides, who'd go along the beach-road such a night as this?"

"It ain't so out o' the way bad now," remarked Robinson. "I'm goin' down."

"I'll go with you," said I.

"Well, I ain't goin' to be left like an owl in an ivy bush," said my aunt. "It's too terrifyin'. I'll go too."

"But the child?" I cried. "Suppose he wakes up?"

"Oh, he won't stir; it's only ten minutes or so. He's old enough to lie quiet if he does wake. He'll see the candles lighted."

So we agreed to run down and see the ghost. The rain had ceased. Escorted by Robinson, who had a lantern, we soon reached the churchyard, which was close by, near the village side, by the inn, where the stream is. In the road and at the stile we found every living soul in the place.

Outside, the night was pitch dark. The great "perpendicular" tower was quite lost in the gloom. The trees tossed about and roared, the ivy fluttered and rustled in a most alarming way; and, sure enough, inside there *was* a light which moved about the chancel and the east window, which was half choked with ivy. But no one would venture near the doors, and we could not hear any sound but the terrible roaring of the wind, and a banging noise at times.

Suddenly the light went out, and we all jumped!

Then, in the darkness and in the middle of the roaring of the storm wind, which seemed increasing, the sound of horse's hoofs were heard clattering down the hill.

"It's the horse, the horse," cried the women, and before you could wink every man, woman, and child present took to their heels and ran for dear life to the houses—anywhere! They had all squeezed themselves into doorways and sheds, like a "general post" in the nursery games at the Manor, in one minute.

The clattering hoofs came nearer and nearer. I was squeezed into the inn door. I couldn't tell what had become of aunt and the keeper. I wished my husband had been there, but it was no use wishing. The hoofs came down the hill faster and faster, banging fire out of the flints as we could see. The ghost rode right up to the road and stopped for a moment. Then he made up his mind and came towards the inn.

The women pushed back and shut the door with a bang in *its* face. Now would it blast us with fire, or come in through the door?

We waited, shaking and quaking, to see what would happen, and then we heard a noise, and a loud kicking or thumping at the door!

Nobody dared to move. Besides it was after closing time. No one could be admitted!

But the rider would not be denied.

"Mr. Hawkin! I say, Hawkin! Open the door, there's mischief about."

"Aye," muttered Hawkin, "and it shall remain outside. Go your ways in peace," he said aloud; "go on, go on."

"Come, no nonsense!" shouted the ghost—if it was a ghost, which I, for one, began to doubt. "Open the door or I'll smash it. Don't you know me; George Syme?"

"George—from The Vicarage!" cried several. "Why, what brings you here at this time o' night?"

"On horseback too," said others.

"Maybe it's only a device of the Evil One," suggested the sexton. "I'd be careful if I was you, Mr. Hawkin."

But a sounding kick and a few hard Cornish words settled the question. Hawkin went to the door, expostulating loudly against violence and ghosts.

CHAPTER III

The Ghost in the Church. A Discovery.

"Ghosts be hanged!" exclaimed George, as he strode into the passage, having slipped the bridle over a hasp in the wall. "What's all this mean?"

"What's what mean?" asked Hawkin, who, with us all, was recovering his composure. The other people who had run away were gradually coming out, like rabbits from their burrow after a shot has alarmed them.

"Why, all this about master and Susan. The house is locked up, master's away, and everyone is not at home. What's up?"

"It's the Vicar's ghost, George. It's in the church."

"Nonsense!" exclaimed the groom.

"We've seen it," cried his audience.

"Seen your grandmother!" retorted the groom, who was perhaps nearer the truth than he knew or suspected. "Where's master?"

"Gone to London."

"Who says so?" asked the man, turning on the speaker. "It's not true; he wouldn't go like that."

"Young man," I said, pushing my way nearer. "I can tell you it is true. Mrs. Jacka, my aunt, and me went up to see your master this day, and that minx, named Susan, said he was packing up. Now you see why. She and he have gone off."

"Why, she was as good as promised to me!" cried poor George. "Some o' ye guesses that."

"Aye, George, we do," muttered some sympathetic voices. "We a'most knows it."

"Well, there, is it natural that she'd go and run away with my master, as honourable a gentleman as ever stepped? No, there's something behind all this."

"It's the Vicar's ghost, George. He came yesternight."

"And let *Comet* loose, I suppose. Rubbish! But why she bolted or how, I couldn't make out, I must say."

"She did bolt then, George?"

"Aye, and opened the stable door into the bargain. I've been after her ever since daylight, and found her in Saddler's farm-yard —off by Ferrybridge yonder. I'd been on her tracks for hours."

"I wish Mr. Mulholland or Squire Driven was home; we could fix up something then. What shall we do, Mr. Hawkin?"

"Find out what's inside The Vicarage, or in the church," said some sensible man in the crowd.

"All very well, but we're incapable of it," said the groom.

"'Sides, keys is in Vicar's study," remarked the sexton. "Drat that ghost, he should be laid by now! Listen to the wind. Some-one's busy to-night!"

"Hush, man, ye can't tell who's listenin'. Let's up to Vicarage, and go in if us can," said the sensible man again.

"That's it," I cried. "Perhaps it's only a trick The Vicar may be playing on you—playing ghost."

"And Susan gone off! Not likely! But come you up to the par-sonage. I think we may get in by the study window. Mr. Atkins, don't call it burglary now!"

"No," replied the sensible voice; "I'll not arrest ye, George. Come along!"

Then I discovered that the constable, the only one for miles round, was the most sensible of all. Certainly we did find out queer things that night, as everyone never suspected Mr. Atkins of such gifts, he being mostly silent. The landlord, who, as the saying goes, could "talk the hind leg off a donkey," was looked on as far the cleverest man and the most gifted. But he didn't hide his candles under a pewter in any way, I could see. And the very idea of candles made me think of Charley in the cottage asleep, all alone. We better go up, I thought.

Just then Aunt Martha came to me and said, "Why, here you are, Lucy! I'm going home."

"Quite right, aunt; it's dreadfully stormy," says I. "Will you find your way easy?"

"Quite easy with the lantern," she said. "There's no ghost, I don't believe; and there is rheumatics. Don't be late, Lucy, now. But bring me the news."

I promised to do so, and she toddled off with another woman who lived top of the hill.

Then, being easier in my mind, I went with the crowd to the parsonage; and the groom, accompanied by the policeman to see fair play, put himself inside the study window, by the light of lanterns which flashed about like big fireflies, throwing queer shadows on the walls, and making giants of small people, sprawling them out on the sides of the house like imps. The constable handed the groom a light into the study, and then the window was shut down. In a moment or two candles were lighted within, and then George came into the hall with a light to open the door to the constable.

"Now, you can't all be comin' in," said he. "The Vicar he wouldn't like his house trampled on. Maybe he's inside all the time. So stand back."

The people didn't like this. They began to grumble. "Parson wouldn't mind," they said.

"Well, then, *I* won't have it," said the constable. "We'll have a few—Mr. Hawkin here, and Mr. Robinson; Mrs. Hawkin and the lady yonder, who's a friend of the family from London, I understand (this was myself). We six will do all there is to be done and let you know. So keep quiet, or I'll have you charged at Truro."

"Six is plenty, sir," we four said, feeling quite certain of our own share in the matter.

"Plenty," assented the groom. "Now, we're four men and two women. Let's divide, and take a lady with each party. Who'll go upstairs and who down?"

His eye happened to rest on mine, so I said, "Let us begin upstairs, and you try the basement."

"Very well," he said. "I, with Mr. Hawkin and the missus, will go below. Mr. Atkins, with you, ma'am and Mr. Richardson will begin at the top, and we'll meet in the drawing-room yonder, upstairs, when we've finished. Now, quiet, please, all of you; any news you'll hear quick enough."

The people in the hall stood quiet, and as we ascended the staircase we could hear the terrible howling of the wind, and fancied that we could distinguish the thunder of the waves beating on the rocky coast as the tide came in. It was a terrible night—for the ghost!

"That's Mr. Penlyon's room," whispered the constable, as we passed a door. "Shall we try it or go on?" he asked, holding up his candlestick.

"Go on, and work down," said Mr. Robinson.

So we went on, and very soon examined the upper rooms. Susan's apartment was first visited. Very few things were visible in it. A dress hanging up behind the door, a trunk and some bandboxes, a pair of old boots, and some other articles, thrown anyhow on the bed and on the floor, didn't look like the trim, tidy, pert maid we had seen that morning. She had evidently been hurried in her movements.

"She's bolted, I should say," remarked the constable. "She's taken light things, and left her box. What's in it, I wonder?"

Clothing such as became a waiting-woman. A few books and some letters. But the clothes were new and clean; a pair of boots attracted my attention. They were rather large.

"A fine foot she had," I remarked, as I took them up. "Why, what's these?"

I stooped again and pulled from under her clean things a pair of trousers, checked pattern, which had evidently been worn a good deal.

"This is a queer start," said the constable; "let's turn out the jade's box at once."

We did so very quickly, and the rest of a suit of male attire, such as might be worn by a lad of sixteen or so—a "flash" suit, the constable called it.

"Well, so Miss Susan was fond of masquerading," said he, after inspecting the clothes. "Did anyone ever see her in boy's clothes, I wonder?"

While he was pulling about the trunk I opened the drawers in the dressing table and found a large quantity of fair false hair nicely done up; in another place were combs and brushes, paste, rouge, and powders, and brushes like painters'—camel's hair things—so she could alter her face as she pleased.

"The hussy!" I remarked. "I saw at a glance that she was a bad one. I told my aunt so! Look at those things! A regular painted Jezebel!"

The men were surprised, I can tell you. "Ay, she is a bad one," said the constable. "Suspect she has bolted with some valuables—not with Mr. Penlyon at all. She's a thief!"

"Never!" said Robinson. "The two was together, that's certain as sin! Come you and see further. Here's George and his party comin' up. What cher, George?"

"Nothing particular. Plate-chest's locked all right, cellar locked too. Can't find the silver candlesticks, though, in the pantry—bedroom pair. Likely in master's room."

"Well, we have found nothing upstairs but Susan's things, including a lovely head of hair," said Mr. Atkins.

George Syme started. "A head of hair!" he exclaimed, staring at the speaker.

"Aye; never mind now. Come into the Vicar's room. Why, it's locked! There's no key!"

"Locked!" we exclaimed, in a chorus. Then he must have gone, we thought. Everyone drew back, and looked in turn at everyone else.

"Leave it until we have searched elsewhere," said sensible Atkins, "and if we find any more suspicious things, or don't find something to satisfy us, then, by George! I'll break the door. Where's the church keys?"

"In parson's study," piped the sexton. "They're a-hanging on a nail behind the press door."

We all hurried into the study. The keys were not there! Curiosity now was getting to a high pitch. We no longer minded the storm.

"They keys is in the church door," squeaked a lad who had just entered. "I felt 'em in the lock, I did."

"You're a sensible idiot, Ben," cried the constable, putting on his hat. "Now, them lanterns. Come along!"

We hurried out and went boldly enough into the churchyard, and up the gloomy path between the graves of the dead—graves of people who had been drowned or cast ashore dead, or who had died in their beds; men mostly, as I had already seen. We reached the church porch, and as the lantern was held up to the lock of the old oak door we perceived the key dangling from the keyhole; the door was locked, too!

By this time our fear of the ghost had considerably subsided, and, notwithstanding the howling of the storm, and the rushing gusts of wind around the church, little hesitation was shown. Mr. Atkins was quite bold, and several of his immediate followers were brave enough; the hinder ones came in with the lights being fearful to remain outside in the dismal darkness and whirling wind.

Mr. Atkins, leading the way and carrying a lantern, stepped up between the old carved pews, on which scenes of Scripture were engraved, with doves and eagles and coats of arms. He stood still near the font and called out loudly:

"Is anyone here?"

No one replied except an echo in the chapel, so he shouted again. This time we heard a moan come from the East end, and a terrible chill struck me. I daresay others felt the same. We had shivers. It was a very weird feeling. The shadowy church, just light enough to make the darkness visible; the howling wind in the belfry overhead, the dangling ropes, and humming bells—all united to make our flesh creep; and then the moan was so sad and weary!

Keeping close together, the men in front, we straggled up the aisle and examined the chancel—no one was there except ourselves. But within the communion rails, near the vestry door, lying prone on the floor quite exhausted, was an elderly woman.

"Why, it's Missus Mumbles!" cried two or three of the spectators. "How did she come here?"

"Never mind how she came, let's get her out. The light is accounted for now," said George.

The fainting woman was raised up and carried out to the inn, where she found voice enough to say: "Robbed—murdered. The master—the master!"

Some of us needed no more. Mr. Atkins rushed away, followed by Robinson, George, myself, and the Hawkins. We all guessed that the secret of Penlyon's disappearance lay in the bedroom which was locked. Robbery and murder are ugly words.

A few well-directed blows stove the door in, and the men entered first with lanterns and candles. Sure enough on the floor under the bed was the old Vicar himself, Mr. Penlyon, dabbled in blood, and apparently lifeless. The private safe was ransacked, the chest of drawers turned out. Many papers and some valuable articles were on the floor, everything was topsy turvy, but some one who knew the place had been there, for the secret drawers were forced open.

By this time the ghost was entirely forgotten, and the doctor was quickly fetched from his house, about three-quarters of a mile away. He came, and having examined the poor Vicar, concluded that he had had a severe blow on the head, but would come round. The gentleman then went and prescribed for Mrs. Mumbles, and the people gradually dispersed—after leaving a nurse with the parson, and George downstairs to see what was missing from the chests, which had been robbed and locked up again.

Mr. Atkins stayed also; but I made my way home with Mr. Robinson, and reached my aunt's cottage as the clock was whirring out One!

"Well," said Aunt Martha, "a pretty time in the morning to come home, and with Mr. Robinson! What's the matter?"

Then I told her, and her face was a caution.

"I knew it—I said so—the ghost did it. Is the Vicar dead?"

"Not yet," I replied; "but I'd have those two villains hanged if I had my way—a pair of ruffians, burglars—both wicked men as ever stepped."

"What men do you mean, Lucy?" she asked.

"Why, the men who robbed and nearly killed Mr. Penlyon Susan and——"

"You said *men*, Lucy," interrupted aunt.

"*And isn't Susan a man?* Of course he is! A made-up young villain, who bamboozled the old Vicar, and nearly canoodled George, the groom. I saw through the paints and the false hair. Yes, I told you *he* was no good."

"Let's get to bed," said Aunt Martha, who never could bear anyone to have praise. If *she* had found it out there would have been hot water and something for a late supper, with chat before bed time. I know; but there was no sign of it then. So we went to bed tired out, and a little thirsty, too.

Next morning we were astir pretty early and in the village, after a short breakfast. Everyone was chattering. Mrs. Mumbles had said something; but, being short of teeth, at the best of times was indistinct, being upset, and no wonder. We made out that a man had called on the previous night—a red-faced man—and made some enquiries. He then must have gone round to the stables and loosed *Comet*, which he galloped up the avenue and off over the hill. At any rate, the mare, being frightened, went off at speed, and when he had "thrown her out" the man must have left her, and made his way back to the Vicarage in the morning early.

With the assistance of "Susan" he seized and stunned the Vicar. "Susan" had previously locked old Mumbles in the church, and said she was away on a holiday. This put people off. George was after the mare, Mumbles locked up, and the burglar, whom *we* took for a ghost, packed up all he could find with his friend's assistance. "Susan" had taken service there as "maid" in order to better carry out the robbery, which yielded a quantity of plunder in silver plate, money, and objects of value, all which "Miss Susan" knew very well where to find, for the Vicar was wealthy.

These particulars came out by degrees; and meantime, while we were discussing the ghost and the robbery, the previous appearances on the same day in former years and their consequences, the men on horseback and on foot were searching roads and paths, sending flying telegrams all over the district, even launching boats when the weather moderated.

We females also tried to find the runaways, and some of us, at low tide, investigated the caverns on the shore, where, in old times, smugglers used to hide themselves and their plunder. And in one of these great recesses the burglars' plunder was found. Worse than that, the body of the pretty, fair-skinned boy who had played parlour-maid, and deceived even George Syme, was discovered dead. He looked asleep, but was cold and stiff. The traces of seaweed, and bits of drift-wood, beside and around him, showed how he had died. The high spring tide had overwhelmed him in his sleep and suffocated him.

In the cave higher up was a bag—a heavy, small sack, containing most of the plunder. Of the older burglar we found no trace. Whether he had escaped or had been carried off by the sea, no one ever knew, and I don't think anyone cared. But many of us were sorry for the lad—a pretty, dark haired boy about sixteen, with handsome features. As we saw him first on the beach, with a dress-skirt on over his other clothes, he looked like a pretty sleeping girl. Some women cried, and not a man said a word against him.

The Vicar would have buried him had he been well enough, after the first inquest-enquiry; but some other gentleman did. "Found Drowned," was the verdict, and the handsome boy was put under ground in a nameless grave. It was very sad indeed, and I'd rather not say any more about it.

Some people came to the conclusion that the Vicar's ghost was all nonsense, but it isn't. The ghost appeared long before the robbers made it an excuse for robbing The Vicarage. We think the burglaries were done by the same man who, made bold by impunity, tried a big stroke at last.

What became of him, we can't tell. Why he left the cave, we can only guess. Perhaps he meant to return, and was prevented by the high tide, or swept away by the waves when trying, or perhaps he fell down the rocks and was washed away. At any rate, we never heard of him again, and don't want to hear.

Mr. Penlyon recovered, but could give little account of the incidents. Mrs. Mumbles told us how she found a piece of candle in the vestry and walked about the church hoping some one would release her. She called out and beat the door, but we were all too frightened to go near the "ghost," as we thought her. We had not a *very* merry Christmas after all these tragic events, but Aunt and I, little Charley and his father (who came down) managed to enjoy ourselves. We left the village (without hearing any more of the Vicar's Ghost) on New Year's Eve, and I was not sorry to be home near Cardewe Manor once again.

Mrs. Henry Wood

THE GHOST OF THE HOLLOW FIELD

I HAVE BEEN ASKED TO WRITE A CHRISTMAS STORY—"something about ghosts." In compliance, I give one that—so far as the actors and witnesses believed—is a real ghost story; not one born of the imagination.

In the parlour of a commodious dwelling house, in the rural village of Hallow, there sat a lady, one Monday afternoon, mending soiled muslins and laces. It was Mrs. Owen, the mistress of the house, and she seemed in poor health. Suddenly the door opened, and a middle-aged woman, with a sensible though hard-featured face, came in.

"I've come to ask a fine thing, mistress, and I don't know what you'll say to me. I want holiday to-morrow."

"Holiday!" repeated Mrs. Owen, in evident surprise. "Why, Mary, to-morrow's washing-day."

"Ay, it is; nobody knows it better than me. But here's sister come over about this wedding of Richard's. Nothing will do for 'em but I must go to it. She's talking a lot of nonsense; saying it should be the turning-point in our coolness, and the healer of dissensions, and she won't go to church unless I go. As to bringing in dissensions," slightingly added Mary Barber, "she's thinking of the two boys, not of me."

"Well, Mary, I suppose you must go."

"I'd not, though, mistress, but that she seems to make so much of it. I never hardly saw her in such earnest before. It's very stupid of her. I said, from the first, I'd not go. What do them grand Laws want with me—or Richard either? No, indeed! I never thought they'd get me to it—let alone the wash!"

"But you do wish to go, don't you, Mary?" returned Mrs. Owen, scarcely understanding.

"Well, you see, now she's come herself, and making this fuss, I hardly like to hold out. They'd call me more pig-headed than they have done—and that needn't be. So, mistress, I suppose you must spare me for few hours. I'll get things forward before I start in the morning, and be back early in the afternoon; I shan't want to stop with 'em, not I."

"Very well, Mary; we shall manage, I dare say. Ask Mrs. Pickering to come in and see me before she goes. Perhaps she'll stay to tea."

"Not she," replied Mary; "she's all cock-a-hoop to got back again. Richard and William are coming home early," she says.

The four children were gathered round Mrs. Pickering when Mary returned. It was something new to them to have a visitor. The two sisters were much alike—tall, sensible-looking, hard-featured women, with large well-formed foreheads, and honest, steady grey eyes. But Mrs. Pickering looked ill and careworn. She wore a very nice violet silk gown, dark Paisley shawl, and Leghorn bonnet. Mary Barber had been regarding the attire in silent condemnation; except her one best gown, she had nothing but cottons.

"Well, Hester, the mistress says she'll spare me," was her announcement. "But as to getting over in time to go to church, I don't know that I can do it. There'll be a thousand and one things to do to-morrow morning, and I shall stop and put forward."

"You might get over in time, if you would, Mary."

"Perhaps I might, and perhaps I mightn't," was the plain answer. "It's a five-weeks' wash; and the missus is as poorly as she can be. Look here, Hester—it's just this: I don't want to come. I will come, as you make such a clatter over it, and I'll eat a bit o' their wedding-cake, and drink a glass o' wine to their good luck; but as to sitting down to breakfast—or whatever the meal is—with the Laws and their grand company, it's not to be supposed I'd do it. I know my place better. Neither would the Laws want me to."

"They said they'd welcome you."

"I daresay they did!" returned Mary, with a sniff; "but they'd think me a fool if I went, for all that. I shouldn't mind seeing 'em married, though, and I'll get over to the church, if I can. Anyway, I'll be in time to drink health to 'em before they start on their journey."

Mrs. Pickering rose. She knew was of no use saying more. She wished good-bye to the children, went to Mrs. Owen's parlour for a few minutes, absolutely declining refreshment, and then prepared to walk home again. Mary attended her to the door.

"It's fine to you—coming out in your puce silk on a week-day!" she burst out with, her tongue refusing to keep silence on the offending point any longer.

"I put it on this afternoon because I was expecting Mrs. Law," was the inoffensive answer. "She sent me word she'd come up to talk over the arrangements; and then I got a message by their surgery boy, saying she was prevented. Don't it look nice, Mary?" she added, taking bit of the gown in her fingers. "It's the first time I put it on since it was turned. I kept it on to come here; it seemed so cold to put it off for a cotton; and I've been feeling always chill of late."

"What be you going to wear to-morrow?" demanded Mary Barber.

Mrs. Pickering laughed. "Something desperate smart. I can't stay to tell you."

"You've got a gown a-purpose for it, I reckon," continued Mary, detaining her; "what sort is it?"

"A new fawn silk. There! Good-bye; I've a power of things to do at home to-night, and the boys are coming home to early tea."

Mrs. Pickering walked away quickly as she spoke, and Mary Barber ran back to the bare, half furnished place where she had left the children.

"Now, I want to go out just for five minutes," she said to them, "and if you children will be very good and quiet, and stop in this room, and not make a noise, or run in to tease your mamma, I shall see what I've got in my pocket for you when I come back. Who says yes?"

The children all said it—said it with eager tongues—and looked surreptitiously at Mary Barber's pocket. But they could only see so far as the outside. She shut the door upon them; and just as she was, without putting on a bonnet, ran down the village street until she came to the place popularly known as "Smith's shop." It sold everything—meat, grocery, hardware, toys, wearing apparel, and sundries. Mrs. Smith was behind the counter,

and Mary imparted her wants—a new ribbon for her bonnet—
white, or something as good as white.

Meanwhile, Mrs. Pickering was walking rapidly homewards.
Hallow was (and is) situated about three miles from Worcester,
and her house was between the two—nearer the city, however,
than the village. She and her sister Mary had been the daughters
of a small, hard-working farmer, Thomas Barber, who died
when they were very young women, leaving nothing behind him
except few debts. The household goods were sold to pay them,
and the girls had to look out for a living. Hester married John
Pickering, Mary went to service. The Pickerings got on in the
world. A cottage and a couple of fields and a cow grew into—at
least the fields did—many fields, and they into hop gardens. From
being a successful hop-grower, John Pickering took an office in
Worcester, and became a prosperous hop-merchant. He placed
his two sons in it—well-educated youths; and on his death, his
eldest son, Richard, then just twenty-one, succeeded him as its
master. This was four years ago. Richard was to be married on the
morrow to Helena Law, daughter of Law the surgeon; and Mary
Barber, as you have heard, considered she should be out of place
in the festivities.

And she was right. Over and over again had the Pickerings
urged Mary to leave service, as a calling beneath her and them,
and to live with themselves. Mary declined.

In the meantime, however, Mrs. Pickering, who understood
very little of the world's social distinctions, and cared less, had
latterly had a great trouble upon her beside which few things
seemed of weight. For some time past there had been ill-feeling
between her two sons: in her heart perhaps she most loved the
younger, and, so far she dared, took his part against the elder.
Richard was the master, and overbearing; William was four years
the younger, and resented his brother's yoke. Richard was steady,
and regular as clock-work; William was rather given to go out of
an evening, spending time and money. Trifling sums of money
had been missed from the office by Richard, from time to time;
he was as sure in his heart that William had helped himself to
them as that they had disappeared, but William coolly denied it,
and set the accusation to his brother's prejudice. In point of fact,

this was the chief origin of the ill-feeling; but Richard Pickering was considerate, and had kept the petty thefts secret from his mother. She, poor woman, fondly hoped that this marriage of Richard's would heal all wounds, though not clearly seeing how or in what manner it could bear upon them. In one month William would be of age, and must become his brother's partner; he would also come into his share of the property left by their father.

Mrs. Pickering went home ruminating on these things, and praying—oh how earnestly!—that there should be peace between the brothers.

The young Pickerings came home as agreed upon: not, alas! in the friendly spirit their mother had been hoping for, but in open quarrelling. They were both fine grown young men, with good features, dark hair, and the honest, sensible gray eyes of their mother; Richard was grave in look; William gay, with the pleasantest smile in the world. Poor Mrs. Pickering! hasty words of wrath were spoken on either side, and for the first time she became acquainted with the losses at the office, and Richard's belief in his brother's dishonesty. It appeared that a far heavier loss than any preceding it had been discovered that afternoon.

"Oh, Richard!" she gasped; "you don't know what you say. He would never do it."

"He has done it, mother—he must have done it," was the elder son's answer. "No one else can get access to my desk, except old Stone. Would you have me suspect him?"

"Old Stone" was a faithful servant, a many years' clerk and manager, entirely beyond suspicion, and there was no one else in the office. Mrs. Pickering felt a faintness stealing over her, but she had faith in her younger, her bright, her well-beloved son.

"Look here, mother," said Richard; "we know—at least I do, if you don't—that his expenditure has been considerably beyond his salary. Whence has he derived the sums of money he has spent—that he does not deny he has spent? If I have kept these things from you, it was to save you pain: Stone has urged me to tell you of it over and over again."

"Hush Richard! The money came from me."

William Pickering turned round; he had been carelessly standing at the window, looking out on the setting sun. For once his pleasant smile had given place to scorn.

"I'd not have told him so much, mother; I never have. If he is capable of casting this suspicion on me, why not let him enjoy it. Time and again have I assured him I've never touched a sixpence of the money; I've told that interfering old Stone so; and I might as well talk to the wind. I could have knocked the old man down this afternoon when he accused me of being a 'disgrace' to my dead father."

It is of no use to pursue the quarrel, neither is there time for it. That Mrs. Pickering, in her love, had privately furnished William with money from time to time was an indisputable fact, and Richard could not disbelieve his mother's word. But instead of its clearing up the matter, it only (so judged Richard) made it blacker. If he had been robbing the office, he had been, legally, robbing his mother; words grew higher and higher, and the brothers, in their anger, spoke of a separation. This evening, the last of Richard's residence at home, was the most miserable his mother had spent, and she passed a great part of the night at her bed-side, praying that the matter might cleared up, and the two brothers reconciled.

The morning rose bright and cloudless; it was lovely September weather; and Mary Barber was astir betimes. Washing-day in those days, and in a simple country household, meant washing-day. It most certainly did at Mrs. Owen's, everybody was expected to work, and did work, the master excepted. Mary put her best shoulder to the wheel that morning, got things forward, and started about ten o'clock. The wedding was fixed for eleven at All Saints' Church, and Mary calculated that she should get comfortably to the church just before the hour, and ensconce herself in an obscure part of it, she meant to do.

She had traversed nearly two-thirds of her way, and was in the last field but one before turning into the road. It was at this moment that she discerned some one seated on the stile at the end of the path that led into the next field. Very much to her surprise, as she advanced nearer she saw it was her sister, Mrs. Pickering.

"Of all the simpletons!—to come and stick herself there to

wait for me. And for what she knew I might have took the road way. They be thinking to get me with 'em to church in the carriage, but they won't. I told her I'd not mix myself up in the grand doings, neither ought I to, and Hester's common-sense must have gone a wool-gathering to wish it. All! she's been running herself into that stitch in her side."

The last remark was caused by her perceiving that Mrs. Pickering, whose left side was this way, had got her hand pressed upon her chest or heart.

And now she obtained a clear view of her sister's dress. She wore the violet silk gown of the previous afternoon, and a white bonnet and shawl. Mary, on the whole, regarded the attire with disparagement.

"Why, if she's not got on her puce gown! Whatever's that for? Where's the new fawn silk she talked of, I wonder? I'd not go to my eldest son's wedding in a turned gown; I'd have a new one, be it silk or stuff. That's just like Hester, she never can bear to put on a new thing; she'd rather——. If I don't believe the shawl's one of them beautiful Chaney crapes."

"I say, Hester," she called out, as soon as she got near enough for her voice to reach the stile, "what on earth made you come here to meet me?"

Mrs. Pickering made no reply.

"Sure," thought Mary, "nothing can have fell out to stop the wedding! Richard's girl wouldn't run away as that faithless chap of mine did. Something's wrong, though, I can see, by her staring at me in that stony way, and never opening her mouth to speak. I say, Hester, is anything—— Deuce take them strings again!"

The concluding apostrophe was addressed to her shoe-strings. She tied the shoe, giving the knot a good tug as additional security.

"Now, then, come undone again, and I'll—— Bless me! where's she gone?"

In raising her head, Mary Barber missed her sister.

"Hester!" she called out, raising her voice to its utmost pitch, "Hester, where *be* you got to!"

The air took away the sound, and a bird aloft seemed to echo it, but there was no other answer.

"Well, this beats bull-baiting," ejaculated Mary Barber, in the broad country phraseology in vogue in those days, "I'd better pinch myself to see whether I be awake or dreaming."

She passed over the stile again, and stood a moment to revolve matters.

"She must have gone off somewhere on the run while I'd got my eyes down on that dratted shoe," was the conclusion the woman came to. "And more idiot she, when she knows running always brings on that queer pain at her heart."

Mary Barber continued her way across the field, and then, instead of pursuing her road to Worcester, she turned aside to the house of the Pickerings. She gave a sharp knock.

"One would think you were all dead," she cried, as a maid-servant opened the door. "They are gone, I suppose."

"Yes, they are gone," was the girl's reply. "My missis left about ten minutes since."

"More than that, I know," was the answering remark. "What made her come and meet me, Betsey?"

"She didn't come," said Betsey.

"She did come," said Mary Barber.

"She did not," persisted the servant.

"Why, goodness gracious me, girl! do you want to persuade me out of my senses?" retorted Mary Barber in anger. "She came on as far as the Hollow Field, and sat herself on the stile there, waiting for me to come up. I've got the use of my eyes, I hope."

"Well, I don't know," returned the girl dubiously. "I was with her at the moment she was starting, and I'm sure she'd no thought of going then. She was just going out at this door, eating her bit of bread and butter, when she turned back into the parlour and put down her green parasol, telling me to bring her small silk umbrella instead; it might rain, she said, fair it looked. 'And make haste, Betsey,' she says to me, 'for it don't want two minutes of the half hour, and I shan't get to All Saints' in time.'"

"What half hour?" asked Mary Barber in a hard disputing sort of tone.

"The half hour after ten. Sure enough, in a minute or two our clock struck it."

"Your clock must be uncommon wrong in its reckoning then,"

was the woman's rejoinder. "At half-past ten she was stuck on the stile looking out for me. It's about ten minutes ago."

It was about ten minutes since her mistress went out, but Betsey did not venture to contend further. Mary Barber always put down those who differed from her.

"After all, she has not took her umbrella," resumed the girl, "I couldn't find it in the stand, off by the kitchen; all the rest of the umbrellas was there, but not missis's silk one, and when I ran back to tell her I thought it must be upstairs, she had gone. Gone at a fine pace too, Mrs. Barber, which you know is not good for her, for she was already out of sight, so I just shut the door and drew the bolt. It's a pity she drove it off so late."

"What made her drive it off?"

"Well, there was one or two reasons. Her new fawn gown, such beauty it is, never was sent home till this morning—I'd let that fashionable Miss Reynolds make me another, I would!—and when missis had got it on, it wouldn't come to in the waist by the breadth of your two fingers, and she'd got her pain very bad, and couldn't be squeezed. So she had to fold it up again, and put on her turned puce——"

"*I* saw," interrupted Mary Barber, cutting the revelation short. I say, Betsey, what's her shawl? It looked to me like one of them Chaney crapes."

"It's the most lovely Chaney crape you ever saw," replied the girl enthusiastically. "Mr. Richard made it a present to her. She didn't want to wear it, she said it was too grand, but he laughed at her. The fringe was that depth."

"And now, you obstinate thing," sharply put in Mary Barber, as the girl was extending her hands to show the depth of the fringe, "how could I have seen her in her puce gown, and how could I have seen her in the shawl unless she had to come to meet me? I should as soon have expected to see myself in a satin train with flounces as her in a Chaney crape shawl; and Richard must have more money than wit to have bought it."

"And where is she now, then?" asked Betsey, to whom the argument certainly appeared conclusive. "Gone on by herself to the church?"

"Never you mind!" returned Mary Barber, not choosing to

betray her ignorance upon the unsatisfactory point. Don't you contradict your betters again, Betsey Marsh."

Betsey humbly took the reproof.

"Why could she not have had a carriage, and went properly?" resumed Mary Barber. "It might have cost him money, but a son's marriage comes but once in a lifetime."

"The carriage came, and took off Mr. Richard, and she wouldn't go in it," said the girl. And then she proceeded, dropping her voice to a whisper, to tell of the unpleasantness of the previous evening, and of the subsequent events of the morning. Mr. William was up first, and went out without breakfast, leaving word he was gone to the office as usual, and should not attend the wedding. This she had to tell her mistress and Mr. Richard when they came down stairs; her mistress seemed dreadfully grieved, she looked white as a sheet, and as soon as breakfast was over she wrote a letter, and sent Hill with it into Worcester to Mr. William. "It was to tell him to come back and dress himself, and go with her to the wedding, I know," concluded the girl, "and that's why, waiting for him, she would not go with Mr. Richard when the carriage came, and why she stayed herself to the last minute. But Mr. William never came: and Hill's not come back either."

"Then why on earth did she come to meet me, instead of making the best of her way to church?" demanded Mary Barber.

"It's what she didn't do," retorted the girl; "she never had no thoughts of going to meet you."

"If you say that again, I'll—— Why, who's this?"

The closing of the little iron gate at the foot of the garden had caused her to turn, and she saw William Pickering. He was flushed with the rapid walk from the town—conveyances were not to be hired at hasty will then in Worcester as they are now.

"What can have become of mother, Mary?" William Pickering exclaimed. "I'm going home to see after her. She's not at Mrs. Law's."

"Why, where's she got to?" responded Mary Barber. "I'll tell you what, William Pickering," quickly added the woman, an idea flashing across her, "she's gone demented, with the quarrelling of you two boys, and has wandered away in the fields! I told you how strangely she stared at me from the stile."

"Nonsense!" said the young man.

"Is it nonsense! It—— Whatever do you people want?" broke off Mary Barber. For the persons she had noticed were surrounding them in a strange manner, hemming them in ominously. The officer laid his arm upon William Pickering.

"I am sorry to say that I must make you prisoner, sir."

"What for?" coolly asked William.

"For murder!" was the answer. And as the terrible words fell on Mary Barber's ear a wild thought crossed her bewildered brain— Could he have murdered his mother? Of course it was only her own previous train of ideas, connected with the non-appearance of her sister, that induced it.

Not so, however. Amidst the dire confusion that seemed at once to reign; amid the indignant questionings of the bridal party, who came flocking out in their gay attire, the particulars were made known. Mr. Stone, the old clerk, had been found dead on the office floor, an ugly wound in the back of his head. Richard Pickering, in his terror, cast a yearning, beseeching glance on his brother, as much as to say, surely it has not come to this!

The events of the morning, as connected with this, appeared to have been as follows: Mr. Stone had gone to the office at nine o'clock, as usual, and there to his surprise, found Wm. Pickering opening the letters. The latter said he was not going to his brother's wedding, and the old clerk reproved him for it. William did not like this; one word led to another, and several harsh things were spoken. So far the office servant testified, a man named Dance, whose work lay chiefly in the warehouse amongst the hop-pockets, and who had come in for orders. They were still "jangling," Dance said, when he left them. Subsequent to this, William Pickering went out to the warehouse, and to one or two more places. On his return, he found that his mother's out-door man-of-all-work, Hill, had left a note for him; a large brewer in the town, named Corney, was also waiting to see him on business. When Mr. Corney left he opened the note, the contents of which may as well be given:

"William! you have never directly disobeyed me yet. I charge you, come back once, and go with me to the Church. Do you know that I have passed three parts of the night on my knees, praying that things may be cleared up between you and your brother!

"Your loving Mother."

After that nothing clearly was known. William Pickering said that when he quitted the office to go home, in obedience to his mother's mandate, he left Mr. Stone at his desk writing; but a short while afterwards the old clerk was found lying on the floor, with a terrible wound in the back of his head. It was quite evident he had been struck down while bending over the desk. The man Dance, who was sought for in the warehouse, and found, spoke of the quarrelling he had heard, and hence the arrest of William Pickering.

Mary Barber's first thought, amidst the confusion and the shock, was of her sister. If not broken to her softly, the news might kill her; and the woman, abandoning cake, and wine, and company, before she had seen them, started off there and then in search of Mrs. Pickering, not knowing in the least where to look for her, but taking naturally the way to her home.

"Surely she'll be coming in to join 'em, and I shall perchance meet her," was the passing thought.

Not Mrs. Pickering did Mary Barber meet, but Hill, the man. He was coming down the road in a state of excitement, and Mary Barber stared in blank disbelief at his news; his mistress had been found on her bed—dead.

In an incredibly short time the woman seemed to get there, and met the surgeon coming out of the house. It was quite true Mrs. Pickering was dead. With her face looking as if it were turned to stone, Mary Barber went up to the chamber. Betsey, the servant, her tears dropping fast, told the tale.

When Mary Barber and Mr. William had departed, she bolted the door again, and went back to her work in the kitchen. By-and-bye, it occurred to her to wonder whether the silk umbrella was safe up-stairs, or whether it had been lost from the stand; a few weeks before, one of their cotton umbrellas had been taken by a tramp. She ran up into her mistress's room to look, and there was startled by seeing her mistress. She was sitting in an arm chair by the bed-side, her head leaning sideways on its back, and her left hand pressed on her heart. On the bed lay the silk umbrella, its cover partially taken off, and by its side a bit of bread and butter, half eaten. At the first moment the girl thought she was asleep; but when she saw her face she knew it was something worse. Running out of the house in terror, she met Hill, who was then returning from Worcester, and sent him for the nearest surgeon. He came, and pronounced her to be quite dead. "She must have been dead," he said, about an hour.

"What time was that?" interrupted Mary Barber, speaking sharply in her emotion.

"It was half-past eleven." There could not be the slightest doubt as to the facts of the case. "It was the oddest thing, and I thought it at the time, though it went out of my mind again, that she should have disappeared from sight so soon," sobbed Betsey.

Mary Barber made no comment; strange awe was stealing over her. This had occurred at half-past ten. It was at precisely that time she saw her sister on the stile.

"Betsey," she presently said, her voice subdued to a whisper, "if your mistress had really gone out, as you supposed, was there any possibility of her coming in later without your knowledge?"

"No there was not; she couldn't have done it," was the answer to the question; and Mary Barber had felt perfectly certain that it had not been possible, though she asked it. The only way to Mrs. Pickering's from the stile was the path she had taken herself, and she knew her sister had not gone on before her.

"I never unbolted either of the doors, back or front, after she (as I thought) went out, except when I undid the front door for you," resumed the girl. "I don't dare to be in the house by myself with 'em open since that man frightened me last winter. No, no; missis neither went out nor came in; she just went upstairs to her room, and died. The doctor says he don't suppose she had a moment's warning."

It must have been so. Mary Barber gazed at all; and an awful conviction came over her, that it was her sister's spirit she had seen on the stile. Never from that hour did she quite lose the sensation of nameless dread it brought in its wake.

"You see, now, Mrs. Barber, you must have been mistaken in thinking my missis went to meet you," said Betsey.

Mary Barber made no answer; she only looked out straight before her with a gaze that seemed to be very far away.

William Pickering was taken before magistrates in the Guildhall for examination, late in the afternoon. His brother attended it, and—very much to her own surprise—so did Mary Barber. The accusation and the facts had revolved themselves into something tangible out of their original confusion; the prisoner was able to understand the grounds they had against him; and the solicitor, whom he called to his assistance, drove up in a gig to Mrs. Pickering's, and took possession of Mary Barber.

"What's the good of your whirling me off to the Guildhall?" she respectfully asked of him, three times over, as he drove back into Worcester. "I don't know anything about it; I never was inside that office of the Pickerings' in all my life."

"You'll see," said the lawyer, with a smile.

One thing was satisfactory—that old Mr. Stone had come to life again. The blow, though a very hard one, had stunned, but not killed him; he was, in fact, not injured beyond a reasonable probability of recovery. He had no knowledge of his assailant; whoever it was had come behind him, as he sat bending over his desk, and struck him down unawares.

The Guildhall was crowded; a case exciting so much interest had rarely occurred in Worcester.

After hearing evidence at the trial, which fully acquitted Wm. Pickering, one of the witnesses named Dance was suspected.

"I have an idea, Richard," said William, "that the guilty man is Dance. Take care that he does not escape. If he has done this, he may also have been the pilferer of your petty cash. Try and get it all cleared up, for the sake of the mother's peace."

"For the sake of the mother's peace!" echoed Richard, with an aching heart. "Poor William little dreams of the blow in store for him."

He did not dream, Richard Pickering; he acted. Giving a hint to the officer to look after Dance, he pressed up to his brother, then being released from custody.

"William," he whispered, "tell me the truth in this solemn

moment—and it is more sadly solemn than you are as yet cognisant of—have you really not touched that missing money? As I lay awake last night thinking of it, I began to fancy I might have been making a mistake all through. If so——"

"If so, we shall be the good friends that we used to be," heartily interrupted William, as he clasped his brother's ready hand. "On my sacred word, I never touched it; I could not do so: and you must have been prejudiced to fancy it. I'll lay any money Dance will turn out to have been the black sheep. Both looks and tones were false as he gave his evidence."

And William Pickering was right. Dance was effectually "looked after" that night that some ugly facts came out, and he was quietly taken into custody. True enough, the black sheep had been nobody else. He had skilfully pilfered the petty sums of money; he had struck down Mr. Stone as he sat at his desk, to take a couple of sovereigns he saw lying in it. The old gentleman recovered, and gave evidence on the trial at the following March Assizes, and Richard and William Pickering from henceforth were more closely knit together.

But the singular circumstances attendant on the death of Mrs. Pickering—her apparition (for it could be nothing less), that appeared to Mary Barber—became public property. People in talking of it, mostly with timid glances backward and hushed voices, grew to call it "The Ghost of the Hollow Field," and for a long while neither girl nor woman would pass through it alone.

Alice Mary Vince

THE WICKED EDITOR'S CHRISTMAS DREAM

H E WAS A VERY GOOD EDITOR, as Editors go, though some of them do not go very far; just a little given to promise where he never meant to perform, which after all is a frailty common to all mankind, and not exclusively confined to Editors, so he must not be judged too harshly. Besides, neither his faults or his virtues have anything to do with his dream. It was his Christmas dinner which brought about all that. He was never quite sure himself whether it was the goose, or the pudding, or the walnuts, possibly the punch. In my opinion the blame should be divided equally between the four, with perhaps a rather sharper reprimand to the punch. It happened in front of a great big Christmas fire in his own dining room, but he did not know that until it was all over. He thought he was in his sanctum at the office, and that the telephone bell was ringing. He never was accustomed to answer the summons quickly, and he did not answer it quickly now. It kept on persistently, and then he looked up and addressed the unoffending instrument as though it were a dilatory office boy. He was just going leisurely towards it when straight from it came something to meet him—something thin, and weird, and wavy—which he instantly recognised as the inevitable Christmas Ghost. He had a great dislike to all ghosts, but a particular aversion to the Christmas species. They were so moral, so improving, so bent on doing good. At other seasons of the year ghosts content themselves with tapping, creaking, and occasionally pulling the clothes off your bed, but at Christmas they always become priggish and apt to rake up things you would far sooner forget all about. The Editor saw that he was about to be bored, and he sighed deeply as he asked:

"Will you kindly give me your name? I do not think I have had the pleasure of meeting you before."

"No," said the Ghost, "this is my first edition. I have been allotted to wait upon you this evening and show you round a bit."

"Thank you," said the Editor, "but the chief reporter generally attends to this sort of thing. You will find him in the other office. Good evening."

"Not so," said the Ghost. "It is to you I am sent, and you know that if I sought the chief reporter, you would make your escape by the back way. You see we know all about you."

The Ghost then moved all the best articles of furniture into one corner, and seated himself in the midst of them. "There is a spirit taking a snap shot of this interview," he explained, "and it will give a better impression down below if one corner of your room is decently furnished."

"I see you are thoroughly up to date," said the Editor; "would you tell me the origin of the Christmas Ghost?"

"Dyspepsia," answered the Ghost, briefly.

"Why is he so much more respectable and tiresome than any of the other kind?"

"There is nothing like the liver," said the Ghost, "for awakening the conscience, and there is no season of the year when the liver is more likely to be out of order, and the conscience correspondingly susceptible. We take advantage of this, and come to earth to administer our rebukes and suggest improvements."

"I suppose you follow the old rules—pictures of the past, present, and future," said the Editor.

"Yes, I work on the good old lines," replied the Ghost, "though I flatter myself I have introduced a little variety into the business. Shall we start? You won't want a catalogue, shall you?"

The Editor groaned.

"You won't think it rude if I don't sit out the whole of the show," he said. "I had an important engagement this evening, and I have a singular repugnance to keeping anyone waiting."

"You shall go at half time," said the Ghost.

Then the room was darkened, and the Editor felt himself swiftly whirled through the air. He shut his eyes and opened them to find himself in a very strange place. He had, as it were, a bird's eye view of a number of houses, all poorly furnished, and filled with men, women, and children, looking scantily fed and clad.

In the centre of the place was a pyramid of used foolscap, dusty with age, at which the people gazed sadly. Some of them held closely-written sheets in their hands, and seemed to be brooding over them despairingly.

"What is this?" asked the Editor.

"This," said the Ghost, "is the Abode of Dejected Men and Rejected Copy. You have largely helped in peopling this."

"Well," said the Editor, "there wasn't room for it all, you know, and I did my best."

"Not always," said the Ghost, in denouncing tones. "Read that."

He pointed to a manuscript over which a very thin, pallid-looking man was leaning, and the Editor read it carefully. It was addressed to him, and bore a date of some weeks ago, but he had never read it before.

"By jove," he said, "that's uncommonly good. I'll use that on Friday."

"Too late," said the Ghost monotonously, "too late. Look into the man's face."

The Editor looked. It was the face of a corpse.

"That man died of want," said the Ghost.

The Editor shivered.

"Shall we move on?" he said. "This place is draughty and I have a slight cold on my chest."

There was another rush through the air, and then they stopped where there was a perfect Pandemonium of movement and noise. All about were hung various copies of contents' bills of the Editor's own paper, and up and down ran boys shouting it out, and offering it for sale. The Editor was proud to see how the people rushed to buy it.

"It has an immense circulation," he said with a smile of satisfaction.

"Yes," said the Ghost, grimly. "It has—down here. Read that bill out to me."

"Horrible murder. Shocking disclosures at the Divorce Court. Suicide of a well-known tradesman. Full details in second edition," read the Editor as well as he could above the din of the boys shouting "Speshul," and the stampede of the buyers' feet. "Yes, I remember that well. We got that murder before anybody."

"Do not boast," said the spirit. "Watch this boy and girl."

The Editor followed the direction of the pointing hand. Both boy and girl were reading the paper earnestly and attentively. The girl who was pretty and innocent looking, was gloating over the story of the Divorce, and the boy was drinking in every line of the Murder case.

"We shall see them again," said the Ghost.

On they went through the Babel and the Editor saw many strange sights as they passed along. Here and there he caught a glimpse of a prison cell, once he saw a gallows, and everywhere his paper was being read. When they got to the extreme end of the place the Ghost stopped.

"There are the two you saw just now," he said. The Editor looked but he would not have recognised them. The girl had grown flaunting and bold, and the boy cunning and wizen-faced. He did not like the change.

"Am I answerable for this?" he asked.

"Yes," said the Ghost. "You and others are answerable for all this."

"But," remonstrated the Editor, "the realistic stuff sells so well now-a-days, everyone goes in for it."

"Even so," said the Ghost, "and that girl is an outcast and that boy is going to the gallows. Have you had enough?"

"I should be glad to go," said the Editor, "if you have nothing pleasanter to show me."

"I was not sent to be pleasant," said the Ghost.

"I gathered that from the very first," said the Editor, for they had left the noisy regions and were ascending again.

"Is it all over?" he asked, for he seemed to be sitting in his office chair once more.

"Not quite," said the Ghost. "You are a little wavering in your politics, are you not?"

"I think you can hardly say that," said the Editor. "It's rather hard to please everybody, you know."

"I understand," said the Ghost, "you are a wobbler. Feel the effects of that."

The Ghost made strange signals in the air, and the Editor instantly found himself seized and shaken roughly from side to side. On his right was a grim apparition all collar and hawk-like eyes, and on his left was one who wore an eye-glass of what seemed at that dread moment to be forty horse-power.

"Who and what are these?" he gasped.

"The one to the right is known as the Grim Old Masterpiece, the other we call the Man of Parts. Have you decided between them?"

The Editor could only just shriek "Yes," so severe was the shaking, and then freed himself with a tremendous effort. The fire was out, and he was in a cold perspiration.

"There was too nutmeg in that punch," he said, as he lowered the gas and went to bed.

Anonymous

THE BARBER'S GHOST

A GENTLEMAN TRAVELLING SOME TIME SINCE, called at a tavern, and requested entertainment for the night. The landlord informed him that it was out of his power to accommodate him, as his house was already full. He persisted in stopping, as he, as well as his horse, was almost exhausted with travelling. After much solicitation, the landlord consented to his stopping, provided he would sleep in a certain room that had not been occupied for a long time in consequence of a belief that it was haunted by the ghost of a barber, who was reported to have been murdered in that room years before.

"Very well," said the man. "I'm not afraid of ghosts."

After having refreshed himself, he inquired of the landlord how and in what manner the room in which he was to lodge was haunted. The landlord replied that shortly after they retired to rest, an unknown voice was heard in a trembling and protracted accent, saying: "Do you want to be shaved?"

"Well," replied the man, "if he comes he may shave me."

He then requested to be shown to the apartment in going to which he was conducted through a large room, where were seated a great number of persons at a gambling-table. Feeling a curiosity which almost every one possesses, after having heard ghost stories, he carefully searched every corner of his room, but could discover nothing but the usual furniture of the apartment. He then lay down, but did not close his eyes to sleep immediately; and in a few minutes he imagined he heard a voice saying:

"Do you w-a-n-t to be s-h-a-v-e-d?"

He arose from his bed and searched every part of the room, but could discover nothing. He again went to bed; but no sooner had he begun to compose himself to sleep, than the question was again repeated. He again arose, and went to the window, the sound appearing to proceed from that quarter, and stood silent awhile. After a few moments of anxious suspense, he again heard the sound distinctly, and convinced that it was from without, he opened the window, when the question was repeated full in his ear, which startled him not a little. Upon a minute examination, however, he observed that the limb of a large oak tree, which stood under the window, projected so near the house, that every breath of wind, to a lively imagination, made a noise resembling the interrogation: "Do you w-a-n-t to be s-h-a-v-e-d?"

Having satisfied himself that his ghost was nothing more or less than the limb of a tree coming in contact with the house, he again went to bed, and attempted to get to sleep; but he was now interrupted by peals of laughter, and an occasional volley of oaths and curses, from the room where the gamblers were assembled. Thinking that he could turn the late discovery to his own advantage, he took a sheet from the bed, and wrapped it around him, and taking a wash basin in his hand, and throwing a towel over his shoulder, proceeded to the room of the gamblers, and suddenly opening the door, walked in, exclaiming in a tremulous voice:

"Do you w-a-n-t to be s-h-a-v-e-d?"

Terrified at the sudden appearance of the ghost, the gamblers were thrown into the greatest confusion in attempting to escape it—some jumping through the windows, and others tumbling head over heels down stairs. Our ghost taking advantage of a clear room, deliberately swept a large amount of money from the table into the basin, and retired unseen to his own room.

The next morning he found the house in the utmost confusion. He was immediately asked if he rested well, to which he replied in the affirmative.

"Well, no wonder," said the landlord, "for the ghost, instead of going to his own room, made a mistake, and took away every dollar of our money."

The guest, without being the least suspected, quietly ate his own breakfast, and departed, many hundred dollars richer by the adventure.

Andrew Haggard

A SPIRIT BRIDE

Part I.

THE ORIGIN OF THE VERY SAD ADVENTURE, which has tinged
my life with grief, was that I went by invitation to a séance
which was held in a haunted house. Although the owner and
his wife had for long been disturbed by horrid shrieks and other
unaccountable noises, and although the servants and themselves
had occasionally had fleeting "rencontres" with flitting shadowy
forms, they had never been able to make out what it was that the
ghosts wanted, as these never stopped long enough to be asked.
At length, however, it became almost impossible to live in the
house, the spirits that inhabited it having developed the unpleasant habit of twitching the bed-clothes at night from off the
living inhabitants. It was of no use putting them on again, they
were twitched off repeatedly. Now, even a worm will turn, and
my friends, Mr. Smith and his wife, who had given the spiritual
inhabitants of the old Manor House a free rein as long as they
had contented themselves with shriekings, tramplings, rattling
of chains, and sudden flittings by in the long passages, drew a line
at twitching of bed-clothes. They therefore determined to obtain
the services of the most powerful medium of the day, and, if possible, make the ghosts materialise fully, give an account of themselves, and say what it was they wanted. Smith was a stockbroker,
without a scrap of superstition in his nature. He had only bought
the Manor House a year or two before, and would not in the least
have objected to buying the family ghost also, on account of the
air of respectability that it would give the place, had he been told
about it. But he had been "done." Instead of one family ghost
there were evidently two or three, and they were, not only not
respectable, but distinctly malignant and spiteful spirits.

"I would not mind them much," said Smith to me, "if only they would treat me fairly; but as they don't appear inclined to do that, I will be even with them soon by pulling the old house down until the site it occupied is as flat and unrecognisable as the place where stood Babylon of old. I will put the plough over it too, and turn it into an apple orchard," he added reflectively. "Apples do very well down there. Not much fun they'll get twitching bed-clothes then," he chuckled vindictively between his teeth. "But I'll tell them all this at the séance, and give them a chance though. Perhaps when I have made it quite plain to them, that if I have to go they will have to do too, they will be a bit more reasonable, and we may be friends yet. But we'll have a nice little party at the séance, even if it is the last party we ever have in my house."

As Smith said, he had a nice little party, but with a view to making the thing a greater success, he had only invited those whom he had heard of as being believers in spiritualism. Some of these he had never even met himself before; thus as a party it was scarcely a congenial one, for very few of those present knew each other,—not that that made much difference to the people, who only went with the object of studying the supernatural.

When Mr. Hawkshaw, the celebrated medium, arrived from town it was eleven o'clock at night. About a dozen of the visitors arrived with him, and as there were several people already assembled we formed quite a large party. When the medium was shown over the house and told to choose a room in which he thought the séance had better be held, he selected a musty old room known as the library. There were not very many books in it, but what there were were large and heavy ones, and there were plenty of chairs, sofas, and settees, quite sufficient, indeed, to accommodate all the guests. As I took my seat on the end of the sofa, I particularly noticed that the chair against it to my right was unoccupied. We determined at first to sit in the dark, so we bound the medium hand and foot and laid him on a sofa, sealed him tight over every knot with many seals, and turned out the lights. No sooner were the lights turned out than a fearful crash was heard behind us on my side of the room. It was the sound of falling books, and as we heard one mighty tome after another being dashed violently on the floor the air became redolent of dust. It was almost stifling.

Suddenly a voice shouted out in an authoritative tone, "You had better all join hands and sing a hymn, there are spirits present."

I knew the voice to be that of John Roberts, the medium's controlling spirit. He had been in his lifetime one of the earliest disciples of John Wesley, and had always shown himself to be a religious God-fearing spirit. In accordance with John Roberts's directions I took hold of the hand of the person on my left, and was leaning across the empty chair on my right to take that of my nearest neighbour, when I found the chair was no longer unoccupied, for a little hand instantly seized mine. I had hardly time for astonishment, indeed only just had time to think that someone must have moved nearer to me, when the din in the room became so terrific that it seemed as if all the powers of hell had broken loose. All the fallen books commenced flying round the room, we were violently lifted up in our seats and shaken, and we could then hear a large table overturned with a smash.

"Strike a light," roared out John Roberts, "or someone will be killed."

Instantly half a dozen matches were lighted, just in time for me to see that a heavy book-case was tottering and about to fall on the heads of several of the people opposite. When the lights were struck, and candles lighted, I was able to see whose hand it was I was grasping on my right. I found it was that of a most beautiful young lady, a brunette, with a perfect figure, splendid black hair, and a pair of lovely and lustrous dark eyes, which were turned somewhat mockingly upon mine.

"Are you frightened," she asked, smiling somewhat sarcastically. "I should have thought, Mr. Ashburton, you were accustomed to the vagaries of the spirits by this time! But never mind, hold tight on to me, I am smaller than you, but I will protect you all the same. The spirits and I are very good friends."

I wondered how she knew my name, but giving her hand a responsive grip, I answered, "Well, really, my dear young lady, you make me feel a little ashamed of myself, but I must honestly own I do not like the idea of being hit in the eye by the brass-bound corner of an ancient bible, or of having my head bashed in by a falling book-case. Still I am glad to find that you are a friend of the spirits," I added, laughingly, "as, then, quite apart from your generous offer to protect me, you will probably run less risk of being hurt yourself."

"Hush," she said, laying a shapely finger on her charming lips, "we must go on with the séance. Don't you know we have come here to see the ghosts? But we will not go on with the business quite in the dark any longer," she said. "It is too rough altogether." Then to my surprise she spoke in an authoritative voice, "John Roberts, we cannot run this séance quite in the dark or there will be accidents. We must have a couple of lamps lit and turned down low, placed at the corners of the room, and you must watch to see that the evil spirits do not overturn them and put them out."

"Very well, Miss Evelyn," answered the voice of the controlling spirit. "I think it will be safer for the medium too."

"Have you any lamps, Mrs. Smith?" said my fair neighbour to our hostess. "If so you had better light them, and place them as I direct."

Neither Mrs. Smith nor anybody else seemed to have the slightest idea who the young lady was who was thus taking the direction of affairs into her own hands, but she replied, "Oh, certainly Miss—Miss——"

"Miss Evelyn," interposed the girl.

"Here are some lamps, Miss Evelyn, just outside the door. Where shall we put them?" For everyone recognised the fact that it was just as well that this very self-possessed young lady should be allowed to take the lead, as nobody else seemed to know what to do.

She lit the lamps and placed them in the corners, turned low; then, coming back to her seat next to me to my great satisfaction she once more took possession of my hand in her firm, but dainty grasp. "There," said she, smiling at me. "Now, Mr. Ashburton, we shall see something."

"I expect we shall, Miss Evelyn," I replied. "And if so, it will be entirely due to you." I only wished I knew Miss Evelyn. Miss Evelyn—what?—but I liked the name Evelyn in itself without any surname.

We had not long to wait. We had scarcely resumed the clasp

of hands all round before the medium was suddenly lifted off the sofa, carried across the room over our heads, and placed on the wide top of the book-shelf which had so recently nearly fallen down.

"He will do there nicely," said Miss Evelyn. "He's in a trance, and they will probably bring him down again if they want him. If not we can fetch him down ourselves."

After the medium, the sofa that he had been lying on followed him on to the top of the book-case. It was placed right over him upside down, but he did not seem in any way annoyed by its weight, or, indeed, aware of its presence. Then the table upon which was one of the lamps was taken violently up, thrown down again and smashed, but the lamp was taken across the room and carefully placed by the other one.

"I saved that lamp," called out the voice of the "Control," John Roberts, as if seeking for approbation.

"Yes, John," said Miss Evelyn, "that was right of you; but all these manifestations are simply rubbish. What we came here for was to see the materialised form of the ghosts that haunt this house, and to find out, if possible, what they want, not to see them play the fool like this."

"I know that, Miss Evelyn," answered John, "but they are bad, unruly spirits, who neither know me nor care for me at all."

"Well, you had better tell them that if they don't show themselves now they will never get another chance, as Mr. Smith is going to pull the house down over their heads. Are you not, Mr. Smith?"

"Yes, I am," answered Mr. Smith, staring with astonishment. "But how do you know this?"

Before she could answer a frightful sound of combined scampering and shouting was heard outside coming along the corridor. The library door flew open, and two hideous beasts burst in. They had horrible human heads covered with long grey hair; one was a male and the other female, and their bodies were those of baboons. Their eyes were fierce, and their teeth long and sharp. They rushed round the room, clawing savagely at us as they passed, but stopped suddenly in front of the terrified Smith. Mrs. Smith and another lady fainted just then.

"You want to see us, Smith, do you? Well, here we are. And the reason that we are here is, that we are the Darwinian ancestors of the Smith family. The missing links, in fact. Do you see any resemblance to yourself?" and they gnashed their teeth dreadfully at him. "Now, say, are you going to keep us, or are you going to clear out and leave us and the place to ourselves?" And they made as if they would tear him to pieces. We were all nearly terrified out of our wits at these awful creatures, when the silvery tones of Miss Evelyn's voice somewhat reassured us.

"You silly people," she said, "don't think anybody's afraid of you, for although you have made such frights of yourselves, you have overdone it so much that a baby could see you are only masquerading. Missing links, indeed! Nonsense! If you really want anything settled, why not appear in your proper forms?"

"She's too clever for us," growled the female missing link. "Who is she? Well, perhaps she's right, so let's change. I am tired of this ugly form, at any rate. But in spite of what she says, we have nearly frightened a couple of women to death. That's some satisfaction."

"Very well, change," said the male being.

The words were no sooner out of his mouth, when two of the handsomest creatures it has ever been my lot to behold stood before us—a gentleman and a lady clad in the court dress of the time of Charles II. But their faces, if handsome, were very, very evil. The lady swept round in front of me, and making a low curtsey, asked, with a hard sarcastic laugh, if I liked her any better so?

"Certainly, madam," I replied, "very much better. But now you have assumed your proper and graceful form, will you not kindly tell us your history?"

They related their history, which, to cut it short, was as follows:—

They had inhabited this house formerly in Charles II.'s days, when the lady had been in the habit of using her beauty to lure the richest gallants of the day under their roof—one at a time. As she had always made absolute secrecy the condition of her favours, when the unfortunate cavaliers had been decoyed by her, and robbed and murdered by the male partner in her guilt, who was her husband, discovery of the whereabouts of the victims when they were missed became almost an impossibility. But the guilty couple had been found out at length and executed, and now they were doomed for ever to haunt the spot where they had committed their crimes. What they wished for, therefore, was to be left in undisputed possession of the Manor House. A compromise was come to by the intermediary of the self-possessed and beautiful Miss Evelyn. Smith agreed on the one side to give up to them entirely the oldest wing of the house. They agreed, on the other hand, never again to twitch at the bed-clothes, or in any way whatever to annoy the Smith family or their descendants. Smith and the male apparition shook hands on the compact, for the two ghosts were fully materialised for the time being. The lady also insisted upon shaking hands with me, as she was kind enough to say she still had a weakness for good looking young fellows. Personally, I did not at all like shaking hands with even the ghost of a murderess, but I thought it best to comply with a good grace. They then bowed politely to the company, and walking arm in arm out of the room, disappeared for ever.

John Roberts and other well-disposed spirits then quietly with unseen hands replaced Mr. Hawkshaw, the medium, and the sofa in their original positions. Hawkshaw was awakened from his trance, and the séance terminated pleasantly. Then we all went down to the dining-room to an excellent supper, of which we stood greatly in need.

During this meal the host and hostess, the latter of whom had quite recovered from her fright, both made a great deal of Miss Evelyn, but imagining, perhaps, that she had come with a friend, they asked her no questions as to her surname, nor how she had chanced to arrive so opportunely on the scene that evening, although I have cause to know that their curiosity about her was very great. But in fact they were just a little afraid of her. For my part, the more I saw of this girl the more I was struck with her beauty; while she continued to glance at me, strange to say, with a look in her grand lustrous eyes which was positively affectionate, and it seemed to me somehow from that look that she wished me to remain near her. It was at the same time a clinging and caressing glance. I did not refuse its unspoken invitation, but kept by her side when we sat down to supper. I found her a most interesting and well-read companion. She seemed to know about everything and everybody, and was just as much at home in Voltaire or Renan as she was in the books of Rider Haggard, or in the ordinary park and society gossip of the day. Supper ended, our host was in somewhat of a quandary. The last train from Kingston, which was the nearest station to the Manor, had gone to town, and he did not quite know how to dispose of all his guests, especially as now he had surrendered one wing to the spirits, he could only offer some of them, Miss Evelyn and myself included, shakedowns upon arm-chairs and sofas. Miss Evelyn, however, spoke in her quiet decided way: "Thanks, Mr. Smith, do not bother about me at all. I must be up in town very early indeed, and intend to stroll quietly along the river and wait for the first train at Richmond. It is a lovely night for a walk, and I feel that the air would do me good. I am quite capable of taking care of myself, unless, indeed, any gentleman"—and she glanced at me—"is dying for a cigar, and would like to come too."

I, of course, took the hint, and offered my escort for the seven mile walk, which she accepted.

"Oh! Mr. Smith," said she, when this was quite settled, "you can, by-the-bye, use to-night without fear the wing you have promised to give up. I can answer for it that you will not be molested at all, for I was responsible for the arrangement being made in the first instance, and I understand the spirits thoroughly. I will, therefore, make myself responsible for them not to take possession until to-morrow night at twelve o'clock."

Her air of quiet conviction brought great relief to Smith and those who wished for a bed to sleep in, for although no one knew who she was, her face was very truthful, and after the events of the evening it was evident that she indeed knew thoroughly well all about the spirits and their doings.

That was an eventful walk I had with this strange young lady by night along the river bank. The harvest moon shone upon the rippling waters, and all nature seemed at peace. She had taken my arm, and in a short time it seemed to me as if our thoughts and minds were blended together—and I felt that she too was deeply moved by the beauty of the midnight scene. Her arm trembled in mine, and presently she said, answering my unspoken thoughts:

"Yes it is heavenly, but do you not think that it is more beautiful in the spheres where the spirits dwell than it is even here to-night?"

"No," I answered gazing passionately upon her. "Nothing in this or any world can be more beautiful than this."

She sighed deeply—then looked up in my face with a sweet smile and said earnestly—"Ah! George Ashburton, that is simply because you think you love me, is it not? You do not even know my name, beyond having heard the spirit of John Roberts call me Evelyn. You do not know where I come from, nor where I go—you have never seen me until four hours ago—and yet now you think in your heart that you love me better than all the world. You would jump into that river for my slightest wish, I verily believe—Say, is it not so?"

"Beautiful Evelyn," I replied, "you are indeed right. I do not think, but know, that I love you as you say, sufficiently to lay my life down for you if need be. Ah! I verily believe that you have bewitched me."

"Perhaps I have," she answered more merrily, "but how do you know that you have not, by some wilful but unforgotten act of your own bewitched me too? I am not in the habit of taking midnight walks with strange gentlemen, you know. How do you know that this is not all a delusion—a dream? What means have you of telling that you are you, or that I am I? After the strange things you have seen to-night, why might not I rather be some vampire or evil spirit, seeking to lure you to destruction for purposes of my own? Do I look anything like an evil spirit?" she asked, looking up at me archly.

"Oh! no," I exclaimed vehemently, "you are no evil spirit, but some good true woman, some woman whom I have known before somewhere, though I know not when or how, for you remind me of someone I seem to have seen in a dream—but evidently you know me, and know me well. Oh! I must tell you that I adore you first—you can tell me who you are or not as you choose." And losing all control of myself I wound my arms around the beautiful girl and drew her to my heart. Oh! never, never shall I forget the exquisite sweetness and witchery of that moment when her lovely lips first met mine,—for oh, rapture, she ardently returned my loving embrace. Presently she threw back her shapely head a little, and I observed that there were tears coursing down her now pale cheeks—her great dark eyes were glistening with the pearly drops in the radiant moonlight.

"I, too, love you, George," she whispered, "love you more than I can tell, with a greater, deeper love than woman ever yet had for man. Were it not so, I should not be here now. But I can tell you nothing now, you will have to take me entirely on trust. Moreover you will have to put up with my involuntary absence from you for thirty-six hours in every week, from every Saturday night until Monday at mid-day, and ask no questions as to where I go or what I do. Some day, perhaps, you may lose me altogether. If you can endure this—if you can stand this tremendous test, then indeed will your love be proved to be great, noble, and true, and as a reward for the sacrifices you make to comply with my conditions, we may be allowed one or two heavenly years of happiness together, we must not expect more than that. I warn you beforehand. Do not decide now. I will see you to-morrow—you can tell me what you have determined on then. One word more; if you think the conditions I impose are hard, know this, that I am utterly powerless to avoid making them, and this it is as painful to me to impose them as it will be to you to comply with them. Further, I may tell you this, although you cannot remember when or where it was, yet we have met before, and, moreover, I have made the most frightful sacrifices to be enabled to meet you again. Now kiss me, and let us be happy to-night in our love, while leaving this matter of your final decision concerning our future till to-morrow."

Silently I enfolded her once more in my arms, and as I did so, I felt even more strongly than before that we were one in heart and soul. And I too knew somehow that it was not for the first time on this evening that I had loved her pure spirit, although the beautiful bodily form that veiled it was new to me.

PART II.

Evelyn and I arrived at Richmond, shortly after dawn, and after merrily partaking of coffee together amid a crowd of workmen at an itinerant coffee seller's stall, we took the first train up to London, where I dropped my companion at South Kensington Station as she said she lived close by. She did not say where, and I did not ask. On parting she promised to meet me at the same place late in the afternoon, when she would learn my decision. But she begged me as an especial favour to go to bed, and sleep for an hour or two before thinking about it; I vowed that I was not sleepy and could not, whereupon the graceful girl, saying smilingly—"then I must charm you to sleep, sir," bent forward and kissed me on both eyes. "Now good-bye, dear one," she added; "go home at once and dream of me." And she left me. I felt drowsy at once, and when I got home slept a sound refreshing sleep until past mid-day. In the afternoon I met her again, when in a pretty summery frock she looked even more beautiful than she had done the day before. She looked up enquiringly when we met.

"I accept your conditions," I said, "accept them unreservedly."

She pressed my arm in a confiding grateful manner, while her face was overspread with such a gladsome look of content, that my own happiness became also too great for words.

"Then now that that is settled," said Evelyn, "we will get married to-morrow, Wednesday"—the séance had been on Monday night—"that will give us three whole days together before I must leave you for the first time. Ah me," she sighed, "I fear, dear one, that you will find these absences heart-rending, but we must not repine, but remember that since there can be no absolutely unmixed happiness in the world, we must make the best of that which we can get while it lasts. Therefore let us waste no time. You can get a special license for me in the name of Ellen Montgomery, and we will be married at St. Paul's, Knightsbridge, as you live in that parish."

For I had a little house close by. It was too big for one, but would do nicely for two. We agreed that I should wire to the Smiths and ask them to come up to the wedding—and also ask Mr. Smith to give the bride away. They were very much surprised, but they were already excessively interested in Miss Evelyn, and suspecting some mystery about her were all the more willing to accede to our request. I got a friend from the Club to act as my best man, the two Miss Smiths were bridesmaids, and we were duly made man and wife. After this quiet wedding we had a delicious and jovial little breakfast at the Albemarle Hotel, where we resolved to pass the three days of our honeymoon. And never has it fallen to the lot of man in this world to pass three days of more complete happiness than did I alone with my wife in that comfortable spot in the centre of London. If I had thought her charming before marriage, I found her an angel after, but not an insipid angel by any means. No, she was the brightest, happiest, most *espiègle* of girls; as I said before, I never knew such a mind, it was stored with everything.

On the Saturday night, when the time came for our first parting, we drove away from the Albemarle along Piccadilly together. She dropped me at my old home, and then after a long and tender embrace, she went on, giving the hansom-cab driver the vague address of South Kensington.

On the following Monday at twelve o'clock she returned to me, when we met with mutual transports of joy. And thus commenced our married life. The enforced absences only made our meetings all the happier, and for a time it was almost heaven. I kept religiously to my compact and never worried my wife as to her doings during her weekly absences from me, although I must own, that my curiosity as to the cause of her weekly departure was excessive. On one occasion, however, I must plead guilty to having played a trick upon her in the hope of retarding her departure. I contrived to put back all the clocks and also her own watch, for half an hour. To my surprise, however, this made no difference to her leaving at the proper time. Glancing at the drawing-room clock that Saturday night, she noticed that it only marked 11.15, when the hour was really 11.45. She merely remarked, "Oh! that clock is half an hour slow, but I must be going." Then she looked at her watch and noticed the same thing. Coming across to me smilingly, she kissed me and said, "You silly boy, you have been doing this, but it is, alas! useless, for I know within myself, without any watches, when the time has come for me to go." I felt ashamed of myself and never tried on anything of the sort again. At last a time came when my dear wife was likely to become a mother. Although I became more and more anxious on her account, this did not make any difference as regards her weekly appearances. She went off all the same, and the months passed by.

I found the Sundays very lonely in her absence, and did not know what to do with myself without her. One Sunday afternoon I went for a solitary walk in Kensington Gardens. Strolling moodily round the corner of some bushes I suddenly came upon an old gentleman and a young lady seated upon a garden seat. My astonishment was very great to recognise in the latter my wife, for she had once volunteered the statement that when she left me she never by any chance remained in town, but always travelled a great distance in the short time. Naturally I went up to her. I noticed that she looked very pale and was crying, and as I approached, I heard the old gentleman speaking to her in angry tones.

"Why, Evelyn, my dear," I said, "it is a very great surprise to me to find you in town to-day. But what is the matter with you, darling, why are you crying like this? And why is this gentleman whom I do not know speaking harshly to you? What does it mean, dear? Tell me at once for it goes to my heart to see you thus unhappy."

I do not know which of the couple looked more astonished when I thus addressed her. Both Evelyn and the old gentleman stared at me in the blankest amazement, Evelyn made not the slightest attempt to recognise me in any way. Indeed she put on an expression as if she really did not know me. There was silence for a moment, and then the old gentleman, turning to my wife, said sternly:

"Evelyn, who is this person who presumes to address you so familiarly."

She replied with an air of truth—"I do not know him at all, Papa. I have never seen him before in all my life."

I staggered as if struck at the lie. I had never known her to lie before, and then such a lie! To disown me like this! But I had not time for much reflection before the old man turned furiously upon me.

"By what right, sir, do you dare to address my daughter when she declares she does not know you"—

"By a very simple right," I replied, "the right that a husband has to address his wife. She has been my wife for nearly a year."

"Her husband! Oh! thank God that she is married," said her father, "then I have been blaming her undeservedly for what I thought her approaching shame. Evelyn, my child, why did you not trust your poor old father, instead of causing all this distress? But why do you disown your husband now you see there is no cause to do so? On the contrary, introduce him to me, and let us all be friends together. What is his name?"

If I had been surprised before, I was much more surprised than ever when Evelyn, instead of complying with her father's request rose from her seat, and angrily stamping on the ground said, looking me straight in the face—"Married! I am not married. Husband! I have no husband, at any rate if so he is not a husband of this world. I have never even seen this man before, and he is a liar if he says that I am his wife."

"But I am not a liar," I retorted. "And I do say distinctly that you are my wife Evelyn, and you have your wedding ring to prove it. Inside that ring is inscribed the date on which you married me at St. Paul's, Knightsbridge, last year, the 13th of July—"

"Now although I don't know how you know my name, I can prove you are a liar," said Evelyn, pulling off her glove. "See, I have no wedding ring—"

"No," I answered, "but see, here is the white mark where it has been, and even if for some extraordinary reason you have taken it off, can you deny to me that you are about to become a mother, the mother of my child?"

"Oh! Heavens, this is too much, father. I repeat to you most positively that I do not know him—and yet in some extraordinary way he seems to know all about me, even that I have been in some awful way the victim of some unintelligible misfortune. But he profits on it, and calls me his wife, well knowing it is false. Can it be that he is himself in some way the cause of all this misery?"

There was no mistake about her voice—it was distinctly my wife's voice.

"What in God's name does all this mean?" exclaimed the father. "True, she has been away week after week with friends or relatives, and may possibly be married to you as you say, but why does she so persistently deny it?"

"Be good enough to tell me your name, sir," I said.

"Thomas Montgomery, sir," he replied—"And yours?"

"George Ashburton is my name, and I insist upon you and my wife here, who is apparently your daughter, accompanying me to St. Paul's, Knightsbridge, to see the register of marriages."

He said he would accede to my request, and Evelyn had perforce to accompany us. He saw the register, and his daughter's name as being married to me. When Evelyn again denied having ever been married there at all, both the clerk and the clergyman who had performed the ceremony told her father they identified her perfectly. After that she became quieted, resigned, and silent, but I insisted upon the father, who was completely dumbfounded, accompanying me to my house, which poor Evelyn declared vehemently she had never seen before. But the servants recognised her without doubt as being their mistress, and her photographs and dresses about the rooms completely convinced the father that she was most undoubtedly my wife. He became perfectly furious with her at length for what he declared to be her double deception, and despite her prayers and entreaties left her with me, saying that I was her husband and her place was with me, and that he washed his hands of her altogether. After he left, the poor girl fainted, and I had to put her in her own bed. She was quite ill and delirious all the afternoon and night, after coming to her senses. At length the doctor who was in the habit of attending her had to be fetched, when he found her declaring that she was not my wife, and that I had no business in her room, and so on—he took me on one side and told me he considered the case most dangerous. There was no doubt, he said, that her mind was completely off its balance.

This was what I feared myself from her extraordinary behaviour. However, although she declared she was perfectly well, and wanted no medicine, he made her take a very powerful opiate, which soon sent her into a trance, like sleep, which lasted until seven next morning. Then she awoke, but alas, no better, for she seemed not to know me in the least, and was perfectly horrified at finding me by her side. She wished to rise and leave the room and the house, and had to be detained by force. At ten o'clock, tired out, she fell asleep again, and at twelve she awoke perfectly cured apparently as far as her brain was concerned, although very weak. She knew me now perfectly, and was most loving in her manner, but asked me how she happened to be in bed, and seemed to know nothing about the day before. Indeed she seemed to think it utterly impossible she could have come to my house on the previous day, until I told her all about the meeting with her father and her strange manner. Then she became very serious, and saying, "I feared something of that sort would happen at last—the end will probably come soon now," she turned on her side and wept bitterly. But she would tell me nothing as to why she wept.

All that week she was in weak health and early on the Saturday morning she was confined of a boy, and a fine little fellow he was too, bright and intelligent looking, with eyes like his mother's. As the evening approached Evelyn became very anxious. She asked for her child, and pressed him to her breast, looking at me the while with the deepest love. I saw there was deep anguish in her glance.

"Do you know, George, my darling," she said, "that this is Saturday, and that I ought to be away as usual at twelve o'clock to-night? But how can I go and leave my sweet young infant, leave him to be nursed by another, who not only will not care for him, but will probably even hate him. And yet what will happen if I do not go, God only knows."

"You are too weak to go in any case," I said. "Why you would kill yourself if you tried even to walk across the room, so that must settle the matter for you, dearest."

"Ah! that would not matter," she replied, "for since what took place last Sunday, my spirit could go, and yet I could leave my body here as it is now. But it would be somebody else's soul that would dominate my body, just as it was last Sunday. She would not in the least understand being ill in bed with a baby, and who knows how she might treat the child? She is an unmarried girl, and might even murder it in her despair. It would be different if I could only see her and explain everything to the spirit form that conceals her identity now—but if we meet and talk it will be death to me certainly, perhaps to her too. No, I must not go, I must take all risks and stay here." And putting her arms around my neck she wept on my heart.

"My darling wife," I said, "I do not wish to distress you, but do you not think the time has now come to tell me all—"

"Yes," said she, "it has. I will disclose everything. Listen my love. When you were very young and first of all began to attend spiritualistic séances, you frequently saw a spirit who gave herself the name of Muriel. I am that spirit— Nay, do not interrupt. In the first instance you could only see my face, then by degrees I used to be able to materialise more and more, until at length I came in the fullest materialised form and was for the time being as much flesh and blood as I am now. And we used to converse together for hours—until at length, you, in your mad boyish fashion, fell madly in love with me—Muriel—the spirit. And then one day, in a séance at which you alone were present, with the entranced medium, you persuaded me to allow you to kiss me. When you did so you embraced me so madly, so ardently, and I was so gained by your love, that I returned your kisses with the passion of the human being I was for the time, not with the chaste salute of a spirit. Then, you remember, to your despair I dematerialised in your arms. I scarcely had the time to whisper, "Farewell, I love you," ere I was gone. And as a punishment, for ten long years I never was allowed to see you again, and with the cares of life you forgot your spirit love completely. However, my love for you had sunk deep into my nature, so much so that when the time came for either my advancement into another and a higher cycle in the spirit world—or else retardation in my former condition for a hundred thousand years, coupled with the temporary possession of you—I chose you, and I thank God, and shall thank God to all eternity that I did so. And this is how it was done. The girl whose earthly form I bear, Evelyn Montgomery, whom I had often met at séances, had lost an earthly lover whom she adored more than life itself. In the world of spirits he made a similar sacrifice to that I have done that he might be allowed to have her with him at times in the spirit. Then it was ordained that while I might assume her earthly form to be near you, she might, for all but thirty-six hours in every week, assume my own spirit form as the ethereal Muriel. But while I, being really a spirit, can

find out, if I like, her earthly doings—she, belonging to an infe-
rior order of beings to myself, cannot tell what I do. Hence her
distress and astonishment when you forced her, in this my body
which is also hers, to accompany you as your wife—also her distress at finding she was about to become a mother. Now to-night,
I ought as usual to yield up to her for thirty-six hours this earthly
frame, but I am physically unable to do so, and should I and she
ever meet and speak of our own free will it has been from the
beginning ordained that she—that is also I, in her earthly form
will surely die. Not that she would mind; on the contrary, it
would be her greatest happiness to join her spirit lover. But to
me, my ever-loved darling, it will mean one hundred thousand
years of regret to quit my earthly husband. But we shall see what
happens to-night. I greatly fear, my husband, my beloved one,
that you will lose me in any case—till then lavish upon me all the
love of your soul. I will cherish its recollection and yours to all
eternity."

That was all her story, wonderful and sad—but true—too
true. Only too well did I now remember my spirit love, Muriel,
and now I understood also why I had loved my Evelyn from the
first. Between eleven and twelve that night, Evelyn dozed with
her infant at her breast. She then woke, and kissing the child, gave
it to the nurse, telling her to take it to the next room and close the
door. She then threw herself into my arms.

"She is come, George," she whispered, "see, there is my own
spirit shape materialising behind you."

I turned, and saw the well-known beautiful spirit, Muriel. She
spoke musically:

"Since you have not abandoned the form of Evelyn Montgomery to-night, spirit Muriel, I have been obliged to come myself
in person and yield up your spirit form to you for the customary
thirty-six hours."

"Alas!" answered my darling wife, "it will not be for thirty-six
hours only, but for ever, since you have voluntarily spoken to me.
Do you forget the ordinance, Evelyn?"

"Ah!" answered the other, "how happy I shall be to regain my
own body and die, sister."

"And how sad I, to give up my husband, for eternity," whis-

pered now my dying wife, "although I know we, too, shall meet
again in the spirit world."

Even as she spoke the spirit form of the real Evelyn, had dematerialised, and passed into the body of my expiring wife. And
then a new Muriel rapidly materialised as the spirit of my wife assumed its own spiritual form, and as the spirit Muriel placed her
lips on mine in one last, lingering embrace, the body of Evelyn
Montgomery gave up the ghost. And they passed away together.

W. L. Blackley

THE HAUNTED OVEN

THADY BROPHY AN' HIS WIFE Bridget wur well-to-do farming people, and worked hard and had good luck. Somehow or other things done well wid them; Biddy would get the butter to come in her churn the couldest day in winter, whin her neighbours would be workin' the dash hour afther hour widout the sign of a thickening till their hearts was almost broke. And Thady's pigs never died, an' his fowls never roosted their breast-bones crooked, and his horses never broke their knees, an' the wireworm never got into his turnips, and all his calves was heifer calves. Everybody said they had the luck of the fairies, and ne'er a thing in the wide world to throuble thim; and so they had till they'd filled a long stockin' with sovereigns, and made their fortune, and thin nothin' would contint them but they must take a bigger farm, and move into a new house. The new house was a fine ould ancient building, fifty or sixty miles from Kilcoskan, where they'd made their money. And what do ye think put it into their heads to go there and set up for gentility? Why the name of the place was Glanbrophy, and Thady made sure that some of his forefathers must have lived there, an' Biddy thought it would sound mighty purty av' he was to buy it, and hear people talkin' of him as Mr. Brophy of Glanbrophy, an' thin she wint on thinking, as we're all apt to do, of how it might go on an' on, from gineration to gineration, an' that maybe in coorse ov time her great-great-grandson might be a magistrate, an' sarve on the grand jury, an' maybe get to be a high sheriff an' have a hand in a fine hanging now an' thin, an' so have something for the family to take pride in. So Biddy set her heart on Thady buying Glanbrophy, an' she sint him over to look at the place. So he rode over quiet an' asy, an' never let on to anyone he was thinking to buy it: an' he asked the neighbours all sorts of questions and came home to Biddy. "Biddy, acushla," he says, "we can get Glanbro-phy for half the valley," he says; "but I don't think I'll take it, all the same," he says. "An' why not thin?" she ses; "didn't I send ye over there just to take it out of a face?" "Ay, but Biddy," he ses; "the raison they have for letting it go cheap is bekase there's a ghost there, an' sure I thought it med be makin' you narvous, you darlint." But Thady's kind tongue was spakin' (as most of us do now an' thin that's got the luck to have a wife) one word for her an' two for himself; for though he was six foot high in his stockin' feet, the thought of a sperrit'd give him an ague as aisy as kiss your hand. "Is it make *me* narvous, acushla," ses Biddy; "sure it's funnin' you are now! The sorra a ghost in sivin counties oud frighten *me,* an' it's kindly obleeged to thim I feel for cheapening Glanbrophy for us, so as to let us into our ould ancient family estate. So jist settle the business as soon as ye can, an' see av' we can't move in three weeks afore Christmas," she says, "an' it's a hearty welcome we'll give the sperrit," she says, "whether they be leprechauns, or fairies, or fetches, or brigaboos. Be off, Thady, hot fut to the lawyer, an' come back to me as Misther Brophy of Glanbrophy, or by the pipers I'll haunt you myself, worse than the biggest old ghost that ever frightened the five small senses out of a fullsized fool before."

Well, Thady knew whin Biddy spoke that-a-way that she meant what she said, an' so, for to save time and throuble, he writ off, like a sinsible chap, and bought Glanbrophy out an' out. Troth, an' if every marrid man in this very room would do like Thady, *some* ov' you, I'll be bound, would have an aisier life than ye have.

Well, the place was theirs', an' they had the mischief's own lot of fuss moving. Biddy hadn't thought of that; an' some of the things was badly packed, an' the breakages wint to her very heart. There was three cups out of seven of her grandmother's tayset all to smithereens, an' she cut the tops of two of her fingers getting the pieces out ov' the hay, an' in short, she had all sorts of worry. But she was a jolly kind ov' a woman, *whin she had her own way,* an' made no more fuss nor she could help. An' by degrees things got pleasanter, an' every day she found somethin' new about Glanbrophy that plazed her, an' the best part of a fortnight passed away, an' they never heard the sound or seen the sign of a ghost, an' they were as proud as Punch ov' their bargain.

Well, wan mornin' ses Biddy to Thady, "There was but the wan thing wantin', Thady," she says, "to make me a happy woman," she says. "All these years at Kilcoskan we had to ate bakers' bread, bekase there wasn't an oven, an' the dickens a chance ov' barm to rise the dough. An' sure I was always havin' the heartburn from all the alum an' stuff they did be puttin' in the bread; but now," ses she, "there's a lovely old oven here, an' there's a big brewery half a mile off, jist beyant our estate, an' I can have barm every day av I want it. An' I've set in a beautiful bakin' of bread, an' now that we've got our ancesthors' estate, an' we're the Brophys of Glanbrophy, wid an illigant outside kyar, an' a beautiful oven of me own, an' home baked bread, I feel somehow, as if I'd be quite contint for to die, so I would, Thady."

"Well, Biddy," ses Thady, "I don't like much to differ wid you; but I'm not sure but I'd feel more contint to stay alive for a while; anyhow, till I tasted the home baked bread," he says, with a laugh; an' so they wint, the two ov' thim, into the bakehouse.

Biddy called the girl to open the oven an' draw the bread. For she'd got up quite airly in the mornin' to surproize Thady wid her beautiful bakin'. An' there was six lovely loaves, lookin' like three dear little pairs of sweet little twin babbies, asleep in all their innocence. "Dear me, O," she says, for she was quite touched wid her success. "What a pity to think that lovely crust'll get soft an' tough before Thursday! An' they're as light as a feather," she says, "an' it's a wondherful fine oven; an' Thady," she ses, "it's not very wholesome, but jist this wanst we'll eat hot bread for breakfast," she says, an' she was in the hoight of good humour, an' ses she, "You're right after all, Thady, I don't want to die jist yet." An' so down they sot to their breakfast.

Well, Thady takes up a loaf to cut a nice piece of undher crust off for Biddy, whin she says, "Stop, alanna," ses she, "May I never, but there's writin' on the bread!"

"Writin' on the bread!" cries Thady, wid a loud guffaw of a laugh, but he turned the loaf up to look, an' sure enough there was some big letthers on it.

Well, they looked an' looked, but they couldn't make thim

out; ould-fashioned looking, upside down, inside out; "Maybe it's French," ses Biddy. "No," ses Thady, "it must be Latin," ses he, "for there's a big B, an' it's just turned right the wrong way; an' there's an R to the left hand ov' it. What does it mane, at all, at all," an' he looked up at Biddy, an' it's startled she was, for all that she was so bould an' brave, her face was as white as the bakehouse wall, an' the teeth was chattering in her mouth. "Sure," she ses, "if it's writing the wrong way, it must be a spell, an' there's something onlooky about. Och! wirras thrice, why did I pass my little bit ov nonsense about the ghosts; there's throuble comin to us out of that oven!"

Well, Thady didn't feel comfortable, but 'twas daylight, an' so he tried to carry it off like a man; so he ses, "Don't be a big fool, Biddy, sure the letthers has no maning; it might be some sort of a rash in the whate, that breaks out on the crust of the loaf." An' then he tried a poor bit of a joke, "the flour was made of *red* whate, an' how could it be *red* without letthers?"

Biddy snapped the loaf out ov his hand in a pet. "Av' there *is* a ghost in it," ses she; "I'll spell it out backwards, and see what he's got to say throublin dacent people." An' on she wint, "B-R-I *Bri*, B-r-i-d *Brid*, G-E-T *get*, *Bridget*," she screams. "Och, Thady, alanna, I'm done for; it's a message for me from the ghost!" Well, they wur like to faint, so they wur, an' they tuk the other five loaves, an' sure enough there was writin' on thim too, an' they turned thim all undhercrust uppermost to read the onlucky backward writing on thim, an' see what was the worst of the spell the sperits was goin' to put on thim. Well, they made it out somehow. The first loaf, as I tould yees, was Bridget —an' that frightened the missis enough—but would ye believe it, the next loaf when they spelt it out was *"Brophy of Glan,"* and the third loaf *"Brophy, died."* When they got this far, they looked at wan another, an' Thady burst out in a fit o' cryin', and Biddy screamed "murther," and caught him roun' the waist, an' tried to get her nose into his waistcoat pocket, for fear of seein' any more of the ghost's message. But 'twas all no use, they couldn't help spellin' the other loaves, an' the long an' the short ov it was, *"Bridget Brophy of Glanbrophy, died Christmas Day,* 1866, *aged 44 years."* An' it wur the very year they wur in, and it wur just ten days afore Christmas!

"Oh, Thady, Thady," cried Biddy, "I'm bespoke!—it's all over wid me!—ten days to live!—and to die on Chrissimas Day!—an' 'twas all your consait wantin' to be Mister Brophy of Glanbrophy that's brought me to this pass! Ochone, for Kilcoskan! I wish I was back! But that's what man's vanity does. Why couldn't you lave me in peace where there wur no ghosts an' warnin' to make my last days miserable!" An' she threw her aperon over her 'ead an' rocked up an' down as if her sorrow was a hungry babby she wur thryin' to hush to slape.

"Arrah! Biddy," ses Thady, presently, quite hearty-like, "cheer up, woman. It's a thrick somewan's put upon you." "How do you make that out, you could-hearted spalpeen," she ses, getting out of the apron mighty quick all the same, for she was in hopes he wed have found a chance for her. "Why," ses he, "do you believe the sperits know whin you'll die?" "Av' coorse," she says, "they know all about everybody, an' they can't be wrong!" "Well, but av' I show you they must be wrong, I 'spose you won't believe them." "Av' coorse not," she says, "but there's ne'er a chance for me, I'm bespoke," an' she took to the apron agin. "Yis there is a chance," ses Thady, "don't take on like that, woman alive; sure the message ses you wur 44 years old next Christmas, an' you're only 39, so it can't be yourself they mane." Wid that Biddy began to screech like a stuck pig. "Och, Thady jewel, its all thrue! They've found me out; och, it's me an' no mistake! Whin I saw you first throwin' sheep's eyes at me, whin I lived at farmer O'Donovan's, I let on I was only 18, an' I was three-an'-twinty, an' I've done you out of five years of my life, me poor fellow, and I've only ten days left for meself." An' wid that down she wint flop, a swoon on the flure.

Thady got her to bed, an' there she stopped; for she felt mighty wake an' poorly, as you med suppose. They had meant to have a housewarmin' and a dance at Christmas, an' word had gone round to all the neighbours. But somehow the story got about one way or another, that there was to be a funeral instead of a dance, and that Mrs. Brophy of Glanbrophy had only a few more days to live. Thady sent for the docthor—he felt her pulse, an' sent a half gallon draught, an' a bastely powder, an' a pill as big as a cannon ball, because they wur rich—but they didn't do her a pin ov good, raison why, she never tuke a bit of them, she knew she would die on Christmas Day. Thady sent for the priest, an' he talked an' he read, an' he sed he'd exorcise the sperits, but he didn't do her a pin of good. Thady sint for the policeman to watch av' there was any ghosts about the place, but he didn't do a pin ov good, for whin Thady stumbled on the step at half-past twelve in the night, the policeman who was in the kitchen cut an' run like a lamplighter, an' was seen three miles off at saven o'clock, an' said he'd chased the ghost that far. So people believed in the ghost all the more, though they did turn the story the other way an' say *he* chased the policeman three miles in twenty-five minnits. So the long and the short of it was that Mrs. Brophy got waker an' waker, an' worse an' worse, till Christmas Eve.

Well, Thady was jist sittin' over the fire in the dusk, an' he was mortial low an' onhappy, thinkin' what 'ud he do the day afther to-morrow an' every day afther that whin poor Biddy would be undher the sod, whin there came a knock to the doore. Thady wint an' opened it, an' seen a pleasant-looking, middle-aged man in the doorway. "Good evenin' to yer honour," ses the man. "Same to you, and save you kindly, honest man," says Thady, "but what med you want, for the house is in throuble jist now." "Och! Misther Brophy," says the other, "I'm Larry Reilly, the fiddler and stonemason, an' I thought to have fiddled for yer dance to-morrow, but I heerd the story of how bad her ladyship was, an' I jist come up to see av' I couldn't cure her!" "Is it cure her?" ses Thady, "I'll give ye a ten pound note av' you do. But I have had the docthor an' the priest, an' the policeman, an' it's all no good, an' she's goin' off to-morrow mornin," he ses. "Nivir mind, yer honour," ses Larry, "I'd like to have a thry for the tin pound note." "An' how'll you do it," says Thady. "O, the best thing in the wor-reld, wid a case like that," ses Larry, lookin' as wise as if he was seven docthors at wanst, "is to show the patient her tombstone, an' let her see it's all in airnest about her havin' to die. Women's so contrairy, that that's the very thing makes them make up their mind to live." "Ah," ses Thady, "you're a stonemason, an' so you think her tombstone would cure her. I suppose you know 'twas a shoemaker who said there was *nothin' like leather!* An' how 'ud you manage to show her her tombstone whin the poor crayture

has to be off to-morrow morning?" "Well, let me thry," ses Larry
Reilly, as bould as brass; "there is a spell about it, an' give me two
hours by meself in the bakehouse, to fight the ghosts out of their
charrum, an' I'll undertake to show Mrs. Brophy the appearance
of her tombstone by nine o'clock, an' maybe she'll be well by
mornin." "It'll be the death of you, honest man," ses Thady;
"you'll never bate the ghosts." "I'll have a thry for the tin pound
note," ses Larry, "give me a pound of candles an' a pint of whiskey, an' lock me in till I conquer them," he says; an' so Thady, as a
last chance, did as he was told. Well, Larry wint in, an' Thady listened at the doore. Presently he heard the sperits an' Larry fightin' hammer an' tongs like one o'clock: smashin', dashin', drivin',
noise enough to finish poor Mrs. Brophy, an' she sint down to
know what it was. Up he wint, an' sed it was a sperit docthor
thryin' to save her life an' fightin' the sperits like mad. Well, this
cheered thim both up a bit, an' much sooner nor they thought all
was quiet, an' presently Larry called to be let out. There he was,
all in a lather, as you med think. "I've vanquished the sperits," he
sed, an' sure enough the whiskey bottle was upside down in his
hand. "An' I've made thim give me Mrs. Brophy's tombstone, to
cure your wife with. Here it is, we'll bring it up stairs." An' sure
enough there was a fine tombstone, six foot by eighteen inches,
with ould writing on it. "Well, that bates all," ses Thady, for he
was dumbfoundhered to think of Larry mastherin' the sperits,
an' they struggled up stairs with the tombstone to Mrs. Brophy's
doore. Biddy was in a blazin' rage at first to think Thady would
get her tombstone cut before she died; but thin she felt flatthered
to think she'd have sich a handsome wan, an' so she read it to see
if it was right about her age, for nobody likes to be dated wrong.
"Sacred to the Memory of Mrs. Bridget Brophy, of Glanbrophy,
who died Christmas Day, 1666." "O ye haythin," she cried, "ye've
put me 200 years wrong! Get along wed ye both ye hard-hearted
savages, av' I must die, let me die in modern times anyhow," an'
as she was wake she began to cry agin. "Mrs. Brophy," ses Larry,
wid a good-humoured laugh on his face; "I'm the best docthor in
the place for your complaint, an' I'm to have tin pounds for curin'
you, an' I'm to fiddle at yer housewarmin', to-morrow night.
This isn't your tombstone at all at all. It's the stone that was over

one of the ould Brophys, 200 years ago, whin the back garden was a churchyard; an' whin the ould oven wanted a new flure afore you come in here, I was set to do it, an' I put in this ould tombstone, an' you set yer bread on it, and got the letthers off; an' you thought the 6 was an 8, for the figures was worn down, an' you read 1866 instead of 1666; an' now that you know the saycret, I'll warrant you'll soon git well." Well, I need hardly tell yez, she did get well, an' Thady ped Larry Reilly ten pounds on the spot, an' they had a tearin' dance on Christmas night, an' Larry fiddled, an' Thady an' Biddy danced as if they was a couple of kittens, an' all the country side took to calling Larry *Docthor* Reilly, for the wonderful cure he made. An' whinever any one talks of ghosts, Thady an' Biddy swagger and scold as if they believed in nothin' of the kind, an' as if they never had been scared by the haunted oven of Glanbrophy.

Lilian Quiller Couch

THE DEVIL'S OWN

WE ALL WONDERED WHY OCTAVIUS NOTTAGE married at seventeen. Octavius Nottage is the youth who drives his father's wagon to fetch and carry linen from our town to the laundry in his own village. An ordinary boy was Octavius until a year or so ago; just ruddy, and grubby, and scented with the boyish scent of brimstone marbles. His name had been bestowed on him by his parents out of compliment to a young gentleman of that family in which Mrs. Nottage had been a nursemaid—the eighth young gentleman in a family of eleven. True it so happened that Octavius Nottage was a first and only child, but there be still some persons living who stride over trifles, and level all difficulties with the besom of disregard; and John and Jane Nottage were of this class.

When first we knew Octavius he was sturdy and mischievous, travelling to and from town and village in the wagon as a sort of unpleasant consequence of John Nottage's rheumatism, fidgetting among the bundles and baskets throughout the journeys for the sole purpose of loading and unloading at the terminus. Then came a time when John Nottage devoted his entire attention to his pain and sat home to give the fiend no cause for jealousy; then were the horse and wagon entrusted to Octavius, who rejoiced thereat, for Octavius was now sixteen, and much preferred the handling of the reins and the breaking of his own record to that forced repose on the uneven surface of somebody's week's washing, to which he had hitherto been doomed. He enjoyed himself, the grinning young ruffian, and we could not find it in our hearts to reproach him for his heartlessness.

But there came a year, a whole twelve months, in which Octavius changed utterly; he grew tall—that, to be sure, was only what one might expect, or at least hope—but in addition to this his face grew white to ghastliness; his eyes stared with a hunted, haunted expression from out his pallor, and he became gloomy as the veriest pessimist. We all noted the change; we all deplored it. Then at the end of twelve months Octavius married, and our regrets turned to prudent disapproval of the imprudence of his act.

"Love" and "ghosts" are superstitions which gain but little credence in these days of science and health exhibitions; but in the story of Octavius Nottage we have to face a strong similitude to both these superstitions; and as yet there is no explanation ready.

On the first morning of that enervating year Octavius drove into town with his baskets as usual, delivered them with a grin and a joke of equal breadth at their respective area doors, remounted his seat on the knify edge of the wagon, and started for home, whistling "Primo" of a duet with the rattle of wheels as he went.

This was pleasant and commonplace enough in its way: but when Octavius reached the margin of the town a strange thing happened. With the wagon still rumbling on, with the rattle of the wheels still in his ears, with the whistle still on his lips, his eyes chanced to glance down at the shafts, and there he saw, clambering up the step even as the wagon went at its full speed, a grimy little child of hideous features, with blazing yellow eyes, and a few tawny rags wrapped round about it.

"Hullo, there," shouted Octavius cheerfully, above the clatter of his own advancing, "get down, you young brat."

But the child neither looked at him nor answered him; it just climbed on persistently, regardless of the wagoner's rights as of its own danger.

"Little beggar, you!" shouted Octavius again, "d'ye hear what I say; get down."

Still the child gave no answering sign.

"Oh, all right; we'll soon see about that," quoth Octavius; and slackening speed a trifle he leaned forward to take the young trespasser by the shoulder that he might drop him over the side of the wagon, with care as with determination; but—there was no shoulder! his hand went grasping air!

Octavius drew back in horror, and the blood ebbed out of his face, while the clutching hand went shaking as with palsy. But even as he looked, there sat the child, grimy and hideous on the foot-board beside his very feet, gazing with those blazing yellow eyes from out its evil countenance at the horse as it ambled on its way.

Then did the heart of Octavius turn to water behind his ribs; then did his tune trail off inelegantly in mid-bar as his mouth drew lax with horror; then did the taut reins slacken in his hands, as his face stiffened coldly. For here in broad daylight, before this ruddy, healthy youth, clothed in corduroy, on a commonplace wagon lacking paint, and hung about with gaudy signs of modern soaps and matchless cleansers, sat a ghost; a grimy, pallid, evil-featured ghost, who asked no permission and heeded no remonstrance.

For a mile or more the horse jogged on unguided, while Octavius stood wide-eyed and horror-struck on the foot-board beside that—thing! and took no count of time or place. It was awful! As the moments went by it seemed to Octavius as if things must always have been in this wise—just he, and it, and the rattling wagon, with no part for him to play but to endure.

Then as the wagon neared the village, from the thing beside him came a short, hellish shriek; and then there was empty space where the thing had sat, and nothing remained but the echo of that shriek in his ears. The sound roused him into some sort of action; he leaned forward, he shouted "Whoa!" to the horse, from his dry throat, though he had no strength to pull the reins, and he staggered down from the shaft to the ground that he might witness the departure of the creature. He looked before him and behind him, but it was not to be seen; then did he stare at the common stretching away on either side of him, at the sky, at the pools; but there was no trace of the hideous thing who had claimed conveyance from him; no echo of footfall, no footprint in the dust.

When Octavius reached his home that afternoon the shock of his journey had already left its mark upon him. His heart cowered within him in childish shame and fear of ridicule, and he said nothing of the horror he had gone through; he, whose communicativeness had driven his father not infrequently to quote copiously from proverbs bearing upon "the speech of fools," and his mother to suggest kindly but daily that it was always as well to eat a dinner while it was hot, and talk afterwards; he, I say, spoke no word of what he had seen, and even unconsciously rubbed his cheeks with his fists to soften that grey rigidity which had fallen upon them. But the terror which Octavius suffered that night when he went to his lonely little bedroom was such as no rubbing of cheeks could destroy the effect of next morning, and it brought upon him Jane Nottage's traditional cure for pallor, a decoction which smelt of many powerful herbs, but was calculated to prove more efficacious in cases of gormandising than of ghosts.

But that terror was as nothing to the terror which followed; for day after day, week after week, did that child-sprite haunt Octavius Nottage; as surely as the wagon reached that spot at the margin of the town on its homeward way, so surely did that hideous ghost child climb to its place on the foot-board, and sit there, ghastly and untouchable, until on nearing the village it vanished with its hellish shriek of woe.

Octavius, erst so impudently satisfied with his fate, grew daily more white and miserable, more nervous and short-tempered; his cheeks fell long and thin, his eyes gazed wide and scared at all things; and by-and-bye old wives of the village shook their heads as he passed by and murmured that "Nottage's boy had been touched by death."

For weeks did Octavius despairingly cast about in his mind for some other road by which he could escape that dreadful spot, or some time at which the spectre would not appear; but there was no other road to lead him to his home, and all times were the same. He might have told of his trouble, one would argue; but there was some fiendish spell, some strange power which sent the trembling words choking back in his throat as he strove to utter them. For eleven months he fought against that power, and then he seemed to conquer; he conquered inasmuch as he forced himself to go to his companions one by one, and bid them meet him by the churchyard wall on a certain evening, for that he had something of importance to tell them. When it so happened that they obeyed him, with curiosity raised and tempers untrammelled by respect of mood or mania, their force did the rest. They questioned him jovially—brutally it seemed—of his "matter of importance"; they twitted him cheerfully on his lady-like complexion, and inquired of his cosmetics; and at last he told them what he had bidden them there to hear. By that churchyard wall in the dim light of a fading summer's evening, with a voice low-pitched and tremulous with the import of his words, he told them his ghastly tale. There was a minute of complete silence as the words ceased, and the heart of Octavius thumped riotously inside him with the fresh pangs of suffering which he endured as his terror sounded on his ears in spoken syllables. Then came the voice of Sam Underdown, the village wag, in tone somewhat muffled, but perfectly solemn and sympathetic in inflection.

"Ocky Nottage," he declared, slowly, "I 've 'eard of that there sort of thing before; 'tis commonly called the 'Jumps.'"

Then followed a full-voiced chorus of laughter, and a general scramble from the hedge, and Octavius stood alone in the grey-ness, with his cheeks throbbing hot at the insult.

From that hour the trouble of Octavius Nottage was bruited about the village with much gusto and little mercy. In the sand-strewn bar parlour of the "Seven Stars," at the gossips' corner by the three cross-roads, at the forge, at the bakehouse, at the post-office; in all of these spots was the tale of "Ocky's ghost" jeered at, while great whole-lunged guffaws went forth at his expense. Even at the laundry, in whose service the poor youth fetched and carried so regularly, Sam Underdown lounged over the window-sill as he passed, and told his humorous tale. There, indeed, it was received with an interest tempered with awe, for the maidens felt more reverence for the unknown than did the men; and they craved more details from the flippant Sam as they bent over their tubs and wrung the snowy linen with their strong red arms. And Sam gave them a sufficiency, elaborated by his own lively imagination, and the maidens shuddered and giggled, turn in, turn out, as they listened, and exclaimed, "Law, now! Sam Underdown, go along with you, talking such stuff," even as they yearned to delay him in their midst.

But down at the end of the row of maidens in the wash-house stood one before her tub who listened to Sam Underdown's repetitions and inventions with straining ears, and spoke no word in return. A large, slow-moving girl she was, with a wealth of shining red hair and a serious face; a girl who joined but seldom in the ordinary frivolous gossip of the laundry, and who had acquired the character of being "a bit pious." Admonition Ellery was her name, and deep down in her heart lay a great simmering love for this youth, at whom they all scoffed in their wicked, careless way.

Up to that day Octavius Nottage and Admonition Ellery had exchanged little more than a few words; for the girl's tub stood at the far end of the wash-house, and her eyes were wont to be sealed upon her work when Octavius or any other village youth lounged near to gossip; for her nature was charged with an overwhelming bashfulness and a shamed consciousness of her fiery hair. But there had been one day, one showery morning, nearly a year ago, when she had broken through her silence somewhat; she had been standing at the doorway with a bucket in her hand, hesitating to run through the heavy drops to the well; and Octavius, chancing to pass by at the moment, and taking in the situation, held out his hand for the bucket.

"Here, hand it over to me, I'll fetch the water," he said in his cheery, off-handed way. So he fetched it, and brought it, and stood for a moment telling of a cow belonging to Farmer Laskey which had fallen over a hurdle; then he jerked a smiling "Good morning" to her, and went on his way, to give many a thought to Farmer Laskey's cow, but never one to Admonition Ellery; while she went back to her tub again and thought of him all day. That had been the birthday of her love, and for almost a year had it grown and chafed in her heart, this mighty young power, this turbulent offspring of a phlegmatic nature.

"The brutes," raged Admonition, inwardly, as she listened now to Sam Underdown's romancing and the comments it provoked, "the lyin', ignorant brutes," and her heart grew fiery as her hair; but still she spoke no word, for habits are not lightly broken; but she bided her time, and she bit her lips as she wrung out her tubful of steaming clothes and rinsed them in the cold blueing water; and then Sam Underdown went on his way, and she grew calmer, and thought and thought again of Octavius and his trouble.

So it happened that same afternoon that soon after Octavius had reached the dreadful spot at which his ghastly passenger climbed to its usual seat, and as he stood there beside it on the foot-board with a wild hopelessness filling his heart, he heard a voice calling his name, and turning his head quickly, always expectant of some new horror, saw a girl standing on the pathway waving her hand to him to stop. It was Admonition Ellery in her holiday clothes.

"I thought maybe you'd give me a lift back," she said, smiling up at him with bashful, deprecating eyes and the blushes flaming in her cheeks. "I'm feelin' dretful tired somehow."

Octavius strove to bend his rigid features into an answering smile as he looked down at her. "Course I will," he answered slowly, his horror still stamped upon his face, "get up here if you don't mind a poor seat; wagons ain't built altogether for comfort, be 'em?"

"The seat's plenty good enough," she answered, "if you've no objection to the company—"

"Ah!" he exclaimed sharply, as she began to climb the shaft and brushed the very shoulders of the terrible child which sat there still gazing intently, with its blazing eyes, into space; then he stopped suddenly, but her yearning heart seemed to divine his pain, for when she reached the narrow seat beside him, she said, falteringly, but with a great sympathy in her voice, "you'm in trouble, I've heard tell; terrible trouble—I'm—I'm mortal sorry for 'ee."

He looked into her face suddenly and longingly, for his own heart ached to give confidence and accept comfort, and his brain grew wilder and less controllable as each day passed; and as he looked he saw great tears welling up in Admonition's eyes.

"How came you to know of my trouble?' he asked breathlessly.

"I'm from the laundry," she said, "and I heard tell of it there to-day."

"And what do they say of me there? Say I'm a mazed-headed fool, I s'pose; and what story do they tell?"

"They say," faltered Admonition, "they say as how—as how— you think you see—"

"'Think I see,'" he interrupted, "'think,' do they say, when I see the thing before my eyes this very minute, a horrible, devil-faced brat, sitting there at your very feet—taking all the blood from my body day after day; there I see it—" his voice rose to a cry as he pointed to the foot-board, and his eyes blazed with wild fear.

Then did Admonition rise from the narrow seat, and clutching the side of the wagon with one hand, raised the other almost tragically to the sky.

"So do I," she declared, "so do I. All that you see I see too."

For moments there was silence, as the boy and girl faced each other, each flushed, each wild-eyed, each trembling with a great earnestness. Then Octavius spoke, pointing to the fearful thing at their feet.

"You see that thing there?" he questioned.

"I see it," she answered; looking at the spot to which he pointed.

"You see its ghastly face and yellow eyes?"

"A face hideous as a devil, an' eyes yellow as burning jealousy."

"You see its dirty rags an' its white body?"

"Rags fit to breed a plague, and body bloodless as a dead thing."

"You see how it sits an' stares, an' now—how my foot goes through it an' never touches it?"

"Starin' like the very congers, an' no solider than a puff of smoke."

"Oh, my God!" he cried, pressing his hands, reins and all, over his eyes, "then I b'aint mazed! I b'aint mazed after all."

"You b'aint mazed no more'n I'm mazed," she cried, with all her shyness wiped out by her great love, and this her great wickedness.

And then he turned to her and caught her hands. "Tell it all again," he cried, "tell of what you see."

And Admonition, the sober, the pious, the bashful, leaned against the ledge of the wagon there as the horse ambled on and the sun went down, and lied to the lad beside her without scruple; and the terrible thing which was in truth invisible to her eyes as the mountains of the moon, sat on in Octavius Nottage's sight as if it listened to her words.

"But what can I do?" he cried, when the torrent of her falsehoods which had flowed so unfalteringly ceased at last. "I can't live on like this always. I'd rather be dead than live like this."

Admonition mused awhile. "Perhaps I can help 'ee," she remarked, slowly. "My grandmother—well, I know my grandmother knows a whole lot of charms—she's done wonderful things sometimes—an' somehow I've felt sometimes as if—as if I could do 'em too."

"I'd give the world, if 'twas mine, to be rid of the devilish thing," he raved.

Admonition looked at him straightly. "There's some as don't want all the world," she answered, quietly. Then as his eyes questioned her meaning, her blushes came back to her. "I'd like to get down here, please," she added hastily, and in another moment she was walking quickly on her way.

For almost a month Octavius Nottage had no word with Admonition Ellery. Day after day he haunted the laundry, or strove to waylay her as she went to and from her home, but she always hurried past him with some shy, murmured word of greeting, and that was all. Then as she grew more distant he became more ardent. She was the one human soul in the village who appreciated his tragedy, and he felt that he could not live without her sympathy; and this was what she longed for, for dearly did she love this lad who heretofore had given her no thought. So all through those days she held herself from him, and went gravely and slowly on her way, to all outward eyes, while his heart swelled within him as the belief was forced upon him that she had fooled with him, and yet—and yet when he remembered her face as it had been that afternoon on the wagon he found it hard to doubt her—he longed so earnestly to believe her, and his eyes grew wilder and his face more white with the suspense, and John Nottage and Jane, his wife, bowed their heads in grief, and sighed with the heaviness of premonition, for, to all appearances their boy, their only child, had truly been picked out by the hand of Death. He was dying before their eyes.

The one evening as Octavius strolled languidly along the lanes he met Admonition, and she stopped before him. She gave him no greeting in answer to his words, and he saw that her face was very white.

"There's a charm—" she began at once without more prelude, "I've learnt it all by myself and nobody knows I've found it out—but you'd never do it. Her voice sank to a tone of helpless conviction.

Octavius clenched his hands. "I swear I'll do anything," he cried. "There's nothing in my power as I wouldn't do to be rid of that ugly child-devil. Tell me the charm," he commanded.

Admonition shook from head to foot as she looked into his face, but she did not blush even now. "An' I must tell of it?" she asked, slowly.

"Yes, yes, be quick, whatever it is."

"This is what 'tis, then, and don't blame me for it when 'tis told."

"Go on, go on."

Then she began with hard, even tones, "You must get your horse an' wagon ready on the night of the full moon, an' you must go the same way where you always see the spirit, an'—an'—"

"Go on," urged Octavius again.

Admonition caught her breath as if in pain, but she continued in the same even tones. "An' your promised wife must be beside you—an'—"

"My promised wife!" exclaimed Octavius.

"——an'—" went on Admonition, heedless of his interruption, "you must hold hands with her when you come to the spot where the spirit appears, an' you must say—

'Spirit, I defy thee.
Spirit, I deny thee,
In the name of all that's holy.'

—an' the spirit goes for ever."

Admonition ceased speaking and clutched her throat as if the words had scorched her. Neither spoke, and Octavius looked at Admonition, and Admonition looked steadily upon the ground.

"But I haven't got a promised wife," he protested, slowly.

Then Admonition raised her eyes to his, and a great hot blush spread over her face and neck till for very shame she raised her hands to hide it and turned to lean forward against a gate for support.

"Admonition! Admonition" he cried, the whole world seeming to open and lighten before him. Then he made a stride to her again and pulled the shaking hands from her blazing face in the wildness of his mood, "what do 'ee mean? Oh, Admonition, will 'ee, will 'ee for my sake!"

And Admonition consented.

On the night that the moon was at its full, Octavius Nottage took his horse and his wagon, and his promised wife, and drove towards the town. Not a word did they two utter, not a sound did they hear, for the wild throbbing of their own hearts deafened them. Then when they had reached the outlying streets of the town Octavius Nottage turned his horse's head towards the village again. In his heart there surged a wild hope of release from his terrible burden; but in the heart of the girl beside him there was nothing but a sickening terror; she knew that she was but juggling with the superstitions which lay so strong within them both, for the sake of her selfish love, she knew that this solemn charm was but of her own manufacture, that by this night's work she must either stand or fall; and for the first time the full sense of her lying crept coldly over her; she realised the sin of it all, but she could only stand there numb and passive, unable to do aught but go through with that which she had undertaken.

As they neared the direful spot the face of Octavius became as a model of ghastly death, and his eyes held in them a feverishness akin to madness; while the great full-faced moon, placid as ever, looked coldly down to witness his defeat or victory, and Admonition still leaned against the side of the wagon, her hands limp with a chilled faintness which had fallen upon her, realising that those daily, routine prayers of hers had been but so much mockery, and waiting for her fate.

"Quick, quick; your hands!" whispered Octavius hoarsely; but she had no power to stretch them to him. The wagon had almost reached the spot, but she made no move to fulfil her share of the rite. So he clutched her damp, chilly fingers, unconscious of their lifelessness, and gasped with a voice almost soundless by reason of the extremity of his excitement.

> "Spirit, I defy thee,
> Spirit, I deny thee
> In the name of all that's holy."

There was a shock, a crash, a confusion of dancing lights, and the boy and girl were hurled from their insecure foothold, the white road leaped to meet the moonlit sky, a roar as of raging oceans filled the air, and for some moments it seemed as if these two defiers had sailed from the petty waters of Life over the great bar to Eternity.

"Is anyone injured?" asked a kindly voice.

There came a faint groan from Admonition in answer.

"There's a girl here," panted Octavius, as he raised himself slowly and painfully from the ground, "come round to this side."

So the stranger went to him, and together they raised Admonition from the ground, and then she lay awhile in Octavius's arms.

"Something frightened the horses; some child or something," said the stranger, "it ran across the road suddenly, and sent my animal swerving into yours. If you will hold the girl I will go now and see what damage is done."

After a few moments Admonition opened her eyes. "I'm all right," she murmured unsteadily. "I'm quite well. I can stand and walk if you'll let me go," and she raised herself and stood trembling upon her feet.

"Come here!" shouted the stranger, and Octavius went to him.

"Ah!" he cried aloud as he bent over the man, and saw what lay in his arms. "Can you hold it? Can you touch it? Oh, my God!" There in the white dust lay the semblance of the spirit which he had defied, the child who had been such a hideous burden in his life, who had changed him from a ruddy, sturdy boy to a picture of living death, who had haunted him night and day, in sight and out of sight, who had drained the courage from his heart and bade fair to steal the reason from his brain; there it lay with its head on the stranger's arm, its grimy rags displaced, its bloodless limbs limp and lifeless, its hideous features distorted, its yellow eyes half-closed—dead.

"Hold it?" cried the stranger, looking up in wonder, "there is no difficulty in holding the poor little fellow now, he is dead. It was quite an accident, I must say; the child seemed to spring from nowhere, and my horse was upon it in an instant."

Octavius made no answer; he stood stunned by the force of circumstances, while Admonition crept slowly to the spot, and stood beside him. Octavius stretched his hand towards her, and she held it fast in hers; and still he gazed down upon the stranger's burden and marvelled, for if he might believe his eyes, the spirit-child was but a creature of flesh and blood, and moreover it was killed. But Admonition did not give so much as a single glance to the dead child at her feet; her eyes were fixed with feverish intensity upon the stranger who held it.

"Well," said the stranger, looking up at them with some appearance of surprise at their strange silence, "there is nothing more to be done for the poor little fellow now. My cart is rather damaged, but I think it will hold together until I reach the town, and I think it will be better for me to take the child's body with me and explain matters when I get there. There is but small harm done to your wagon. Just tell me your name that I may be able to communicate with you."

And Octavius told his name as in a dream, and as they stood, he and Admonition, and watched with wide, hunted eyes as the stranger laid the little corpse in his cart, examining the damage done to that vehicle, bade them "Good-night," and then drove swiftly from them along the moon-lit road.

The "Good-night" echoed in their ears unanswered, and still these two lovers stood there watching. At last Octavius turned to Admonition, and there was an awful look stamped upon his face.

"What does it all mean?" he asked hoarsely.

" 'Tis the devil carrying off his own," she answered solemnly.

Then the horror of it all came rushing over her, she turned and clung to Octavius, and there came such a storm of tears as her calm eyes had never known before.

"Let us go home," she sobbed, "let us go home."

So he kissed her and comforted her, and the doing of it steadied his own reason as nothing else could have done; and with the moon still flooding the world, and shining on their white and horrified faces, they journeyed home.

From that night no sight nor sound of the stranger, nor of the spirit-child, ever reached Octavius or Admonition.

The marriage took place a few weeks later; and since hearing the story of their wooing, the imprudence of the alliance appears less inexcusable.

Anonymous

A CHRISTMAS GHOST STORY

THERE WAS NOT A PRETTIER PICTURE anywhere than the water mill, where the country people in the neighbourhood of Darnforth took their wheat to be ground. It was worth a long walk to see the Old Brook, as it was called, turn the great wheel, and dance in a thousand glittering drops from every mossy timber; and to hear it, after it broke away from the task and darted off under the great black arch below, was to be deafened with wild and turbulent music.

Frank Underwood, the owner of the Old Brook mill, and the proprietor of the fine house close by, was once very poor, and, paradoxical as it may appear, was suddenly ruined by becoming very rich. When he was a young fellow, the pride of the neighbouring village, the hope of the adjacent town, and the betrothed of Alice Martin, a rich uncle died and left him heir to a fine estate, upon which stood the Old Brook mill.

With an approved worldliness that you might hardly have looked for in such a quiet rural district, young Underwood broke off the engagement between himself and Alice; but he was punished for his perfidy. Riotous living and unfortunate speculations soon reduced him to ruin and bankruptcy, and, like many another, when he lost his gold he lost his friends too. The only being who did not desert him in affliction was the sweetheart of his boyhood. When those who had been his companions in the days of his wealth had left him, she hastened to him to be a comfort and solace in his misery. But Alice Martin fell a sacrifice to her devotion and her lover's insincerity. Scandal wove its meshes about her fair fame, and deprived her of the shelter of a father's roof. The blow fell too heavily for her weak nature to bear, and a frozen corpse, taken from the Old Brook soon afterwards, told her sad story of suffering and woe.

After this, Frank Underwood stood alone in the world, a friendless and wretched man. Securing by loan enough money to purchase the mill where his uncle had made his money, Frank left the big town where he had been unfortunate, and, as years rolled on, he regained nearly all the lost estate. By-and-by everything he touched seemed to turn to gold. The country people said he had sold himself to the devil. He became a thorough money-grabbing, snarling skinflint like old Scrooge, and he had the same hatred of Christmas, and, indeed, for every other festival which in any way interfered with his worldly arrangements. What Scrooge was to the city of London, Underwood was to the Darnforth district; and I can vouch for the truth of every detail connected with this history of his love affair with Alice Martin.

It was evening. The Christmas chimes were ringing in the villagers, and the dear, old-fashioned music came sounding through the air from Oldbrook.

For an hour or more the miller sat rocking himself to and fro in his chair. At length the night grew darker and darker, until, save now and then in the flicker of the firelight, he could scarcely see across his little room. The noise in the village grew still, the bells ceased telling their "tidings of great joy," and the regular "tick-tack, tick-tack" of the old clock on the stairs became more distinct. The fire was low, the wind was high, and now and then a hiss on the smouldering ashes told of the falling snow without.

Presently old Underwood looked up, and found that he was not alone. A figure was seated opposite to him, watching him with a huge pair of lustrous eyes, which, for a time, held him in motionless fascination. But the miller had a stout heart. He soon rallied, and demanded the business of his mysterious visitor.

The shadow with the eyes informed him that he was the ghostly representative of his uncle, who, when he died, fearing that his heir might be a spendthrift, had buried a large amount of treasure near the oak tree on the common. He felt, now that his nephew had gone through the fire of adversity, seen the result of extravagance, and had turned out so excellent a money-getter, that he could not rest in his grave without Frank dug up the hidden treasure.

"I'll do it, I'll do it, if it's all fair and no humbug, Mr. What's-your-name," said the miller, trembling before the shadow.

"Then follow me," said the visitor.

"To-morrow," replied old Frank, the miller; "to-morrow I'll dig it up."

"To-night you shall do it—to-night!" said the spirit.

The window shook, a gush of wind rushed down the chimney, the doors opened with a bang, and the miller followed his ghostly leader into the freezing Christmas air. The miller saw nothing but the glaring eyes of the ghost, and he followed them until he stood by the old oak tree on the common.

A spade and a pick-axe were lying by the tree, and the miser, despite the coming infirmity of age, went lustily to work. For an hour the spirit stood by, glaring at the gold-finder.

Suddenly the axe struck against a hard substance.

" 'Tis there!" said the spirit.

" 'Tis there!" went echoing over the common.

" 'Tis there!" was repeated by a thousand voices in the air.

The miller would have fallen, all but speechless, had he not suddenly discovered that his visitor had departed. But he soon rallied again. The passionate craving for gold was upon him, and he resumed his digging. The substance with which his axe had come in contact was an old-fashioned urn, full of guineas, notes on a local bank, and precious stones. It was all the miller could do to lift it.

"Oh, oh," he chuckled, as he feasted his eyes upon it. "I can satisfy my grudge against Simpkins and Co. There shall be a run on the Oldbrook bank to-morrow. Why should I help the poor?" he continued, as if answering a question suggested by the inward monitor; "I was poor myself. Nobody helped me. The poor, indeed, with their 'Merry Christmas!' "

Until the perspiration rolled down his face, the miller laboured to put the urn and its treasure on his shoulder, and at last he succeeded. But why does he tremble? Why do his eyes appear to be starting from his head? Why does he sink to the earth, and cry for mercy?

The urn has changed. On the miller's shoulders crouches a demon, fearful to contemplate! It is peering into his face with a fiendish grin. The old oak tree, too, is changed. Jabbering sprites are swinging about in the creaking branches, and swarming around the supplicating miser. They hiss at him, and the air is filled with their fiendish laughter.

At this moment the miller would gladly have given up one half of his wealth to have been once more at home at his mill. He prayed loudly and fiercely for mercy, and, hoarse with crying, he fell senseless to the earth, at the foot of the old oak tree. By-and-by he was raised from the earth. At his side stood the figure which had first lured him from home, but without that terrible appearance which it had at first assumed. The tree had disappeared: the common, too, was gone; and there was a weight upon the miller's back which needed no care on his part to keep there.

"Where are we?" asked the miller, turning to his ghostly attendant.

"Ask no questions, but pay attention to what thou seest. I have driven hence the fiends who terrified thee, and am now here, at the command of my master Time, to show thee pictures of the past. The veil of the future will also be partially lifted to thy gaze, but it is in thy power to alter what I shall there show thee. Thy deeds in the past have been judged. Thy yesterday, a furrow on the sand, has been washed out by the returning tide of to-day. The future alone is open to thee," said the ghost.

They were at the outskirts of a beautiful village. There was a fragrant smell of newly-mown hay in the air. Trees, clothed in all the beautiful verdure of refulgent summer, stretched long, leafy arms over the spot where Frank and his companion stood. The shades of evening hung a misty mantle around them, which the pale moon, just rising, strove in vain to disperse. A youth was walking in the moonlight, and a gentle girl leaned lovingly on his arm. The garb of a peasant set off the manly form of the youth. The maid was also clad simply, and her long brown hair fell in careless tresses over her shoulders.

"It is! it is!" exclaimed Frank, much agitated.

"Silence!" said the ghost. "Listen!"

"Alice, dear Alice," whispered the youth, "when we have money enough, marriage shall free you from his persecution.

Fear not. Ere long I shall earn more; and some day, when poor old uncle leaves this world, I may be rich."

"Hush, dear Frank! We will not build our hopes on the dead. I have saved a little, and we shall yet be happy. I do not desire that we should be rich."

"But that fellow James is wealthy, and he would marry you to-morrow. He loves you, too, and might make you happy. He can give you comforts which you may never look to have with me, dear Alice."

"If you love me, Frank, is that not enough for me? Could I not suffer, if it were necessary, and be happy still if you were by my side?"

"Bless you!" exclaimed the youth, clasping the hand of Alice with fervour, and pressing a hot, burning kiss upon her forehead. "You shall never regret your love, Alice."

And they walked slowly away beneath the elm trees.

"Oh, let us follow them! Good ghost, pray let us follow them. I know them well. We are in my native village. The beautiful girl is Alice."

"And the youth is Frank Underwood," replied the ghost.

"I would follow them," said the miller.

"'Tis useless. Whomsoever you see, they cannot see you. We are to them no more than air; these are the shadows of the past," said the ghost.

Frank attempted to follow the lovers, notwithstanding, but the weight on his back pulled him to the earth.

"Take it away—gold or diamonds, remove the weight!" groaned the old man; but still it pressed heavily upon him.

"I meant to be true to her, I did indeed," said the old man, as the scene changed again.

Frank Underwood, Esq., once the peasant youth, now the wealthy manufacturer, sat at the head of his own table in his own dining-room. Around him were a crowd of sycophants, male and female. The master of the house was carrying on a pleasant flirtation with an ogling, painted beauty.

Ere the miller could speak, the village was before him again. He stood on the same spot where he had seen the lovers only a few minutes before. Alice, grown into womanhood, was there—alone with her sorrows.

"I saw him, but he never heeded me. He turned from me in scorn, and the servants drove me from his door. I will never go again. Now that he is rich, it is not likely that he can love a poor girl like me. No one loves me now. Tired of asking me to accept the hand of Mr. James, father scarcely speaks to me save in anger; and when poor, dear mother died she would not have her broken-hearted Alice near her."

Thus, between sobs and tears, spoke the beautiful Alice, as she glided slowly past the miller, and his unearthly guide.

"Poor soul! God forgive me!" exclaimed Frank on his knees. "Take me away; I can see no more. I'm going mad!" almost shrieked the old man. "I loved her again—I did, I did!" he continued.

Once more the scene changed. They were within the walls of a prison. Frank Underwood was in a debtor's gaol. By his side stood Alice.

"I could not desert you when I heard you were in distress, although you drove me from you in your prosperity," said the girl.

The man groaned audibly, and big tears were in his eyes.

"I repent—I repent! but 'tis useless now. You can never love me again. You can never forgive me."

"I can!" said the girl.

"You cannot love a prisoner, a bankrupt, an outcast from society."

"Ah, you do not know a woman's heart! I can love you now more than ever, if that were possible. Can *you* love Alice again?"

"I can—but I have said so before and proved false to you. I hate myself; I am wretched, miserable, mad. Go home, poor girl, go home!" said the man, in terrible accents.

"I shall soon have no home except in heaven. This visit to you which has cost me a day and a night of hard walking, may rob me of the last spark of a father's love. Think of your younger days! Think of your promises! Think!" said the girl, looking earnestly into the prisoner's face.

"I do, and am mad with remorse; but I may yet atone."

At this moment a turnkey bade Alice depart.

"Stop, stop!" cried the miller. "I loved her—I loved her then—I meant to atone. Let her know that, at least," he said; but the prison and its occupants vanished.

Once again the village appeared. It was a cold winter night.

The snow was on the ground. No living form, save that of a woman, was visible.

"I cannot bear it," said Alice, as she hurried by the spot where the miller and the ghost were standing. "Driven from home, footsore, disgraced by the tongue of scandal, weak, cold, houseless. It is too much for me; and how do I know that he will even now love me again? Oh! no, no; I am going mad."

"He will—he does!" cried poor old Underwood, the miser miller.

"Follow her, and see still more of the effects of riches. Go, man, and see thine own handiwork," said the ghost; and the miller hastened after the wretched woman.

The noise of the Old Brook was heard in the distance, as it fell from the mill-dam and roared beneath the water-wheel. Louder and louder became the noise of the torrent. Nearer and nearer approached the woman towards the river.

"I could save her now but for this horrible load," cried the miller, satisfied of her wild intent. "Take it away—take it away!" he shrieked; but the demon sat still more heavily upon him.

The ghost was by his side to taunt and to warn.

"'Tis the gold you dug out of the common. You'll want it; gold is your idol, old man."

"Not now—never again," shrieked the miller. "O Heaven, remove this weight!"

They were now close to the mill-dam. A gleam of moonlight played upon the river. The water-wheel clicked in solemn regularity. Old Underwood was within reach of the flying maiden. He put out his hand to save her—once more his load of riches dragged him to the ground.

"Save her! oh, save her! dear, dear, Alice!" rang over the waters; but the Old Brook had received the suicide, and the mill-wheel went round, and the water rolled on as before.

"Take away the weight! it burns me, it pierces my heart—I am dying! Mercy, mercy!" cried Frank.

"Why, whatever's the matter, Mr. Underwood?" cried Sarah, his housekeeper, who had just returned from an evening visit, and found her master lying on the floor gasping for breath. "Whatever have you been a-doing, sir?" she said, as she proceeded to lift him up.

"Oh, Sarah, Sarah—where am I? Take off the weight—take it off!" cried the terrified miller.

"Why, you're where I left you, sir. Dear-a-me, where do you think you are?"

"Light the candles; but don't leave me," he said, seizing her by the arm.

"I'd sooner be poor Sarah Maggs than rich Mr. Underwood, after all," thought Sarah.

The candles lighted, Frank shook himself, pinched himself, stood upright, sat down, walked, stamped, and went through other similar investigations into his physical position, and at last came to the conclusion that he had been released from the ghosts—for he would never believe that he had only been dreaming.

Perhaps it was all the better he should discard the dream, and adhere to the more terrible idea that he had been in ghostly company; for from that moment he became a different man, and he has now the credit of being the best and most hospitable landlord in the neighbourhood. The year after he went out with the ghosts, he built that fine house on the hill yonder, where Christmas now brings some of its happiest moments. The genius of Christmas Past presides there, bringing every year its sirloins of beef, its pies and puddings, its capons, its turkeys, its geese, its wassail bowls, its yule logs, and its thousand other good things, all to the big house of the old miller. The great festival is observed in every detail, and there are little presents for all who call there on Boxing Day.

A handsome tombstone has arisen over the grave of Alice Martin, five miles above the dam; and every Christmas Eve an old man is seen in the churchyard, some say upon his knees. Old Sarah knows that there is a great deal of truth in the report; for ever since that evening when she found her master in such a dreadful fright, Frank Underwood, the miller, always quietly disappears for several hours on every successive Christmas Eve. The white mare and the well-known phaeton may invariably be seen tethered in a by-way near the turnpike, waiting for their grey-headed owner when the bells were ringing in honour of Christmas Eve.

CPSIA information can be obtained
at www.ICGtesting.com
Printed in the USA
LVHW081148021121
701928LV00035B/1089/J